THE ANTISOCIAL MAN

Borgo Press Books by FRÉDÉRIC BOUTET

The Antisocial Man and Other Strange Stories
Claude Mercoeur's Reflection and Other Strange Stories
The Voyage of Julius Pingouin and Other Strange Stories

THE ANTISOCIAL MAN

AND OTHER STRANGE STORIES

FRÉDÉRIC BOUTET

Translated by Brian Stableford

THE BORGO PRESS

MMXIII

CLASSICS OF
FANTASTIC LITERATURE
NUMBER TEN

THE ANTISOCIAL MAN

FIRST EDITION

Published by Wildside Press LLC

www.wildsidebooks.com

THE ANTISOCIAL MAN

CONTENTS

INTRODUCTION

This volume is the first of a set of three showcasing the work of Frédéric Boutet, the other two volumes being *The Voyage of Julius Pingouin and Other Strange Stories* and *Claude Mercoeur's Reflection and Other Strange Stories*. Viewed as an ensemble, the collections illustrate the range and development of Boutet's early work, and provide a few representative samples of its later evolution. Although several stories by Boutet were translated into English in the 1920s, especially in America, they were selected from his later works, when he was mostly writing sentimental stories and crime fiction for popular magazines; no examples of his early work, most of which consisted of offbeat supernatural fiction, have previously been rendered into English (although his work of that sort became quite popular in German translation, where it retains a higher reputation than it does even in France). This set of three volumes will hopefully serve to introduce the work of a highly distinctive writer of weird and baroque fiction to a new audience.

Frédéric Boutet was born on 5 November 1874 in Bourges. His father, Charles Boutet, was an engineer working for the *Ponts et Chaussées* [Bridges and Highways agency]—the governmental department in charge of the construction and maintenance of roads and associated structures—who is still remembered as the author of two ambitious plans to build a bridge over the English Channel, for which he failed to obtain finance from Napoléon III.

Unfortunately, Charles Boutet died not long after Frédéric's birth, leaving his widow to care for four children: three daughters and one son, Frédéric being the youngest child. One of the daughters, Elisabeth (1871-1964) eventually became a writer of children's books, using the signature "Valdor" in the 1920s and early 1930s; she appears in the Bibliothèque Nationale catalogue as "R. Valdor" but various other bibliographical sources include her real name. The family left Bourges to take up residence in Auteuil, but financial difficulties eventually forced them to move to what was then humbler accommodation in the Rue de Bac in Paris.

In the early 1890s Boutet began to frequent literary cafés, including Le Chat Noir, keeping company with numerous contributors to the Decadent and Symbolist movements, among whom he quickly acquired a reputation for sarcastic wit. He also cultivating a strong interest in occultism—which was, at the time, very easily combined with such literary interests, as there was more than one notable salon in which occult fascinations and literary ambitions were central topics of concern. His earliest works of fiction were dark allegories combining the themes of sex and death in a conscientiously Decadent fashion. He developed the habit of working at night, by candlelight; a habit that presumably reflected and alimented his typical themes but did not help his eyesight, which was never good and deteriorated considerably during his lifetime.

Boutet is now most frequently cited in Britain because of an account he wrote of an accidental meting with Oscar Wilde in 1899, when he was able to do the distressed writer a small favor; he became one of Wilde's most loyal friends during the desperate final year of the latter writer's life, and was one of his coffin-bearers when he died. He is closest literary friends were the novelist Paul Adam and the poet Jehan Rictus but he also befriended the young Guillaume Apollinaire, who expressed considerable gratitude for his kindness in the fulsome dedication to *Le Poet assassiné* (1916). The circles in which he was moving were also subject to fierce tensions and rivalries, however, and the sometimes-barbed character of his wit presumably did not endear him to everyone; he does not appear to have got along well with some of the other influential figures in his initial field, including Remy de Gourmont and the circle associated with the key Symbolist periodical the *Mercure de France*; Boutet was one of the few significant contributors to the Decadent/Symbolist Movement to whom Gourmont never offered any critical praise, and that exclusion, as much as the subsequent changes in direction that his career took, has led to his rarely being given any substantial attention in modern critical works on the Movement. Even so, his first collection of stories, published in 1898, *Contes dans le nuit* [Tales in the Night], is set solidly in the tradition of Symbolist prose, and is thoroughly Decadent in its style and attitude. Henri de Régnier, the most successful writer of Symbolist prose in the 1890s, praised his work.

After writing the stories in that first collection Boutet developed a fascination with a literary method that mimicked dramatic form, although few of the pieces he wrote in that manner were capable of being staged, and few appear to have been composed with that possibility in mind. He was obviously aware of the opening of the Théâtre du Grand-Guignol in 1897 and must have been conscious of the kinship between the material in which it specialized and his own interests; if he ever submitted anything to the theater in question, however, it never reached production. He published two volumes of stories in quasi-dramatic form, *Drames baroques et mélancoliques* [Baroque and Melancholy Dramas] (1899) and *Les Victims grimacent* [The Grimacing Victims] (1900). Some of the items included therein are earnest allegories in the same vein as the stories in the first collection, but others develop a conscientious staginess that coverts them into graphic black comedy.

Boutet's first three collections were all published by Chamuel, whose primary specialization was books on occult subjects, for whom literary material was very much a subsidiary sideline. The books remained relatively obscure and undoubtedly sold poorly; their lack of commercial potential was evident, not only by virtue of their esoteric form but the darkness of their subject matter, but they did attract some critical attention. His next endeavors, however, exhibited a further and more calculatedly sardonic evolution in the direction of black comedy, and he produced two remarkable novellas in "L'Homme sauvage du Quai Rue Bois-l'Encre" and "Le Voyage de Julius Pingouin," which were published together as *L'Homme sauvage et Julius Pingouin: Deux petits romans fantaisistes* by Juven in 1902; the former is dated March 1901 and the latter December 1901.

Translation of the former title is difficult because the French word *sauvage* has a considerably wider range of meaning than its English derivative "savage," and is more often used to mean "uncivilized" or "antisocial" than "wild" or "violent." Indeed, the story hinges on that multiple not-entirely-translatable ambiguity; essentially, it is about a man considered by his neighbors to be antisocial, who turns out to be extremely, if absurdly, uncivilized, wild and violent. The painstaking development of that ambiguity develops the baroque elements of the story in a surrealist and absurdist manner that has a marked kinship with the literary direction taken by Alfred Jarry and Guillaume Apollinaire, the two writers primarily responsible for the evolution of Symbolism into Surrealism. Indeed, Boutet could easily have figured in the Surrealist Manifesto as one of the significant precursors listed by André Breton, although the fact that he had become a thoroughly commercial writer by the time the manifesto was produced in the 1920s presumably militated against his nomination.

When Jacques de Gachons provided a brief introduction to the much later novella "Le Reflet de Claude Mercoeur" (translated as the title story of the third volume in the set) for its publication in *Je Sais Tout* in 1921 Gachons did not hesitate to say quite frankly that "Frédéric Boutet est un sauvage," evidently having the much earlier novella in mind, although he explained the remark, lightly, by citing Boutet's reclusiveness and nocturnal habits—tendencies that Boutet had already begun to develop in

1901, although he was, at that point, far from taking them to the extreme that he subsequently cultivated. At any rate, "L'Homme sauvage du Quai Rue Bois-l'Encre" is very much the fantasy of a man regarded, somewhat resentfully, by his neighbors as a curmudgeon, who might very well have had got into an argument similar to the initiating incident of the story, prompting the intervention of a bailiff—without, of course, the ability to react in the same magnificently perverse fashion.

In a similar spirit, "Le Voyage de Julius Pingouin" (translated as the title-story of the second volume in the present set) is a modern escapist fantasy that immediately crosses the boundary of the absurd and keeps on going, taking an initially placid nonsensicality to a wild and violent extreme. Although the story identifies itself as a travesty of the Greek myth of the Golden Fleece, as retold in Apollonius Rhodius' epic *Argonautica* in the third century B.C., it also has obvious affiliations with works by two of Boutet's favorite writers, Edgar Allan Poe and Jules Verne.

Verne had recently published a sequel to Poe's *Narrative of Arthur Gordon Pym of Nantucket* (1838). *Le Sphinx des glaces* (1897; tr. as *An Antarctic Mystery*), in which, typically, he had attempted to provide naturalistic explanations for the mysterious events and entities tantalizingly glimpsed by Pym, but that kind of reduction was entirely contrary to what were then Boutet's inclinations; although his account of Julius Pingouin's explorations of the same regions are more caricature than sequel, they nevertheless attain a fantastic extreme of which Poe— who considered his own works to be "tales of the grotesque and arabesque and had a taste for absurdist comedy as well as grim horror—would undoubtedly have approved wholeheartedly. Many readers presumably thought in 1902 that the crazy admixture of methods, attitudes and themes contained in Boutet's novella was too odd to be considered successful, but it remains a unique literary work in its unrepentant eccentricity and bizarrerie. The Juven volume was reprinted by Flammarion in 1922, when it probably sold far better.

In spite of its modest critical success, the Juven volume did not pave the way for Boutet to continue working in that direction. He was, however, able to reissue a "revised and corrected" selection of his earlier works, with a laudatory introduction by Paul Adam, via another publisher, the exiled Englishman Charles Carrington. Carrington was no nearer to the heart of the Parisian literary establishment than Chamuel, and probably deserves to be considered even further away; his principal reputation was for publishing pornography, and many observers suspected that his occasional publication of serious literary works by writers like Oscar Wilde and Anatole France was merely a mask for his other operations, but in fact, the lavish editions he produced of those upmarket works testify to a genuine interest and considerable respect, and he might have done far more in that vein had circumstances and sales given him more encouragement. At any rate, being published by the man notorious as the promulgator of the long-running series *La Flagellation Travers le Monde* and the dubious classic *Raped on the Railway* (1894) cannot have helped Boutet's reputation.

Boutet is not known to have written any pseudonymous pornography for Carrington, whose primary source of such material was Hugues Rebell, but Guillaume Apollinaire and various other post-Symbolist writers dabbled in erotica, and it would not have been very surprising if Boutet had done so too, and that the publication of the second edition of *Contes dans le nuit* in 1903 was part of his recompense. He did do some translation work for Carrington but the only item he signed was a French version of John William Harding's thoroughly respectable Old Testament epic *The Gate of the Kiss* (1902). The 1903 version of *Contes dans le nuit* is translated in its entirety in the present volume, along with a translation of "L'Homme sauvage du Quai Rue Bois-l'Encre." Six of the items that the 1903 collection contains were manifestly reprinted from the original *Contes dans le nuit*, presumably in revised versions (I have not had the opportunity to compare the two volumes), while three are new versions of items taken from *Drames baroques et mélancho-*

liques, one with a variant title; two titles appear in the 1903 collection for the first time, but are probably revised versions of stories from the first collection.

After the publication of the Carrington collection, Boutet's work changed direction again, although, once again, it was more of a swerve than a break. By 1903, a considerable and fiercely competitive market for short fiction had developed in the French newspapers. French newspapers had made an institution of *"feuilleton* fiction," mostly consisting of long rambling serials, since the 1840s, when the leading papers of the day had found it possible to develop their fierce rivalry by offering readers the circulation-boosting inducement of daily serials by Alexandre Dumas and Eugène Sue. Although much less significant by the 1890s, the tradition still continued, and *Le Matin*, one of the two leading dailies of the era, had the most popular *feuilletonist* of the day, Gaston Leroux, on its staff. In the 1890s, the editor of its chief rival, the slightly more upmarket *Le Journal*, decided that instead of trying to compete directly with Leroux, he would attempt to cultivate the rival form of the short story, with a particular focus on the subgenre of the *conte cruel*, previously developed in *Le Gaulois* and *Le Figaro* by such writers as Jean Richepin, Octave Mirbeau and Léon Bloy, usually in a somewhat haphazard fashion. Once *Le Journal* had started promoting such fiction as a regular weekly feature, however, *Le Matin* swiftly joined in with a similar feature billed as "Le Mille-et-un Matins," and the contest moved into a higher gear in the first few years of the twentieth century.

Writers who could churn out such fiction on a regular basis over a considerable period of time were, however, few and far between; even Richepin and Mirbeau, who provided the most prolific and accomplished production lines, eventually faltered, and their endeavors increasingly required supplementation by other hands. "Literary supplements" issued by other rival papers, including *Le Gaulois* and *Le Petit Parisien*, also stepped up the competition. *Le Matin*'s publisher decided to intensify it even further by introducing a short fiction feature to its evening companion, *Le Français*; in 1903, Boutet became one of the principal contributors to that particular slot. He then followed the example of many previous aspirant writers who found the business of making a living challenging, launching a career as a journalist that ultimately displaced his more pretentious work, and gradually converted him, at least in the eyes of his detractors, into a crowd-pleasing hack. Some of his early contributions to *Le Français* were reprinted in the collection *Histoires vraisemblables* [Plausible Stories] (1908), all of whose contents are reprinted, along with other material, in the second and third volumes of the present series.

There were other developments in Boutet's life at this time, which made their own contribution to the subsequent development of his career. The most important was that he became enamored of Lucienne Million-Drisx, the step-daughter of the Symbolist writer Gustave Kahn; he married her in 1908; the necessities of establishing a household obviously played a considerable part in his determination to concentrate more intently on commercial work. There was, however, a rather curious and unfortunate incident that might well have added impetus to his subsequent withdrawal from the Parisian literary community and his deliberate cultivation of the lifestyle of an *homme sauvage*.

Among the Symbolist writers Boutet seems to have offended was the poet Laurent Tailhade. Claude Deméocq, who has made a concerted attempt to revive Boutet's reputation in France, writing a detailed biographical and critical article in his work in the literary periodical *Le Visage Vert* in 2002, which was adapted for use as an introduction to a new edition of *Histoires vraisemblables* in 2004, alleges that the animosity was contrived by a salon-keeper, Camille Prévost-Roqueplan, who attempted to pay back a grudge against Tailhade by engineering a liaison between Boutet and Tailhade's wife in 1900. That allegation is apparently based on an episode in a satirical *roman à clef* written by Tailhade's brother-in-law, Fernand Kolney, *Le Salon de Madame Truphot* (1904), although it is by no means obvious that the episode in the novel can be taken at face value, given that many of its other scurrilous accusations are pure fantasy. For whatever reason, however, Boutet was vitriolically pilloried in the novel, along with Jehan Rictus, Léon Bloy, Octave Mirbeau, and several other habitués of Camille Prévost-Roqueplan's salon, as well regulars at the occult-leaning salon hosted by Henriette Maillet, who provided one of the models for Joris-Karl Huymans' Madame Chantelouve in *Là-Bas* as well as for Kolney's Madame Truphot.

Some of Kolney's victims had previously thought that they were Tailhade's friends, and never spoke to him again, assuming—probably correctly—that he was responsible for the raw material developed by Kolney. Jehan Rictus sued for defamation of character, and contrived to win a judgment removing the novel from circulation, at least temporarily, but that only enhanced its *succès de scandale*. Whether or not the specific allegation it made against Boutet was true, and whether or not, even if true, it really reflects all that badly on his character, became irrelevant in terms of the sneering gossip stirred up by the novel, and the damage done might well have contributed, as Deméocq suggests, to Boutet's virtual withdrawal from society and his retirement to his study, where he continued to write by night until his eyesight finally gave out, a few years before his death in 1941. That gradual consummation of a lifestyle that was already in the process of evolution before 1904, however, did no harm at all to his productivity, and he continued to pour out short stories, articles and novels in profusion. He joined the staff of *Le Journal* in 1909, and remained a regular contributor for the next two decades.

Boutet obtained his greatest popularity, and also his greatest critical acclaim, during the Great War. In 1914 he was still theoretically eligible, if only just, for mobilization, because the war broke out shortly before his fortieth birthday, but he would probably not have been called up even if his poor eyesight had not rendered him unfit. The war restricted his publishing opportunities severely, as regards fiction, as it did for every other writer in France, but it did leave him a margin in which to operate, which he exploited to the full. His work had already began to move in the direction of naturalistic *contes cruels* describing the vicissitudes of life in the Parisian "underworld" of poverty-stricken drunkards, prostitutes and petty criminals, and he had compiled a first collection of such works, *Le Lantern rouge* [The Red Light, which translates metaphorically as well as literally] (1914), before the war began. Such work only needed a slight adjustment of context to add the circumstance of the conflict to the relevant plague of troubles.

Boutet followed *Le Lantern rouge* with three further collections in a similar vein, in which life during wartime became the central feature: *Victor et ses amis* [Victor and His Friends] (1916), *Celles qui les attendent* [The Women Who Wait for Them] (1917) and *Douze aventures sentimentales suive d'Autres histories d'à present* [Twelve Sentimental Adventures, and Other Stories of the Present Day] (1918). The second of the three, focusing on the arduous trials of women whose husbands were away fighting in the war, was particularly successful, because rather than in spite of the fact that it did not strive as hard as many contemporary works to support the cause of propagandistic morale building by "putting on a brave face."

After the war, Boutet felt free to indulge his own penchants a little more evidently in occasional works, but most of the fiction he produced was aimed at such popular magazines as *Je Sais Tout*, which preferred upbeat material. Even so, many of his love stories and much of his crime fiction continued to develop distinctly cynical, and even macabre, twists; some of the stories in such collections as *Aventures sombres et pittoresques* [Somber and Picturesque Adventures] (1921), *Le Reflet de Claude Mercoeur* (1921) and *Le Spectre de M. Imberger* [Monsieur Imberger's Ghost] (1922) retain a sardonic spirit not too far removed from the black comedies in *Histoires vraisemblables*, and even an occasional delicate hint of absurdism, although he was careful to distribute more *outré* material rather thinly.

The bibliography appended by Deméocq to his *Visage Vert* article includes further thirteen-story collections published by Boutet after 1922, but might not be complete even with regard to books (Google Books lists a few titles not included therein or in the Bibliothéque Nationale catalogue), and does not even attempt to tackle unreprinted material in periodicals. In between, Boutet produced novels on a regular basis, most of the later ones being crime novels, and he also did a considerable amount of work producing scenarios for silent movies; one of his most successful books was *L'Orphéline* [The Orphan] (1922), an early novelization of a scenario whose film version was directed by Louis Feuillade. Toward the end of his life he exploited his early interest in occultism by editing a *Dictionnaire des science occultes* [Encyclopedia of the Occult Sciences] (1937), which turned out to be his final work; it recycled and supplemented the research he had carried out for his earlier *Tableau de l'Au-Delà, étude sur spiritism et l'occultisme* [The Catalogue of the Beyond; A Study of Spiritualism and Occultism] (1927), whose second volume was separately titled *Les Aventuriers de mystère* [Adventurers in Mystery].

Perhaps Boutet would have attracted more attention from literary historians and modern critics had he not been so prolific—the task of locating a full set of his works would be very daunting, as many of them have become extremely scarce, and reading through them, if such a set could be accumulated, would require a considerable investment of time. The works that have remained available, however—or have once again become available thanks to electric copies—testify to the fact that he was an accomplished and interesting writer whose contributions to supernatural fiction, offbeat crime fiction and Great War fiction are all significant. This set of translations will allow his contribution to the first-named genre to be measured, and also provides a handful of sample texts—including two science fiction stories—that allow some appreciation the greater breadth of his endeavors.

The translation of the 1903 version of *Contes dans le nuit* featured in the present volume was made from the electronic copy made available on-line by the University of Toronto, available via *archive.org*. The translation of "L'Homme sauvage du Quai Rue Bois-l'Encre" was made from a copy of the 1922 Flammarion edition of *L'Homme sauvage et Julius Pingouin: Deux petits romans fantaisistes.*

PREFACE TO
THE 1903 EDITION
of *Contes dans la Nuit,*
BY PAUL ADAM[1]

At a time when new miracles are pullulating; when the Hertzian waves are transporting human thought beyond the oceans with the promptitude of magical events; when a ship can plunge beneath the ocean with its "subtle and powerful" machines, deadly weapons and skilled crew, and then swim in the depths, a monster unexpected by the marine gods; at a time when the sovereignty of nascent trust is perhaps effacing from history all the ancient prides of monarchs, peoples and clergies; at a time, finally, when the old Adam formed of planetary clay is transforming himself, an entire literature, in France, is singing exclusively about bread and wine, the little white house decked with foliage, the odor of ploughed fields, the savor of naïve kisses, the timidity of simple souls, the bliss of ignorance, and the petty sensations dozing in the corner of the modest hearth. Far from choosing for the object of its preoccupations and its songs the formidable new gods and genii unsuspected by the legends of defunct ages, the youth of poets roams the meadows,

---

1. Paul Adam (1862-1920) achieved his greatest fame with a series of historical novels set during and after the Napoleonic Wars, begun with *La Force* (1899). He had earlier collaborated with the Symbolist poet Jean Moréas on the novel *Les demoiselles Goubert, moeurs de Paris* (1886), which was specifically intended to fuse the supposedly rival schools of Naturalism and Symbolism.

clutching the moist fingers of lovers. It grows tender before the happy cottage, like sensitive women a hundred years ago. It seems to want to ignore the Messiahs or the Scourges that are resplendent on the horizon of the future.

It is necessary to admire that faculty of reaction in an entire laborious and enthusiastic generation. Already, excellent works honor it. Francis Jammes, Saint-Georges de Bouhelier, Fernand Gregh, Maurice Leblond and others have expressed in the best fashion the reveries of their musical art. But it is surprising that a constellation has not assembled alongside them that aims to proclaim the epoch of mechanical and fluid forces. I am astonished that Alfred Jarry can have no rivals.

It is important that a literary school should form, somewhat akin to those Oriental poets whose magnificent amazement admires the combat of giants, the apparitions of lightning, the wrath of the firmament and the emotions of mountains. We lack bards capable of crying their emotion before the awakening of Prometheus in sublime verses, of showing him breaking the chains of the Caucasus where he was once crucified by the jealous gods, then killing the vulture that kept him weak and sterile, and finally surging forth to manipulate imponderable and prodigious fluids once again. Here he is, ready to vanquish distance and space, to unleash upon the planet a livestock of iron and steel, capable of running vertiginously over the ground and of plunging profoundly through the waves. We lack temple-poets who will sing the new mystery, in the fashion of a Firdaussi. We are awaiting our Ramayana, which will praise the Titans of science, prophesying their victory over the gods of anthropomorphism and their return to the Maternal dwelling: those whose name alone terrified Faust; those who are the guardians of generative fire, of the great Agni.[2]

Whatever attacks might be directed today against Symbolism,

---

2. Adam did make some attempt to found such a school; the works he produced during the 1890s have a significant concern with futuristic utopianism, although it usually remains subsidiary to story-lines set in the present day.

it had, at least, the merit of attempting a leap toward the comprehension of Platonic Ideas, of their willful individuality, of their eternal evolution under the successive appearances of races. The taste for magic, for ancient science, the care to link it to the modern conception, to marry the two, to demonstrate their relationship by literary rather than philosophical means; those were noble hopes. I regret that that task, of reaching for difficult and arduous truth, seems to be neglected by youth. I once imagined that the beauty of the contemporary struggle would inspire a few Latin Edgar Poes, that it would incite them to resume the efforts of Arthur Rimbaud and Jules Laforgue, of Francis Poictevin, of our modern mystics, rather than abandoning to the overly objective talents of Rudyard Kipling and H. G. Wells the honor of immortalizing the gigantic combat of contemporary humankind against the natural powers, and conquests unparalleled in the history of anterior epochs.

So, when a writer becomes manifest whose audacious talent is not discouraged by the quest for the strange, for that which our unconscious divines beyond the reflections that agitate on the walls of the cave, an excessively rare joy enchants my mind.

Frédéric Boutet appeared in the world of letters a few years ago. His *Drames baroques et mélancoliques* were, if I am not mistaken, among the first gestures of his salutation. I believe that it remains the best, although, since then, other notorious books have won their author legitimate admiration. The temerities of an excessive Romanticism have not prevented the appreciation of the beautiful philosophies inscribed in the symbols of those tragic tales. Frédéric Boutet's pessimism is not languid and nonchalant. It is a kind of continuous snigger. If the macabre were not rattling his bones and his fleshless jaws, one might think that Leonardo da Vinci's John the Baptist were becoming transparent in the mist of unique and precise nightmares, his divine smile wickedly indulgent to human faiths. That enigmatic face is present is present in the room where the prostitute and the two undertakers mutes converse, and the resuscitated man whom they so bravely, in order not to give way to the treachery of the illusory, pack away in the coffin, the matter having been agreed and decided by the physician of the dead, the agent of the civil estate and the drunkenness of the vigil-keepers. That enigmatic face presides over the natural and atrocious sciences that enjoy themselves in the tavern where, in a foreshortening that one might call Shakespearian, all the essentials of hellish life agitate.[3]

Among the other fables in that extraordinary collection, I firmly believe that those two demand, by their robust, extraordinary artistry, the legitimate applause of the most meticulous critic. There are essays in high literature there. Certain passages evoke in the memory the words of Ahasverus, as Quinet relates them in the course of his illustrious poem. It is outrageous, for the renown of our theater, that no one has attempted to make the public appreciate the life and forms of these two parables, their profound meaning. Furthermore, I do not know a book in which superior irony plays more cruelly with out paltry lives, our precarious virtues, our egotisms concocted with the antidotes of sentiment.

These *Contes dans a nuit* owe their excellence to analogous merits. The same taste for the strange appears there in a fashion that fortifies the mind. Oedipus and the Chimera are at grips on every page. Anxiously, human curiosity interrogates the aspect of the mystery that deceives us.

Behind the ordinary actions and events of life, common to all of us—love, illness and death—our mind suspects, and, at certain times glimpses, the mocking personality of unknown laws called gods by religions, physical forces by modern occultists, errors by the naïve pride of scientists incapable of admitting the reality of what their instruments do not register, of that which their meticulous and myopic observations do not grasp. Plato and Iamblichus explain, the former directly and

---

3. It is perhaps odd that Adam should select for special praise two of the stories from the collection in question that are not reproduced in the sampler that he is introducing. I have, however, included translations of both of them in the second volume of the present set.

the latter subtly, by means of theological figures, the probable vigor of those whims that one sometimes senses nearby, even in an empty and silent room. Thus we allow ourselves to be persuaded that far from us, in a suprasensible world, either good or ill fortune is developing with our intention. The anguish sometimes becomes strong enough to render us breathless, or the hope sufficiently ridiculous to constrain us to quit our seat and stir in a singular fashion, as if we were already holding the object of our desire. We discern even in the appearance of material things—furniture or walls—certain fugitive signs of hilarity or hatred. The eye of a keyhole imposes itself upon us. The gleam of a bronze fist mocks. Portraits lavish the clear and worthy gaze of their defunct mentalities upon us. The feeble armchair consoles us with its welcoming gesture and invites us to meditate, in accordance with the theory of Epicurus. The window becomes Spinozan and the chair Darwinian, while the door allows the impenetrable mask to remain on the face of the unknown that it dissimulates, and which might come in and reveal itself at any moment. The door remains, eminently, the emblem of religions.

If we go outside the dwelling, people's faces and the actions of passers-by similarly betray the mysterious actions of the hyperphysical. In a tumult of various facts, either the fatality of ancient tragedy or, when the drama put on the false nose of vaudeville, the irony of John the Baptist always appears. Shakespeare has established these two faces miraculously, the face of mocking laughter and the face of fear, appropriate to all the expressions of life. In the dread shadow of every murder, an irony slips away. There is no masquerade without consumption coughing, fever wandering, debt gnawing, envy biting and hatred breathing beneath the disguise. Between the joined lips of lovers, there is room for the ignominies of cupidity and the murderous appetites of jealousy. It is already their blood that they are licking, beneath the epidermis of the mouth, while awaiting the veritable tally-ho of the end of passion, anticipating the cynical moment of treason, abandonment and vengeance.

The contrary god always breaks through the enchantments of merriment, the crêpes of despair. Janus is the veritable effigy of the humanity that understands itself totally, as a complete phenomenon, with neither affirmation nor negation, in the hyperabstract identity of its contrariety.

The art of Frédéric Boutet is marvelously obstinate in making felt, and even understood, the veritable life that parades beneath the ephemeral masks of individuals, behind the conflicts of beings, the emotions of groups. He is a Janus of letters himself. singular, troubling and magnificent. He is a son of Shakespeare, Goethe and Quinet, who fills his puppets and phantoms, his fleshy humans, his adventurers and whores, and his Julius Pingouins with divinity.

The task seems to devolve to him of some day undertaking the miraculous poem that will be sung of the reawakening of Prometheus, the revenge of the Titans against Olympus. He is, at this moment, the French writer most apt to earn us the triumphs that the Poes, Kiplings and Wellses attribute to their homelands. Here, I think, are the preliminary and suggestive verses of that poem.

THE LAST ADVENTURE

The sand of my life has run out;
the thread of my days is woven;
this prodigy is gazing at me....
Thomas of Erceldoune[4]

On the night of the solstice, the first snows enveloped the country.

The snow, flying from the black sky in light swirls, rose up virginal and mute over the limitless plain.

Along the road bordered by fir-trees, black and white phantoms, a fully-armored knight was driving his weary horse, and the flakes wove them a heavy robe.

Alone in the magical silence of that darkness, enveloped by diffuse gleams rising from the ground, the man was deeply sad. He was returning from Egypt, after years of massacres and perils. He was returning, a stranger to his own homeland, sick and poor, and the hope in God that had sustained him for so long had gradually withdrawn from his soul, leaving despair and regret.

The horse slackened its pace, and the rider, allowing the reins to hang loose, lulled by the rhythmic movement, sensed

---

4. The Scottish laird Thomas Learmonth (c1220-c1298), alias Thomas the Rhymer or True Thomas, obtained a contemporary reputation as a prophet, reputedly producing many prophetic verses, but the published examples are probably all apocryphal. His greatest fame is that of being the hero of one of the greatest Scottish ballads, whose story is either an adaptation or the source of the similarly-famous English ballad "Tam Lin."

the soft white deluge drawing around and over him like a fugitive and endless net. The cold intoxicated him, in the dazzle of luminous waves that quivered beneath his strides. He felt weary and languid, gripped by an unknown charm, and he dreamed without fear of the sleep of death....

Suddenly, in the distance, a flamboyant light appeared, like a beacon fire lit between the fir-trees.

Immediately, he was torn from his torpor. The instinct of life gripped him again, in the terror of that mortal solitude; he spurred his horse toward the light and human existence, in order to ask for shelter.

He reached a castle outlining its slender forms against the sky. A narrow window at the top of the central tower was projecting an intense light. Suddenly, it went dark.

In the powerful wall of the façade there was an iron door at the top of broad steps, which the horse climbed. The man drew his dagger and knocked with the hilt, producing a resounding noise that bounded through the icy air to fade away in the distance.

Then the heavy metal jaws parted, and the newcomer was dazzled by the yellow light of twenty torches carried by valets between the red walls of a stone vestibule. On the threshold, in front of squires armed from head to toe, was a tall old man clad in a black robe open over a coat of mail. The cold night air, entering with snowflakes, stirred his white hair. He made a gesture of genuflection before the cavalier and said: "Oh my Lord, greetings to you! Until the hour when the winter flowers turn to spring flowers, the hours are yours. Until the hour when hope turns to snow, the pleasure is yours. When you see the night flowing away, it is your death."

He turned round and, gripping the horse by the bridle, tilting back his head and throwing his arms wide, he cried beneath the sonorous vaults: "The Master is here! The Master is here! Our Seigneur has come!"

The entire castle was filled by his powerful voice. The joyful sound of bells burst forth from turrets, and the valets in the vestibule waved their torches, and the squires brandished their sparkling swords. They all cried: "The Master is here!" And they hastened around the man, who was rendered mute by astonishment.

He dismounted, and the old man led him through a stone gallery, escorted by seven torch-bearing valets, to an ebony door that opened wide.

There was an immense, solemnly magnificent hall. The high walls and the majestic dome of the ceiling were covered in red velvet, bearing stars and crescent moons in its higher parts, with zodiacal figures mingled with arabesque designs on the walls, all in embossed red gold, as were the carved crampons retaining the fabric whose heavy folds fell to a cedar-wood parquet. At the back, the vast steps and winding banisters of a stairway rose up in the midst of waves of velvet disposed as an awning. To the right, beneath the sculpted mantel of a gigantic fireplace, the moving splendor of blazing logs flickered above mighty andirons raising the heads of gilded serpents hieratically.

Amid the tumultuous, illuminating and sparkling flames, like a wild flash in the living light or like a pale gaze in the parted half-light, the strange figures on the walls and the stars on the ceiling caught reflections. Above everything else, at the summit of the vault, there was a great globe of burnished gold, like a sun surrounded by mist.

In the center of the hall there was an oval table. On the embroidered linen of the dazzling cloth, a profusion of rare victuals was offered on golden plates, among the candelabras from whose long wax rods gleams erupted, multiplied by the polychromatic faces of goblets and the transparences of crystal glasses.

There were bloody meats, roasted game and fat poultry. There were fish, skillfully filleted and ornamented, pink hams, thick sauces, pâtés of spicy mincemeat. In white and veined faience there were perfumed creams and aromatic preserves; in light baskets freshly-tinted fruits and bloody oranges were stacked. Numerous bottles stood there, full of the bright ruby and topaz of precious wines. And the aroma of the foodstuffs exasperated the voyager's hunger.

At the table, surrounded by pages and attendants, a prodigiously beautiful young woman was sitting. Her black hair, bound up in bands of gold alternated with pearls, undulated over the pallor of her temples, and was gathered at the nape of her neck. A double flat-linked chain, emerging from the headdress, supported a limpid emerald that sparkled on her white forehead, beneath the dark hair, above large eyes as green and radiant as itself. A similar stone sealed the golden girdle around her waist, tightening a scarlet velvet tunic that parted in elongated curves over a satin dress the color of water, decorated with darker flowers, over which, at every undulation, a fugitive and charging reflection ran. The corsage, of the same glaucous satin, fitted exactly to the upper body, opened in a sharp, low-descending slit, bordered by soft lace clouding the warm whiteness of near-naked breasts, from which rose a troubling perfume, as fresh as those of the fields, as voluptuous as those of the Orient. And there, a third emerald, on a necklace of golden beads, scintillated in the moist shadow. Scarlet sleeves pinned by diamonds on the shoulders and draped in long folds uncovered arms molded to the elbows in white silk, which terminated in a flood of lace falling over ungloved hands, and sometimes, during elevated gestures, turning back in such a manner that the slender lightly-ringed fingers and the slim wrists circled by sonorous bracelets, emerged like a flower from its calyx.

Meanwhile the old man cried in the vast hall: "The Master is here! The Seigneur our Master has come!"

The young woman stepped forward and said, with a smile in which the flash of her teeth lit up her lips: "Be welcome, my dear Seigneur! You have been away from me for a long time."

The cavalier did not speak, for he knew that he had never seen the woman before, and believed that he was being suborned by the Devil.

"Must I believe that you had forgotten me, or that you have preferred another?" she added, with a movement of the head that troubled the voyager's soul, into which the caresses of the voice and the eyes descended like a powerful narcotic, numbing surprise and dread. "I know, however, that that is impossible!"

He put his hand in the chatelaine's hand, and allowed her to guide him. In a neighboring room ornamented with tapestries and bright furniture, servants washed him with scented water, perfumed his beard and hair, and replaced his heavy breastplate with a robe of black silk ornamented with gold, red and silver embroideries.

"Behold, my dear Seigneur," said the young woman. "I am the one who embroidered all the designs for you—all the elaborate and mysterious designs! Oh, very mysterious, in truth, but not as mysterious as my soul. Does it not please you?"

"Yes, truly," he replied, having now lost all astonishment, "it pleases me. But are your beautiful eyes not weary?"

"My eyes are not weary," she said, leaning over and dazzling him, through her long lashes, with her large irises, in which the fires of all the torches were golden dots.

She led him to the table and he sat down. A squire, his arms at full stretch, brought a golden platter bearing a majestic roasted peacock, ornamented with its deployed plumage.

The feast was prodigious, and the voyager lost all memory of the past in the heady aromas of old wines and succulent meats, in the aphrodisiac perfumes of unknown beverages, the delicious excitation of which invaded his brain.

Afterwards, climbing the stairway illuminated from the height of bronze torch-holders, he was conducted to a round room situated in the middle of solemn apartments—a room without windows, in which soft, diffuse and indolent light expanded from globes scarcely-visible beneath green scarves, like vapor on a lake, rolling its warm and musky waves beneath the ellipse of the padded ceiling.

The decoration of the room was entirely green, with bright or changing colors, profound or light, dressing the walls with cameo shades, lacquering the sides of voluptuous items of furniture with gleams, reflecting infinities of glaucous pools in large mirrors, constellating the soft crushed velvet wall-hangings with buds of aquamarine and chrysoprase, quivering over the silky plush and marbled satin. Roses were dying in jade urns.

And she was lying softly naked in the caressing silks of the bed, her face drowned in dark hair, in the vaporous light that bathed her beauty.

In that love-making, the voyager discovered superhuman joys. He savored subtle caresses the she alone knew, silent kisses that resorbed life, profound embraces in which he wanted to die. There were astonishing returns of sensations already experienced, once lived, and now possessing him again, tenaciously and sensibly manifest, in the same décor.

He thought he was in a wood beside a cool spring on a spring evening, breathing the fresh perfumes of flowers, mingled with the aromas of fermenting seeds. He was at the commencement of his youth, and sensed a new life swelling his muscles and lifting his breast. An invincible need for love invaded him with a cruel and delicious ardor. Lying on the living ground, he sobbed, strangely proud of being a man, full of imprecise sadness and joy, aware of nothing but the powerful tenderness of the spasm in which nascent nature was quivering around him.

He thought he was on the soft sand of an Egyptian beach, at the end of a night of which the marvelous charm and the adorable silence, over the serene sea, had gradually overwhelmed him with a mad desire, as strong as the sea, as unfathomable as the night, to abandon his terrestrial life to melt into the radiant oblivion whose majesty was crushing him…and he was ready to die when the first splendors of the sun streamed forth, hurling him back to existence, frightened by having desired death, desperate at not having dared to grasp it.

Then there was the nave of a Roman cathedral, full of religious song and the vapors of incense. He received the host and sank into a plenitude of hope and faith, which raised him up toward the heavens with the liturgical purity of the hymn and the perfume.

Lust came: a Jewish prostitute he had known in Jerusalem

for seven days, and whom he had fled in a moment of satiation. In an oriental chamber, he found himself drunk on a mysterious brew of aromatic plants, the taste of which was still on his palate. He stretched himself out on the musky-perfumed tiger-skins covering his divan. The courtesan caressed him. He contemplated, with his visionary eyes, scarcely-veiled dancers, plump and hairless, swaying to the rhythm of monotonous music in the heady effluvia emerging from golden incense-burners in the hands of naked girls....

Then he had impressions of childhood, impressions of dreams. He saw his life again, and beyond life....

In those kisses, in those embraces, in those perfumes, his soul, becoming delirious, hesitated on the threshold of a mysterious world, an enchanted Eden, which the love of that woman revealed to him as in a dream, the veil of which she lifted with her marvelous hands, with caresses gentler than those of flower petals....

His mistress covered him with her profound hair, drew his weary head to her quivering throat, cradled him with amorous words. She fixed her magnificent eyes upon him, full of desire and languor. Her smile was a lascivious charm. She leaned over her lover and enchanted him with the adorable caresses of her silky lips, her snowy hands and her supple naked body...impregnating his entire heart with a divine perfume of irresistible voluptuousness and triumphant amour that was her own, rising from herself, born of her transports, floating in her embraces....

He slept, however, without knowing how many hours passed.

When he awoke, he found himself in the banqueting hall. The hangings were now pink moiré silk, the fireplace was curtained and, between its pillars of white marble there was a profusion of flowers, gathered like an immense and delightfully odorous bouquet.

Before the traveler, his mistress, smiling, was leaning on the mantelpiece. Over her shoulders, her hair, speckled with white roses, flowed in free curls. Her body seemed naked beneath a long dress of white silk, lined with swansdown and garnished with pearls, open in a square over the bosom, fitted to the breasts and hips, and from then on reminiscent of an inverted tulip, falling in straight and ample lines to the ground.

On her forehead there was a lactescent opal; another clasped her pearl necklace, and a third fastened her silver girdle.

At the back of the room, two large windows were wide open. Soft light breezes came in. Outside, it was a spring noon.

The traveler was suddenly gripped by a great desire to savor the charm of the day in the countryside. He said so to his mistress. She sighed and smiled, replying: "Yes, you ought to go down into the valley now—into the valley, where the sun is bringing the woods into flower. For myself, I shall stay here, and ornament myself for your return, my beloved."

He left on horseback, in spite of his regret at abandoning, for however short a time, the woman he loved more than anything else. He rode forth, looking around, and the tender freshness of the new foliage saddened him, although he did not know why.

He saw that he was in a profound valley, the only exit of which was blocked by the manor. He contemplated the high hills outlined against the clear sky. None of that astonished him, for no memory of his past life existed in him any longer.

He wandered for some time, and finally came to the foot of one of the hills, not far from a torrent, the foaming waves of which were howling in the depths of a ravine. The cavalier attempted to climb up to the summit of the mountain, climbing the steep slopes. He climbed for some time, with ever-increasing difficulty, amid the fir-trees and livid rocks, the mocking faces of which frightened him. The memory of his mistress faded within him as he advanced, and the old reality returned and grew in the torment and the fear. Soon, it became impossible to continue his ascent, the rocks being vertical and bare. He turned back in order to look for another way out, for he was agitated by terror and utterly resolved to flee, that same day, what he regarded as the death of his soul.

He went back down, therefore. Then, the memory of his love came back to him, becoming stronger at every step, causing the desire to flee to decline along with the fear. So, when he was in the valley, he did not attempt a further climb, for he thought that on the heights he would forget his mistress again, and might be able to escape. And he would have preferred eternal damnation to that, for she was his God.

Darkness was already occupying the gorges and climbing the foothills, gradually rising up toward the sky. The cavalier made haste, in order to return to his amours sooner. On the pathways, surrounded by flowering bushes, light perfumes floated around him. White petals were strewn on the ground everywhere, and their rain, fluttering in the breeze, covered him. Soon, ablaze with the last gleams of a sunset as sumptuous as the sunsets of autumn, the manor appeared to him.

On the threshold, he dismounted. Serving men and women, pages and squires were standing in large numbers in the vestibule. Weeping and lamenting, they were crying: "The Master is dead! Our Seigneur is dead!"

The traveler spoke to them, but they did not reply and did not appear to see him. Alone, he followed the marble gallery, marching in the mortal cold falling from the high walls, assailed by a melancholy he could not dispel. The great hall appeared, as if buried beneath a somber violet velvet, which bore, in silver, the knight's coat of arms and motto. The ebony parquet was bare. In the center there was a great catafalque.

On the funereal bed, the form of a coffin was discernible beneath the drapery.

Around it were a dozen squires carrying gigantic torches with ruddy flames, burning without glare, with a singular livid glow that lingered upon the somber velvet, further emphasizing its obscurity.

Twenty guards, helmeted and armored, with bucklers on their arms and swords in their iron-gauntleted hands, surrounded the torch-bearers. At the front, the old man who had greeted the traveler the day before was standing in his iron armor and his black robe.

Beside him, upright in a tunic the color of night, streaming without attachments from the neck to the ground, stood the young woman. A large violet veil was before her face, only allowing a glimpse of her beauty, ornamented with the sickly gleam of three identical stones, round pale amethysts attached by black pearls.

Beneath the resonant vaults, the sound of a bell, striking resounding notes at equal intervals, tolled in the silence, fading away to be born again, and dying once again. As the traveler advanced into the hall an aromatic odor penetrated him, and he recognized the perfume of tombs. At the same moment, the old man cried at him, in a terrible voice: "The Master is dead! The Master is dead! Here is the man who was the Seigneur our Master, now defunct and buried!"

The squires waved their torches. The guard, striking their bucklers with their swords, made a great din. They all cried: "The Master is dead! The Master is dead!"

The man, witnessing these things, felt his soul upraised by a prodigious emotion, by the consciousness of an inevitable destiny. The words with which the old man had greeted him came back to his memory for the first time, and he realized that they were prophetic.

He penetrated the augury of the white petals of the bushes of the pathways, the opals that his mistress had worn. He looked at her, and understood the livid amethysts, emblems of mourning. He gazed at the hall, the guards, and the torch-bearers. He looked at the old man. He contemplated once again, through the veil, the pale visage of the woman he adored. But a strange anguish rent his heart, for the mouth had an expression of bitter grief, and the divine eyes, lowered until then, looked up at him without seeing him.

Now, those eyes had also taken on, marvelously, the veridical and fatal color of amethysts…and, burning with passion, drowning in joy, they seemed to be swooning in voluptuous intoxication.

He marched toward the catafalque. He climbed the steps and threw back the mortuary cloth, uncovering the bier, which was empty. He lay down upon it. He placed his sword alongside him, beneath his hand. He pulled the velvet folds over his weapons. Thus, he buried himself, and, with his eyes closed, his face turned toward the heavens, he remained lying, without moving.

The monotonous knell rolled under the vaults. With a martial racket, the swords collided with the bronze bucklers. The old man, the guard and the torch-bearers all cried in unison: "The Master is dead! The Master is dead!"

After them, the Lady spoke. Her voice was desolate but, to the buried man, it seemed to be fainting with love, and identical to the one she had manifested when she moaned voluptuously in his kiss.

She said: "Oh, my beloved, come back...death cannot match my love...."

He died.

THE VERITABLE VICTORY

And I struggled desperately in
spirit with the grim Azrael....

Edgar Allan Poe, *Ligeia*

In the darkness, the man, hidden by his black cloak, marched along the deserted quay beside the river.

To the right, at the bottom of the riverside walls, the water ran, as deep and tranquil as that of a canal. In places, oblique staircases descended. Red beacon lights blazed on moored boats. The opposite bank was only indicated by the distant patches of yellow lanterns and the illuminated windows of invisible houses.

Bordering the broad quay to the left, the old houses loomed up, with their gray façades, their iron-barred doors and their long, narrow windows, mostly dark or shuttered. In the shadow of the ensemble, a faint light filtered from some through thick curtains or cracks in Venetian blinds. At intervals, the dimly-lit corner of a solemn room could be glimpsed, with its large severe portraits and its profiled oak furniture.

Sometimes, separating the old houses, there were long dilapidated garden walls, above which the grimacing branches of trees seemed to be gazing curiously at the passer-by. Occasionally, set back in an obscure side-street, a hanging lantern projected its moving light over the top of a wall; here and there, at the top of a flight of steps, a bronze door surmounted by a motto or a title carved on a coat of arms, marked, along with the morose grandeur of the edifice, the hereditary palace of one of the noble families of the old city.

Dusk had not long fallen: a foggy November twilight in which livid clouds ran across the moonless sky, pursued by gusts of wind, like large fantastic flocks emigrating precipitately.

And beneath the clouds and the nocturnal wind, in the barely-troubled silence, the city of ancient splendors rested in its mysterious and venerable antiquity.

The man, however, contemplating all of that as something familiar, increased his rapid pace. He passed a bridge and soon, stopping on the threshold of a narrow house, opened a low door with steel bolts.

The vestibule was vast, illuminated by a ruddy lamp suspended from the vault. At the back, a stairway extended its flat banisters and is broad steps. He went up to the third floor, which was the uppermost. Approaching the arched door beneath the lamp and the sculpted lintel, he knocked three times. A moment went by. He knocked again and, as a dull sliding sound was heard inside, he threw back his cloak and took off his hat. His features were visible in the faint light. His face was pale, but his eyes, eyebrows and beard were entirely black.

A Judas-hole opened, and then the door, with the numerous sounds of locks and chains.

He went in. In front of him was an old woman wearing a nun's head-dress and habit. As she took his cloak, the newcomer appeared, clad in black; on his white hands, from which he removed his gloves, rings sparkled with the various gleams of their stones.

He pushed back the long hair covering his forehead and looked at the old woman.

"Yes," the woman said, "she's waiting for you. She's waiting for you in her shroud. But why must I repeat that every time? Don't you know, then, that she's waiting for you—in her shroud, alas? That she's always ready, and that it's me, a poor old woman, who always prepares her, and who will burn with you for centuries in hell because of it? But who can resist you, and why do I bother to say that? You're not listening to me! Take care, though—there might come a night when it's true!"

Paying no heed, as if to vain words heard every day, the visitor went past. In a small dressing-room, lit by long candles between mirrored panels, he got undressed, put on a long robe of black silk, perfumed himself, and quit the place.

A violent emotion agitated him. He seemed paler; his lips were taut and his hands tremulous. And the opium he had taken before coming began to invade his brain with a dreamlike and concentrated ardor.

Now he found himself in a square room garnished with broad divans and ebony furniture. Pale, brocaded with silver corollas, the violet silk of the wall-hangings dressed the ceiling, hung down in curtains over the windows and hid the door. To the right, there was a vast draped mirror; to the left, a silent clock; sheaves of roses inclined in bronze vases; the carpet reproduced the ornamentation of the drapes. A lamp on a side-table spread a vaporous light through a globe tinted with pink and mauve.

Going to the back of the room, the man moved one of the wall-hangings aside, uncovering a deep alcove draped with white velvet attached by silver cords. It was occupied by an ivory bed, completely white, with lace pillows and satin sheets, its curtains made of immaculate batiste.

A young woman of great beauty was lying there, motionless. The snowy quilt rose to the undersides of her beasts, whose firm roundness stood out beneath the silver silk tunic tightened and wrinkled around the bosom. The delicate neck was surrounded by a triple row of pearls; a silk headband framed the translucent pallor of the face and veiled the hair.

She remained motionless, her hands folded beneath the throat that did not appear to be agitated by any breath. White roses were scattered on the bedclothes; an ivory crucifix had been placed between the breasts. A silver night-light illuminated her beauty softly. Perfumes saturated the warmth.

The visitor contemplated the woman, and an immense grief was born within him, and the violent disturbance of sensual emotions, for she was desirable beyond all expression, and offered the perfect image of death. It seemed that those long eyes would never raise their translucent lids again, that those pink lips, so slightly parted over the gleam of teeth, would never open again to kisses. It seemed that the bare arms, circled with pearls and silver, would never uncross their delicate hands in order to embrace the man she loved…that she had loved.…

Under that lamp, had her life not yielded its last sighs? Were the flowers that covered her not the flowers of death, the crucifix the one that would go with her into her coffin, and her adornment that which would prepare her for the eternal marriage with the Angel of Death?

Gradually, he submitted to the illusion. Kneeling beside the bed, looking at her passionately, he lost consciousness of the reality. The opium and the perfumes in the warmth of that closed alcove enveloped him like vertigo. Despair descended upon his heart, and also a sensual desire that grew with every passing second. He wept; he had seized one of the woman's hands and was caressing her bare arm. And in his soul, lust and despair, love and death, intermingled.…

He undid the headband over the black curls. He contemplated the beautiful visage, and, within the illusion to which he had surrendered complete credulity, a vehement hope rose up, redoubling the irresistible desire—the sacrilegious desire, now. He was beside her, kissing her slightly parted lips, recklessly embracing the supple and slender body. And the hair spread out like a flood over the lace, and the parted tunic uncovered all the secret beauties.

He thought: *What does tomorrow matter? She is beautiful tonight; she is all mine; and I shall love her until I vanquish death!*

He possessed her in a voluptuous delirium multiplied tenfold by opium. Now the lips parted further to render kisses and moan with love; the supple arms reached out for reckless embraces; the translucent eyelids allowed the blue of the large eyes to pass through, and voluptuous tears to flow. And from her entire being, a divine perfume of love rose up.…

For him, hallucinated by powerful sensations, sensing life born beneath his kiss, he swooned, in a boundless voluptuousness, in an extraordinary pride, and thought:

My love has been torn from the tomb! Once again she is alive! Once again…and I am the master of death!

What the man was doing that night he had done on many previous nights, always drunk on opium, in that white alcove, with that woman waiting for his kiss in the languorous ambiguity of her beauty, ornamented for the tomb like a virgin dead before her first taste of love. And in truth, he must have accomplished it several more times, since it was not until the last evening of the present year that he came for the last time.

A mystical snow was falling over the old city in the darkness. The flakes were dressing everything in virginal robes; their fluttering fall was engulfed in the black waters of the river, as tranquil as a canal—and the old city was utterly mute.

Through the snow he walked, already invaded by the opium, whose strange visions populated the moving curtain gliding around him.

He went into the house beyond the bridge and climbed the stairs. He knocked and, as usual, the old woman opened the door. She seemed agitated by terror and more troubled than usual, but the visitor, occupied with his thoughts, did not notice anything.

She said: "What, it's you! I hoped that you wouldn't come… but I don't know why I hoped that, for I knew full well that tonight, she was to wait for you, and I know full well that you always come…but it's necessary that you not go to her. She's in her shroud, she's ready for the tomb, and this evening, it's the truth. It happened a short while ago. My God, a very short while ago. Alas, it's me, poor woman, who has laid her out, and who'll rejoin her in eternity where she'll burn, if I let you in. But you will go in, for I'm talking in vain; you're not listening to me at all, and who would dare resist you? But know this: tonight, it's the truth...."

He did not hear and had already gone past. She was left to her lamentations.

He was in the violet room, then the alcove. Everything was exactly as it always was.

The woman who was still lying in chaste whiteness, under the nebulous lamp, looked like a statue lying on a tomb. She had the same pallor, the same immobility. She was what she was every time. If her lips were less rosy, her eyelids whiter, her bare arms colder in spite of the perfumed heat, her lover did not realize it. So he did what he always did; he sought and found a limitless despair—a despair that he succeeded in rendering veritable. Desire gripped him....

She was in his arms and beneath his kiss....

But he exhausted himself in vain in gluing his lips to the pale mouth; she did not part her own any more. In vain, he caressed the voluptuous body passionately, but she did not quiver and her arms did not return the embrace. The translucent eyelids remained closed over the large blue eyes, the little feet were icy, the limbs became ever colder, ever heaver. And the veridical power that she had formerly simulated for the man's pleasure reigned over her beauty irremediably.

Perhaps it was because that night, in spite of the voluptuousness of his caresses, he was unable to love her enough. Perhaps, instead, it was because she, who had played dead so many times, was finally curious to know it in reality; or even because, plunged in the horror and terror of her game, she wanted to make it a reality by way of expiation....

At any rate, the visitor was obliged to recognize that the old woman, in the words that he had misunderstood, was not mistaken, and that it was the truth. Then, without illusion, he permitted himself to experience the heart-rending distress of that which is irreparable. And the desire was dead, slaked.

Thus were abolished the last links that retained that man in life. He opened one of his rings and took the poison that he kept in it like a faithful hope. He embraced the woman who was no longer lying. He kissed the lips that he had loved so much…and his weary head fell upon the bare breasts, in the final vertigo, the final intoxication.…

And for his definitive and veritable victory, the Angel came.…

FLORENCE

Turn to me your eyes full of azure and stars!
For one of those charming glances, balm divine,
On pleasures more obscure I shall lift the veil.
And I shall go to sleep in an endless dream....
Charles Baudelaire, Delphine et Hippolyte

Florence went down the broad marble perron and, turning round, glanced momentarily at the château filled with light. Through the wide open windows she saw the ballrooms with their torches, their hangings of iridescent silk, their flowers in bouquets and garlands, with beautiful and ornamented women. The strains of the orchestra vibrated, softened and lulled by the night....

Alone, Florence plunged into the pathways of the old park, She walked nonchalantly, her satin shoes gliding over the fine sand and her white dress scarcely rustling. Her blonde hair, speckled with pale pink, descended in mobile curls over her shoulders. Her arms were bare under the gauze, and the pearls of her necklace were caressing her neck with a lactescent light. In the centuries-old shadows, she resembled some romantic apparition of another age.

She was only a child, though. Dazed by music, perfumes and light, she allowed herself to be cradled by confused pleasures, by new and profound charms. The sounds of the orchestra could hardly reach her any longer, and everything around her was tranquil and obscure. The odor of acacias and orange-trees enveloped her in a slight languor; the warmth of the night floated over her skin, and all the mysterious melancholy that dwells in old parks, which is the eternal and primitive soul of great trees, descended upon her like the revelation of unknown sentiments. Vague emotion stirred within her.

The château was a long way away, but Florence did not give any thought to that, and, without knowing exactly where she was headed, she followed the paths that she had not seen since infancy.

After a bend, she found herself confronted, at the bottom of a grassy bank, by the lake that occupied the center of the estate. She went down the slope and sat down on a seat of rocks at the very edge of the water.

The lake, a glaucous and somber expanse of velvety appearance, extended in an elongated curve, becoming confused with the darkness in the distance. There was no moon, but a diffuse light emitted by the stars mingled with the mist. The banks, planted with poplars and willows, were strewn with large rocks; reeds, bulrushes and water-lilies flourished in the waters, and far out on the water, a little islet was half-drowned in the dim light. Two white swans floated majestically by, and then disappeared. Everything was delightfully tranquil.

Florence contemplated the nocturnal scene, breathed in the fresh breeze coming from the water and the heady scents of the flowers. She remained motionless, her feet extended on the grass and her head resting in her hand. The seduction of the night penetrated her like an intoxication, and the time went by without her finding the desire to go away, like a virgin retained by an amorous charm.

Then, on the almost-invisible island, she perceived a white form, which became gradually more distinct, advancing over the lake. Soon, she recognized a woman clad in long veils, which were undulating behind her like a wake.

Florence sat still, surprised and tremulous. The woman who was walking over the water was here now. Her face was marked with passion and melancholy, with her large sad and ardent eyes, her red mouth and her pale complexion, surrounded by her black hair, which flowed in waves over her shoulders and breasts, mingled with scarlet flowers.

She knelt down and took the child's hand in her own cold hands. She fixed her dark and passionate eyes upon the blue eyes, and her irises became dolorous; tears flowed, and the unknown visitor buried her face in the little hands she was gripping. Florence felt a warm flood filtering relentlessly between her fingers. A profound emotion penetrated her, and her own tears flowed too, fugitive and brilliant, into the undulating ebony hair on her knees. And they wept together....

Finally, the young woman lifted up her mysterious visage again, smiled in a tender and melancholy fashion, and then drew away toward the island, a white form fading into the bosom of the vaporous night.

Florence fled toward the château.

Three days passed, and on the third night Florence knew that she had to return to the lake.

When she was sitting on the rocks, the one for whom she had come appeared, walking over the immobility of the velvety transparent water. As on the first occasion, she knelt down, placed her arms on the child's knees, and looked at her for a long time, passionately. She put her hands on the blonde hair, murmured some indistinct words—and that was all.

Another three evenings. This time, on the edge of the shore, in the light falling from heavy white clouds, her unknown friend was already there.

She put her arms around the child's neck, and sat down beside her, and spoke to her lovingly.

"You're more beautiful than a radiant night in spring. You're as sadly silent and gentle as the enchanted moonlight; you're as perfumed as the breath of hyacinths. Your face is like an Oriental pearl; your eyes have the depth of a tranquil sea, in which the light of the stars are reflected; you hair has the adorable shade of pale amber and the undulation of waves. Like a flowering rose-bush, your figure is slender and supple. You're completely beautiful, O my soul! No beauty can be proud beside your beauty. I see you like an unparalleled star rising in a sky of hope; like a divine rose growing serenely in the most beautiful country of the land of Love! You come toward my affliction, toward my desire and my solitude, like an angel holding in her marvelous hands the flowers of dreams and ecstasy...."

Thus Florence came to the lake, and the woman who walked on the water uttered particularly delightful words, gentle and tender symbols, in praise of her beauty, to tell her marvelous stories about the unknown or lost magnificences of the land, the sea and the sky. She spoke about real things and unreal things. Her stories possessed the charm of dreams....

She evoked magical landscapes in which monstrous flowers bathed in pools with iridescent reflections, the gardens of Paradises of troubling delights, of unknown Edens full of enchantments that lull the soul with perpetual and ever-changing pleasures.

She talked about the fabulous radiations of subterranean grottoes whose walls are jewels carved by dwarf laborers, the primitive grandeur of solitary forests, the charm of hidden valleys where the perfumed warmth of spring reigns in perpetuity. She described isles of crystal, cascades of silver, singular countries that exist beyond the world of humans. Her voice gave birth to magical palaces, the languorous enjoyment of perfumes, the splendor of light, of fabrics and adornments.

She also spoke of the love whose voluptuousness is boundless and cannot be abandoned by those who know it...but she did not speak about the love of men and only mentioned the unions of eternal virgins who are daughters of the night and the heavens, the great woods, lakes and fountains....

She evoked their kisses and their embraces, the jealous fêtes of their sensualities, their transports, their sobs, their intoxications....

And into Florence's heart, her voice descended like a philter....

The summer ended, however, and Florence was obliged to leave the estate.

The last evening was the eve of the autumnal equinox. The woods and the gardens had taken on the reds of decline. Through a light mist, the moon appeared, round and bright.

Florence shivered in her long cloak, but her unknown companion hugged her and said: "Don't tremble, my love. It's the day of farewell, but after the winter, you'll come back, and we'll love one another more. Remain faithful to me. I shall always adore you, uniquely."

Now, when Florence came back, she was engaged to be married. Until the day of the marriage she did not return to the lake, but on the very evening of the marriage, she could not help leaving the festivities at the château in order to go and see her unknown friend.

Florence loved the man she had married, and loved him as much as the woman whose soul and existence were enigmatic. Her love for the former was simple, gentle and timid by virtue of her virginal innocence. Her love for the latter was profound and confident, also timid, but perhaps of a more immaterial timidity. It was more intimate and more complete, and possessed the charm of secrecy. And that evening, Florence was troubled.

Gliding over the water, the inhabitant of the lake appeared.

"Oh my friend," she said, "so you have finally come back to the one who has remained in sadness, far from your eyes. I have suffered a great deal from your absence, but let us forget past dolors, let us forget solitary despairs; we're together again. You shall accompany me this evening; I want to show you my domain on that island, from which I have so often come to see you. Come—don't be afraid; I'm with you...."

Taking Florence's hand, she drew her on to the motionless water, and, side by side, they walked over the lake, sparkling in the moonlight.

Soon, they reached the island. The banks were overhung by a dense curtain of bushes and trees. The two visitors went along a path that guided them to a large rock. An opening appeared in the wall of stone, and closed again when the visitors had passed through. They followed an inclined gallery in the darkness. Passing through a heavy door, they came into a room of limited extent and not very light. The walls, covered in orange plush studded with silver, inclined at an angle six feet above the ground to form the ceiling. In each corner, a sculpted silver column rose up, extending to the center of the vault. There was a similar ledge at the place where the walls ceased to be vertical. The extent was occupied almost entirely by a vast divan covered with plush similar to that on the walls, supporting a host of crimson cushions. The perimeter of the floor disappeared under similar carpets, with golden arabesques. On the columns hung little lamps, scarcely luminous, and warm perfumes floated in the half-light.

Florence's companion lay down in the middle of the cushions, and drew her toward her. She caressed her slowly, with words of love. She took off hr garments one by one, hugging her to her naked breasts and burning her with her magnetic eyes. Intoxicated, Florence abandoned herself to long kisses, which penetrated her to the heart. She quivered, breathless, swooning on the cushions under the mouth of the woman who was searching for her own joy in hers, who was swooning herself in making her swoon, panting and delirious in a reckless voluptuousness....

Florence, however, remembered her real existence, and wanted to leave. Her friend, without saying anything, guided her to the place where she had approached her for the first time, and watched her draw away, with a singular smile.

In the darkness, Florence, without being aware of the time passing, invaded by a voluptuous lassitude and unable to think, was still shivering with a prolonged frisson.

She saw the château; it was placidly dark. Astonished, she

climbed the perron. The large door opened magically before her, as did the others. She did not see a living soul, and her surprise was mingled with anxiety, but she was still drowning in the seduction of her memories.

Half unconscious, Florence headed toward the nuptial chamber. She crossed the threshold and recognized the furniture and the wallpaper. She saw the bed, lit by a night-light—and lying on the bed was the man she had married, the man she loved. He was asleep, and a woman was lying in his arms who was exactly similar to herself, who was another Florence, sleeping in a disorder of lace, with an expression of confident happiness upon her parted lips.

Then, Florence felt the indolent languor that possessed her vanish. With a bitter dolor, she understood that her real life had ended for her; she understood that she was irredeemably separated from the existing world.

Florence left the room and the château; she fled toward the Lady who lived on the island in the lake, the one in whom her only hope resided.

The night was coming to an end; the trees were exhaling more vibrant scents, and the birds were greeting the daylight, which was already illuminating the high windows of the manor although the park was still dark.

Florence thought despairingly of all those she loved on the earth and whom she would only love in future in another self. She thought about her past existence, about her dreams of the future, which were irrevocably detached from her…and she walked, weeping, along the paths.…

But the memory of her mysterious companion, whom she would never leave again now, made her shiver in the depths of her heart, and she hastened in order to be consoled.…

Having reached the lake, she embraced its extent with a glance, which the first light of morning was bathing with a translucent mist. The undulating waves, the flowery banks, and the shadows of the island were deserted. Florence felt a sharp anguish born within her. She walked fearlessly over the glaucous velvet of the water. She reached the island, and then the rock—but it presented an impenetrable wall to her, in which she searched in vain for the opening that had welcomed her only a little while ago....

She collapsed on the stone in order to sob, a desperate child, imploring from the depths of distress the one who did not come. And in her broken heart, there was no more hope.

At that same moment, in the nuptial chamber of the château, Florence awoke in the arms of the man she had married—and she told him her own story, the story of Florence; she told him about her secret love, her adventure and her abandonment....

But her husband did not believe her, and for him, she was still the one he had chosen, and whom he loved more than himself.

And Florence, the little desolate shadow wandering over the lake and in the park, without hope, without respite, continued to search, always in vain, for her inconstant companion of yore, who no longer loved her, after loving her so much.

THE IDOL

Your joyous speech has despotic words;
Your eyes are so powerful, your aspect so strong,
That the kings of the Orient have said in their hymns
That your redoubtable gaze is the equal of Death....
—Alfred de Vigny

Singularly wild and desolate was the aspect of that forest in the autumnal dusk.

Jean Falmor, urging his horse along indecisive roads, found himself invaded by sentiments of anxiety and melancholy, which, in the darkness that was gradually taking hold, attained an almost superstitions intensity.

The livid light that still lingered here and there left the distances drowned in obscurity, while things close at hand seemed to grow and take on a particular significance. The traveler was unable, without anxiety, to contemplate the old trunks reaching for the sky with their gnarled and leafless branches in all directions, multiplying, gigantic and similar, as far as the eye could see, with an immemorial aspect, with the semblance of knowing all the mysteries of the night and the woods, or the inextricable tangles of brambles and thorns, creeping toward the roads like unknown enemies—and above everything, the enormous crags, whose forms borrowed a human appearance from the vague shadows that hid them, convulsive stone features beneath their tresses of lactic plants and ivy.

In the trees, the cold wind of the November evening howled

without interruption. Heavy fuliginous clouds raced relentlessly over the dark sky, still blood-stained toward the horizon.

The dead leaves heaped on the ground constantly rose up in rapid eddies, some precipitating themselves in unison to the side, while others headed for unknown and various goals, falling slowly back as if too weary ever to set off again—little inconstant things appearing, in their puerile agitation, immediately turned aside, to be feeble creatures in search of happiness.

The centenarian pines scattered their eternal verdure in the wind. Profound groans emerged from the tormented branches, whose stiff and identical movements solemnly cursed the triumph of some unknown enemy. Sometimes, large branches broke. It seemed that the end of the world was nigh.

In the darkness, however, amid the gusts and the melancholy noises, Falmor continued to advance, penetrated by sadness and anguish. Ravines cutting the road obliged him to make continual detours, and soon he could no longer find his direction. Then he wandered at random, oppressed by fear.

He emerged from a profoundly enclosed path and found himself close to a large fire lit against a rock. Several individuals were gathered around the blaze.

The traveler dismounted. In the distance, he could see other similar fires, in a line curving to the right. The beings gathered by the fire did not move aside for him; they did not look at him and did not address a single word to him. He saw them, clad in rags, with unkempt hair and beards. A continual tremor agitated them, like that of senile old age, and yet, for the most part, they did not seem to be very old. They all wore the same expression on their faces, of unconsciousness and imbecility. Some were voraciously eating roots or wild berries. Others were asleep and shivering. Several were sitting down, eyes wide and drooling; sometimes, they grimaced odiously against the flames.

Jean Falmor watched them attentively and experienced a strange impression. The features of all those people displayed the image of lost intelligence. It seemed as if a vigorous genius must once have inhabited those heads and enspirited those now-vacant eyes. In spite of their degradation they inspired the respect that an empty temple soiled by the stigmata of a filthy destination inspires in the midst of disgust.

The traveler remained plunged in thought for a while, and finally touched the arm of the man who was closest to him.

Raising his head, the individual allowed a slow gaze to wander over him. He shook his head and resumed eating. The second did not even make a movement; his tearful eyes continued to stare at the flames while a lamentable laugh twisted his face. Another tried to speak, but only proffered disconnected sounds. Finally, an old man whose long white beard was blowing in the wind exclaimed, in a shrill voice: "Oh, I'm cold! Oh la la, I'm cold!" Then he sobbed, brokenly. Two or three of them threw themselves on the ground then, howling.

The traveler, penetrated by astonishment and horror, left them. With the bridle of his horse wrapped around his arm, he marched toward the second fire. Those in its vicinity were just as miserable and degraded. One was singing a plaintive refrain, another was growling dully like an irritated beast; a few, lying face down, were drinking from a pool of stagnant water. Falmor renewed his attempts, but again obtained nothing but silence or incomprehensible words. Several manifested an evident ill-humor, and one of them showed him his fist, with frightful facial contortions.

He went to the third fire. There, near some of the unknown creatures, was an old man, who was studying them. He was dressed in a monastic habit and holding a horse by the bridle. When Falmor approached him the old man took a few steps toward him and asked him what had brought him there.

The traveler told him about his interminable walk through the forest, explaining how he had got lost, and asked the old man to give him, if he could, an explanation of the strange beings they had before them, and then to put him back on his road. He added that he was a good Christian and strongly inclined to recognize, in the deplorable condition of these people, a particularly odious manifestation of the Devil's malice.

The old man invited him to sit down next to him on a fallen tree-trunk, and began by saying: "You're conversing with the monk Marestote."

The traveler greeted his companion respectfully, for the name of Marestote was attached to a man whose profound virtue and vast, clear-sighted wisdom was famous and venerable.

Marestote continued: "I am Marestote. Those who surround us were the intellectual luminaries of all nations." He indicated the creatures sleeping around him like beasts in their lair. "They include saints who have seen God and philosophers who souls have penetrated the secrets of all ages to create a new wisdom. There are scientists, whose works have driven back mystery, whose words are law in schools. There are artists who were marked by divine genius, prudent and rigorous legislators, erudite doctors who plumbed the secrets of the minds and bodies of human beings.

"I tell you this: those who surround us were the first among men—that is true; as true as it is that they are now the least. All their power has vanished. Nothing remains but the body, deserted by the soul and reverted to the instincts. Nothing exists for them beyond the satisfaction of the primary appetites. The rain falls upon them, the wind lashes them and the cold tortures them. They scratch the earth to find roots and drink from pools. When they suffer, they are content to moan, devoid of the energy to struggle. And they do not even regret what they were, because they have forgotten everything."

Marestote paused, and then continued: "All these men were defeated by the same adversary. The same force broke their prodigious faculties. The same voracious monster has devoured their souls, abandoning their bodies to the condition in which you see them, for the greater power of its fatal power—an eternal enemy, ever vigilant in her perversity: Woman!"

He had pronounced these words with great anger, and Falmor was afraid.

The monk went on: "It is Woman that has made them what they are now. It's her accursed kiss that has vanquished their energies and their thoughts. It's in loving her that they have descended lower than the worst of beasts.

"Alas, since the days of *Genesis*, things have been thus. Why was Man not left solitary? Why that faithless companion, so different and so attractive? Without Woman, everything would be pure and harmonious; voluptuous sobs would no longer trouble the meditations of philosophers and the songs of poets; the perfume of oblations would no longer be combated by the odor of bodies in heat, and the mind of Man would progress in liberty toward the gaze of God without the torment of the flesh.

"Now, the same creature, beast of lust, queen of debauchery, has destroyed all those who surround us. Armed with the lascivious splendors of her body, the perversity of her caresses, the power of her fatal beauty, armed with all the power of love, in the enigma and mystery of her retreat, she has reckoned with their strength...and it is her that I, Marestote, a black monk commissioned by the Pope, must combat in her own domain, and vanquish, if it please God!

"The woman in question lives nearby. In a marvelous palace, the infernal glory of her beauty blossoms. A labyrinth surrounds and defends her habitation, and no one, if he does not have a guide, can cross the entanglement of its similar avenues, or even get out of its monotonous maze. However, I'm convinced that I can reach her, for her pride has never recoiled before a power and a challenge. She has a supernatural knowledge of those who travel to see her, and she never refuses to meet them.

"Men have come from all points of the world. Alerted by dreams or by apparitions, armed with the various forces of their beliefs, of their genius, they have risen without fear to the conquest of the kiss, and their souls have been lost. The most celebrated philosophers and prophets of all religions have come from overseas. I have seen fakirs whose spiritual strength was boundless, whose entire lives had been concentrated in thought, and even they were vanquished.

"I know the story of an Arab magician who knew the most terrible conjurations to command material and immaterial forces. He came, served by two enchanted figures who marched before him. He wore a golden breastplate consecrated to the Angel of the Night and presenting his redoubtable emblems. Serpents coiled around it like tresses of flame, and the center was occupied by a magical visage, the gaze of which no one could support. In his left hand was a lamp taken from the tomb of Solomon. On his head, his black and red cap bore a phoenix plume and the pentacle of Good and Evil.

"So he came, boasting of enchaining that woman by means of invincible charms and reducing her to slavery forever, but no artifice was effective against her. The enchanted figures were immediately subdued, the serpents were annihilated on the vain breastplate, where the redoubtable face remained dead—and the magician was seen walking on his hands and knees and grazing the grass like a beast. He joined those she had already enslaved and who retained, in their stupidity, the sole desire not to leave the vicinity of the place where that woman and her souls dwell.

"Thus, she is haunted by her victims, who maintain fires circling her domain by day and night, and their lugubrious fires burn for her triumph, and their smoke rises up like an incense to her omnipotence....

"I shall destroy these things by constraining her to obedience, for I have come bearing on my breast the image of my crucified God, carved from the wood of the True Cross—and against that, no power will be able to prevail.

"If you want to march with me, man whom celestial foresight has placed on my path, your presence will be salutary for me; your prayers will protect you from any danger and reinforce mine; you shall witness the triumph of the faith and, with me, you shall purify by fire the accursed seductions of which we shall render ourselves masters. You shall be my companion for the battle and for the glory. God will name you among his elect, and when they speak of my victory, men will celebrate your name with mine, saying: that man has also fought and vanquished for the cause of the Most High!"

The old man fell silent.

"I will go with you," said Falmor. "I too have suffered at the hands of a woman. I will go with you, and I shall die, if necessary, in order to serve God and vanquish the sacrilege."

They mounted their horses.

Side by side they advanced, remaining silent. The wild desolation of the country enveloped them with an unquiet sadness.

They reached the foot of a hill and saw a great red wall extending to the right and the left in a long curve. They went along it and came to a vast open gate. Beneath the lintel, an oval violet flame remained suspended in the darkness without emitting any light. As they approached, it descended to within ten feet of the ground.

"This will guide us," said Marestote.

Going through the gate, they followed the fire, which moved horizontally. They were riding over polished scarlet stone between similar walls, vertiginously high. The sky disappeared behind stormy clouds. Sometimes, the moon's wan light shone momentarily, immediately veiled. Enveloping the riders, a furious wind howled along the walls and eddied in the intersections, but the guiding flame was not tormented by it. Thus, they went along oblique, sheer-sided paths, with innumerable turnings. Similar intersections succeeded one another, in which identical avenues opened. Here and there, bridges traversed the meanders of a rapid river, whose obscure waves flowed between red banks.

After more than an hour, they came into a semicircular area cut by the pink marble façade of a château occupying the summit of the hill and presenting a bizarre and elegant style, with numerous sculptures, delicately-excised battlements, an extended peristyle and sculpted silver balconies that sparkled in the sparse rays of moonlight.

They left their horses behind and, guided by the flame, climbed a huge perron, passed through a silver doorway and then, at the far end of a white vestibule, climbed a similar stairway.

In front of them stretched a spacious gallery illuminated

by a multitude of flames of every color, from the brightest to the softest, the palest to the darkest. They floated lazily in warmth saturated with musk and attars of roses, gliding along walls made of ivory, which bore the encrusted images of enormous sulfur-yellow, mauve or sea-green flowers, interlaced arabesques, around indecisive blue-tinted pools populated by fabulous birds, amid lacustrian plants and flowers.

The floor, half-covered in carpets of ermine and glaucous silk, was tiled with ivory. Large corollas of the same substance composed the ceiling, displayed upside-down, attached by their rims, bearing golden pistils. Most of them held a tiny flame. Along the wall to the right was an immense divan draped in pale satin. At the back stood a mirror with three faces, framed in silver. There was an organ to the left, between high windows, whose stained glass, reproducing vague landscapes of walls, was buried beneath silks tinted like the carpets.

As they went forward, the two men saw a somber form leaning against a panel at the extremity of the gallery, toward which the guiding flame floated. They recognized a woman draped in a cloak of violet satin. With her hands, she brought the dark folds back toward the lower part of her face, invisible beneath masses of burnished golden hair, encircled from the temples to the nape by a silver band terminated by two large sapphires, leaving the forehead uncovered.

The flame became immobile above her forehead.

The monk marched resolutely toward her. He stopped, standing up straight in his habit.

"I come," he said, "on behalf of God, the creator of human thought. Woman, I have come to defeat your influence and destroy your power. No adversary, until now, has been able to resist you, whatever his force and whatever his armor. Know that I shall triumph, for I am invincible. I have the chastity of my age; I have the energy of those who count life for nothing; I have the calm and the confidence given by just causes. I am invincible, above all, because I am protected by Jesus, the son of God, God Himself. A piece of his holy and sacred cross, on my breast, reproduces the sign of the Redemption, against which the gates of Hell can never prevail…and I fear nothing.…

"I tell you this: in your palace, which will fall, your glory will be abolished, for you are material, and the spirit of God, which has created you, will destroy you! But it is necessary that the souls that you have enslaved in the bonds of your vices should be liberated. It is necessary that the world's thought be restored to the world. It is necessary to abdicate your hatred and your pride, in order finally to adore the power that you fear and venerate in your rebellious jealousy, which you are avid, above all else, to prostitute, knowing that, alone in the world, it is capable of dethroning the ignominy of your despotism!

"Woman is shame incarnate. Her passions are puerile, her dreams perverse. Promised to Hell, she wants to drag us all thereto by means of the ascendancy given to her by the voluptuousness of her body and the tenderness and cruelty of her heart. She has damned angels. She gives birth to all our dolors and can put them to sleep. There are moments when her embrace becomes the supreme goal. Accursed, and a thousand times accursed are you, prostitute beast, on earth and in heaven!

"For you who are listening to me, the measure is complete. The time of expiation has come. I am your master. It is necessary to obey. Hell burns, life is effaced! Prostrate yourself before the Judge!"

The black monk fell silent.

The woman said to him, with a soft harmonious voice: "I don't understand your words. I only know beauty, my beauty—that alone is important. The souls you demand are not captive, madman! They remain in me of their own accord, in a permanent, every-increasing bliss. They have definitively abandoned their carnal shackles. Various flames, according to their various essences, you can see them floating in this palace—their palace—and I do not want them to leave me, and they do not want to leave me. I can tell you that they are incarnate in me, and also that my beauty is made of their beauty. The weaknesses of the flesh do not exist for us. I am a virgin, and will be forever, and we love one another uniquely. What god would be worthy to move us? What amour could equal our marvelous amours?

"I tell you this: they are speaking to you through my mouth; my beauty is the garden of their delights, and I hold in my hands the keys of Paradise. Do you understand me?"

She raises her head and, parting her arms in a slow gesture, she draws the edges of her somber cloak back to the ivory wall with her fingertips, thus resplendently displaying her naked beauty, her miraculous beauty....

The whiteness of her skin is mat and polished, with a gilded roseate translucency. Above her arched feet, resting on a swansdown carpet, the slimness of her ankles elongates and folds back lazily. Then, there is the gracious grasp of the knee and the voluptuous plenitude of thighs; the skin is as delicate as the most adorable silk, seemingly warm and perfumed, and the delight of its touch must be superior to any other.

The polished curves of the abdomen rise above, without a shadow. The amplitude of the hips widens its roundness to diminish on the slenderness of the waist. The torso swells, and the two breasts extend their pure contours, with their rosy and distant tips and their moist cleavage caressed by the curls of her hair. The arms part in a supple movement, developing their tapering lines as far as the small, half-open hands.

The blonde hair is gathered in undulating masses around the throat; allowing nevertheless a glimpse of the gracious bearing of the neck, it surrounds the pale and symmetrical slightly-elongated oval of the face. Of the forehead only a small section is perceptible, blossoming like the profile on an inverted cup beneath the undulation of the tresses circled by the silver headband, whose sapphires reflect sparkling gleams. The straight and slender nose presents nacreous translucencies.

Between the red lips, of an exquisite precision, the enamel of the teeth is scarcely illuminated. The eyebrows are thinly and emphatically arched. The eyelids, half-raised, disclose the unfathomable light of the gaze that attaches to that of the old man.

The eyes are long, perfectly divided, surrounded by serried blonde lashes curved at their tips. The irises have an astral radiance, and the velvet of flowers. They are violet, changing and profound. Their expression is proud and candid, voluptuous and infinitely soft. Nothing can be compared to them.

Flames come in number and form a suspended, swaying aureole around the woman's body and visage.

Thus she poses, divine.

Jean Falmor did not receive the gaze of the eyes, which were pouring all their light into the eyes of the monk, but, torn by a prodigious emotion, he contemplated such superhuman beauty passionately, and, kneeling down without knowing whether it was to pray to God or to pray to her, in the chaos of his soul, he prayed. Meanwhile, he darted a glance at his companion.

Now, the monk Marestote was lying on the ground. His eyes were fixed on the radiant eyes and his hands were clasped, and his voice rose up in a pathetic cry.

"I renounce the World, Man and Christ! You alone exist! You abolish everything before your glory, O Woman, supreme marvel, only God!"

These words, spoken by Marestote struck Falmor with an immense terror. He seemed to find himself at the center of a cataclysm. Without raising his eyes again, he fled. He went down the marble steps and, recovering his mount, drove it into the labyrinth of red stone.

There, he wandered for a long time through the similar junctions, the identical avenues.

It was not until the middle of the following day that, guided by hazard, he reached the gate, still open. Exhausted by fatigue, he lay down on the dry leaves outside and went to sleep.

When he woke up, it was dark. As he detached the bridle of his horse in order to leave, he heard footsteps behind him and saw a human form emerge from the long scarlet maze. It was an old man, marching with a shuffling gait.

Jean Falmor had difficulty recognizing Marestote, the black

monk commissioned by the Pope, for the old man's soul had quit his body, in which nothing any longer remained but base desires and instincts. He interrogated him, but obtained no response other than a peevish clucking and vague complaints regarding cold and hunger.

Side by side they walked until they reached the nearest of the fires, and cries broke out because the old man had immediately hurled himself upon one of the miserable creatures to snatch away the root that he was gnawing.

Falmor could not bear to watch the savage struggle. He fled.

He galloped all night, in a delirium and terror of doubt, through the desolate forest, the menacing rocks and the trees convulsed by the wind. As day broke, his mount fell dead, on the threshold of a monastery.

Having fallen unconscious, Falmor woke up in a monk's cell, and, regarding that as an order from God, he never returned to the world of men.

Thus, for having approached the idol that he could not comprehend, he was obliged to spend his life.

Fifteen years later, he died in a state of sanctity, in despair and terror, because, since the very first moment, he had adored with all his soul the woman whose beauty he had seen unveiled, and who had not deigned to take possession of his credulous and uncertain soul.

VISIONS IN THE SILENCE

Mistrust décor…do not be deceived
by the appearances of things.
Paul Adam

There were, ultimately, powerful dilapidated walls, centenarian trees and the gate of the old park that Sardal had sought for such a long time.

He turned his horse round and studied his surroundings.

To the left, descending from west to east, a river passed by, hidden behind the trunks of the tall fir-trees looming up on its banks. An uneven chain of hills, veiled by a light mist, stood on the horizon. In front of him, he distinguished in the distance the black masses of woods covering an undulating terrain. Closer, a vast plain extended, bordered by the sinuous line of the waters, which disappeared to the right in the ancient darkness of the forest.

Dusk was falling. Through the confused curtain of trees, already beginning to shed their leaves, Sardal saw the setting sun above the river, crimson and tawny, the sky stained here and there by gleams of a more luminous gold or a brighter red, covered at intervals by silvery flakes or violet clouds. Toward the zenith there were large clouds the color of flesh, and narrow strips, pink, mauve or snowy, floating in the green-tinted sky, where a single star trembled.

A sharp perfume came from the pines and the heather. Swallows were swooping over the river, but their shrill cries were not troubling the silence. The solitude established itself more perfectly. The décor of the clouds died with the sun; a slate-hued vapor emerged from the forest, and the moon emitted a yellow light between the fir-trees. Night-birds saluted it with their cries.

Sardal savored the charm of the time and the place voluptuously, and he thought about how uniquely appropriate the remote château would be to his amours.

The old man had closed the gate again and was standing before the visitor. His bald head was gleaming in the moonlight, and his bearded face expressed a dull surprise.

"Why have you come?" he said.

There was a silence. The old man went on:

"Do you know that today is the only day, in the entire year, when I can open that gate, and that at midnight you would have found it obstinately closed?

"Know this: that for many days, many years, many centuries, no one has come...no one! And I have not opened that gate.

"Why have you come? Why is it you? But in truth, why should it not be you? And yet...and yet...it has been there for such a long time But why is it you? In truth, I tell you, it has been there for hundreds of years!"

The sound of his voice made an unpleasant impression on Sardal, who interrupted him by repeating his request.

"Yes," said the old man, "yes, you can visit the domain today. You can...but you'll go alone. I won't go. I'll show you the way to the door in the wall, but after that, you'll be alone."

"That's fine," said the visitor. "Which path should I follow?"

"How should I know?" cried the old man. "Go forward, keep going forward, that's all."

Dismounting, Sardal tied the bridle of his horse to a tree, and accompanied the old man.

By means of a narrow path through the woods, the two men reached a concave circular wall that made the part of the park in which they were into a small section isolated in the unknown domain.

With the old man's unusual farewell still ringing in his ears, Sardal had traversed the obscure grotto and gone into the driveway. It was straight, broad and long. A high grassy bank rose up on each side, like the banks of a river, dominated by immense oak trees, which rounded the arches of their foliage overhead. The moonlight filtered through that vault on to the sandy ground.

Aligned at the foot of the bank, white marble statues represented strange monsters or gracious feminine figures. Between them, on granite plinths, were huge vases crowned with stout plants, which hung down on every side like spiny serpents. There was no wind. A slight aroma trailed under the branches, and a profound silence weighed upon the park.

Sardal was penetrated by an abnormal emotion. The old man's terror, the unexpectedness of the double enclosure, and, above all, the décor of the regular driveway and its branching paths, maintained with so much care in that long-deserted domain, gave him a strange impression of unreality. He thought that the gardens bewitched by the enchantresses of ancient legend must have had an analogous beauty, and must have respired that same atmosphere of mysterious and attentive enchantment....

In order to convince himself, he attempted to utter a cry, but the sound of his voice did not seem to exist, any more than that of his footsteps on the gravel. No sound struck his ears. He observed the fact and was not troubled by it. His mind accepted the marvels by which he believed himself to be surrounded, and he enjoyed it without any terror, with the curious expectation of what he might discover combined with an afterthought of incredulity, like that which sometimes mingles with a dream.

Suddenly, an immense yellow light appeared before him, with a fulgurant glare. His dazzled eyes closed momentarily, and then saw this:

Set across the driveway was an immense golden bed, magnificently sculpted and encrusted with precious stones. In that bed, half-covered by a crimson satin quilt and lace sheets, lay a fat and gigantic pig, crowned with a sparkling three-pointed diadem. The beast was sprawled on its belly, its snout buried in the embroidered pillow.

Two naked negroes extended their colossal stature at the bedhead, each armed with an enormous scimitar of dull steel.

This time the light was red and shone behind him. He turned round.

In a blood-colored aureole a gibbet stood. One of its arms held by the neck a large white swan, with its wings hanging down, the other a mitered bishop in a violet robe. Sardal was able to make out his dilated eyes and swollen tongue, protruding between his teeth. The hanged man was, however, gesticulating in his direction, while the bird was beating its wings.

Everything disappeared again. He resumed walking.

A woman came along the path to meet him. She was clad in a long white silk dress that left her arms bare and was only attached around the bosom. Beneath a toque of swansdown garnished with silver, brown hair covered her forehead all the way to the eyebrows, mingling with pendants garnishing her coiffure. Descending no lower than the shoulders, it fell upon her breast to frame her face, which Sardal could make out, pale, symmetrical, almost child-like with its harmonious contours, its pink lips, its delicate nose and its large blue-green eyes, ingenuous and indecisive in their nacreous rings.

She advanced toward him, and he saw that, with her fingertips, she was lifting up the hem of her white skirt, which was lined with black velvet. Beneath it she was naked and, already, the feet in little ermine slippers, the slender ankles and the tapered roundness of the legs were unveiled. Her dress was still rising up and, her innocent and vague eyes fixed on Sardal without appearing to see him, she walked with a swaying stride, uncovering her voluptuous body from her feet to her breasts, illuminated by the moonlight filtering through the foliage.

Still shivering with unslaked desire, he walked along the second half of the driveway, where giant horned frogs fell mutely from the top of the bank. First two came, then two more, another two—and suddenly, there were seven. The last one, the largest, guided the troop. Parting its large jaws, it seemed to be uttering a formidable croak, but no sound was perceived by the visitor who was drawing nearer, with the three small black eyeless cats still following him, trotting and hurrying in order to remain on his heels.

Obedient to a signal, the six frogs lined up behind their conductress. The latter, turning her head alternately from right to left, periodically looked at Sardal, coldly. The others imitated her precisely, and the first, raising herself up in a lazy hop, traveled ten feet. Scarcely was she in the air than the band launched forward with the same movement, covering the same distance—then a glance at the visitor—then another hop.

Thus they all advanced, soundlessly, in the half-light.

Contemplating the high wall of chaotic rocks and the bay open before him beneath the hanging curtains of verdure, he remained hesitant momentarily, but, mocking his anxiety, he followed the frogs, which plunged into the subterranean passage.

He went down a steep slope in darkness and discovered a grotto illuminated by red light. The rapid seething waters of a river flowed, rising to the level of the rock ground, and, to the left, plunged in a cataract into a gulf. They disappeared from sight, and a thick vapor swirled over the falls, indicating its prodigious depth—from which, however, no sound emerged.

In front of the visitor was a wooden door, and on the other side, in a hollow, there was a large fire around which three old women were sitting.

The frogs looked at Sardal one last time and leapt into the river. Their fall made the water splash in all directions, but inaudibly.

The visitor crossed the bridge and was able to see the three old women at close range. One had a dog's muzzle, the second an owl's beak and the third the maw of a pike. Each of them wore an immense bonnet pretentiously ornamented with blue, yellow or green ribbons. With the tips of their clawed fingers they were clutching sparrows to their bosom and plucking them, devouring them as they went, shaking their heads and clicking their jaws. The three little cats, leaping on to their shoulders, disappeared, and when Sardal went past them, they turned round, showing him their fists.

He finished climbing the slopes and finally reached the château, massive and somber in the moonlight.

The visitor climbed the perron, went through three arches devoid of doors and found himself in a red stone vestibule, vaulted and punctuated with columns between which bronze lamps with scarlet flames were suspended by loose chains. Three ebony doors, surmounted by sculptures, were locked by heavily silver bolts. He could not open the first but looked inside through a judas-hole built into the batten. There was a cemetery covered with grass, where, over multitudinous mortuary stones and crosses, hundreds of morose fire-follets were floating.

He traversed the vestibule. The second door, also closed, permitted him to see, inside, a lake draped with blue-tinted veils beneath which swans floated amid monstrous flowers.

He was able to open the third door, at the back of the vestibule, and was on the threshold of a sparkling banqueting hall whose walls were hung with tawny leather encrusted with gold, with panoplies, trophies and luminous ornaments.

In the center of the room stood a huge table covered with candelabras, magnificently supplied with food but in total disorder and surrounded by guests: men dressed in silk and velvet, wearing poniards or épées, apparently having arrived at a high degree of excitement and drunkenness. Some, standing up and singing, were leaning their fists on the stained tablecloth and lifting crystal glasses or silver goblets, which they emptied in a single draught. Others, their eyes half-closed, were swaying on their leather chairs. A few were brandishing their glittering swords with threatening gestures.

A man with a gray beard occupying the top of the table stood up with a grave expression. He took off his boot, poured four bottles of wine into it, and, saluting his guests, emptied it completely without drawing breath.

Then he perceived Sardal and extended his arm toward him. Suddenly, they were all on their feet, seemingly uttering a formidable cheer—but the newcomer heard no sound, for a deathly silence weighed upon the banqueting hall.

The gesticulating guests, however, were manifestly demanding an anticipated event. They were served. Two valets brought a vast silver bowl, which they placed in the center of the table, and two others brought a child, a naked little girl who was struggling in terror. Above the bowl, a sweep of a cutlass cut her throat; blood sprang forth, steaming, between the metal walls. Then they emptied floods of red wine into it, and filled their glasses to the brim with the mixture. The man at the top of the table seized a great crystal chalice, filled it, and, approaching the visitor, presented it to him with a gracious and noble smile.

Sardal dared not refuse.

As he raised his glass the guests did the same, and seemed, before drinking, to toast his health with further cries.

Silence, however, continued to reign, and the visitor drank, as they all did. The insipid and heady taste of the liquor tautened his nerves. He threw the glass down on the tiled floor; it shattered soundlessly.

He ran out, abruptly shoving the door, which seemed to be turning on oiled hinges and falling into padded grooves.

Devoid of pillars, oval in shape and constructed in green stone, illuminated by bronze lamps—such was the vestibule on the first floor.

At each extremity there was an arched ivory door, Sardal opened the one on the right and went into complete unfathomable darkness, which the light of the lanterns could not overcome, and a humid atmosphere charged with frightful odors.

He saw vague white gleams moving a long way away; a sticky touch brushed his face....

He fled toward the second door.

There was a vast room, dilapidated and unfurnished. On the disjointed floor-tiles, under an old lamp hooked on to the ceiling, there was a coffin of black wood. The lid was half-raised over a human head; an emaciated hand covered in scratches was clutching the rim. A deformed being was creeping around it. His face was thin, with a snub nose, immense ears terminated by tufts of hair, and a bushy red beard, trimmed and twisted into a stiff point. Enormous protrusions swelled his breast and his back. His legs were severed half way down his thighs, but he was hanging on to the coffin with long, muscular arms and moving rapidly. He had a red silk bonnet garnished with mute bells, a woolen waistcoat checkered green and blue with canary yellow ribbons. An enormous hammer was passed through his belt. A gold chain hung around his neck and plunged into a pocket set over the heart, to attach a vast watch, which he took out incessantly in order to consult it, grimacing anxiously. He was making great efforts to pull down the coffin lid and imprison completely the individual enclosed therein, who was resisting with a desperate energy.

The dwarf forced him to let go, however, and with the aid of long nails, hastened to secure the lid. The hammer rose up rhythmically and fell vigorously, but made no sound. Soon, one end was nailed down, and the workman, having looked at his watch joyfully, was actively working at the other. He was troubled by the prisoner, who, succeeding in loosening one side, stuck out a large pale head covered in yellow hair, bloody and ripped by the points. The bare shoulders attempted to follow, but already the dwarf, crawling along the floor, was there, and, only pausing to consult the time, struck the skull with all his might, in which the hammer made a dent.

The victim turned his large eyes, full of anguish and supplication, toward the visitor, whom the torturer summoned with a gesture at the same time, showing him the dial of his watch authoritatively.

Sardal advanced to help the buried man, but when he reached the bier he put all his weight on it and knelt on the lid, suppression all rebellion, while the delighted dwarf checked the time and drove in the nails, his long beard stranding up victoriously with every effort.

When it was finished, without knowing why he had acted as he had, Sardal got up and went to the door. And as he went out, he saw the imprisoned man, who, having dislodged the lid from within, was still trying to escape, while the cruel dwarf, full of anger, was attacking him, crushing the enormous skull with great hammer-blows and desperately consulting his watch.

The room formed a vast oval. The center of the ceiling was an ebony vault of the same shape as the whole, but considerably smaller. Around it, on three sides, seven Gothic vaults were delimited by arches and columns, each presenting a different color: sea-green, orange, dark violet, silver, scarlet, mauve and pale pink.

Each ceiling, polished and encrusted with arabesques in the colors of the other six, bore a large number of small lamps of every color, which did not hang down more than a foot from their point of attachment, thus leaving the floor in an iridescent half-light.

The walls were hung with supple velvet, colored and ornamented like the vaults. Sardal, leaning against a side wall, could feel that it was soft and elastic behind the broad creases. His feet sank into a thick carpet of silks, combining the seven hues against a black background with gold arabesque, which covered a floor as soft as a divan. Thick cushions and profound furs were scattered everywhere.

The reserved space at the back of the room was covered by a dome of pure gold, sculpted at the sides and polished at the summit. A similar brocade coated the walls. And there, a rounded golden platform was erected, provided with steps and encrusted with jewels. A large crystal throne with a reclining back surmounted it, beneath a similar cupola, sparking in the shadows. And on that seat, voluptuously sprawled, were two women, their arms around one another, kissing one another on the lips. They had all the splendor of life, but the eternal immobility of statues. Their beauty was divine.

Meanwhile, a large number of beautiful young women were distributed about the room: women of the every type and every beauty in the world, including black women, red women and yellow women, although those in the greatest number were white. Their adornments were various. Many wore nothing but jewels over their bare flesh, but some had threads of red or gold weaving down over their bodies. Others were displaying their delicate skin through clinking silky webs. Several wore robes of transparent lace or tunics slit down the sides. Some were wrapped in scarves of silvery gauze, draped in elegant cashmeres or were incompletely veiled by strips of spangled fabric.

They glided through the dim light, intermingling in idle and lascivious dances, seemingly following the mute rhythm of strange instruments played by squatting musicians.

With voluptuous poses and cadenced undulations they passed by, joining together in meandering chairs, brushing one another with rapid caresses, separating from one another for other kisses, and other equally temporary embraces....

Around the golden throne seven women were kneeling, each enveloped in a large cloak of silk colored like one of the chapels and sprinkled with embroidered flowers. Gems were sparkling in their hair, and their religious hands swung the perfumes of golden incense-burners toward the symbols of their divinity....

Under the ebony vault, beneath the multicolored lamps, the dancers were still twirling, causing their breasts to jut out and their hair to float, but the caresses with which they were brushing one another were more tremulous now and their kisses extending to the point of swooning...and on the profound furs and cushions, they fell together, side by side with those who were already lying there, fainting with voluptuousness.

The groups melted into the nebulous shadow, where gleams

of white flesh suddenly shone. The redness of lips parted over teeth. Enlaced forms were panting to the rhythm of kisses. The perfume of amour floated over their transports....

A furious desire had seized the visitor. He marched toward the extended, offered bodies—but the priestesses who were kneeling around their divinity got up and came toward him.

They were the only ones standing in the room, and Sardal saw all seven of them, made up and bejeweled, voluptuously beautiful with their gem-studded hair and their long cloaks undulating as they walked. They advanced, forming a semicircle. The two positioned at either end had black hair with blue or bronzed tints; their eyes were dark; they wore nothing with their heavy jewels but Chinese silk scarves, broad, dark and fringed with gold, knotted around the waist so as to make the throat stand out. One of them wore a sea-green cloak, the other a cloak of ancient rose.

Those who came after them displayed their nudity against mauve and orange satin backcloths, interrupted solely by circlets of pure gems wound around the neck, the waist, the breasts, the thighs and the arms, crossing over the feet and rising over the face to maintain the coiffure, spiraling around the entire body in a scintillating line: burned topazes matching the irises of the one on the right, whose hair was chestnut-brown, emeralds as transparent as the eyes of the other, who was red-haired.

Then came two blondes; one, as blonde as gold, had a scarlet cloak, and the other, as blonde as amber, wore violet. Their bodies, from their feet to their waists were exactly fitted with nets, black velvet studded with rubies for the first, red velvet with diamonds for the second; and one had large gray eyes, while those of the other were black. There were heavy necklaces on their bare throats.

The visitor paid particular attention to the one who occupied the center of the semicircle, directly facing him. Beneath a narrow diadem she had brown hair mingled with pearls and massed to either side of her face. Her deep blue eyes were luminous. Her silver brocade cloak hung down in heavy folds, and her marvelous body showed off her splendor fully, without a single gem.

Thus they came, and their cloaks fell like wounded birds. And Sardal realized that he was naked, and they embraced one another around and upon him, making love to one another. Hands and lips slid over his skin; tresses full of perfume enveloped him. The scent and contact of palpitating bodies set his senses ablaze to the point of delirium.

He lost consciousness of everything that was not sensuality; every part of his flesh was maddened by a delight and a dolor. He choked, writhed in a vertiginous spasm, as if he were coughing up his soul under the kiss and caress of the woman with blue eyes, under her cruel mouth....

And silence reigned.

Sardal climbed the somber staircase for a long time and finally emerged on to the crowning platform of the château.

It was completely dark, the moon having disappeared behind the clouds. And someone was there on the high platform overlooking the tops of the tallest trees: in the middle, an old man was sitting in a stone seat. His arms were resting on the granite supports; his head was slumped forward over his breast. He was clad in a coat of chain mail, rusted and corroded by time. To his right stood a tall clepsydra, to his left a gigantic hour-glass. In front of the old man, in the depths of a niche hollowed out in a loophole, was a bronze clock.

The steel needle was moving around the vast dial, but no sound emerged from the machine. The habitual and monotonous tick-tock, the course of time itself, could not trouble the profound silence, which—here more than anywhere else—was burying life.

The visitor approached. On the stone spheres at the summit of the armchair, two owls were sitting motionlessly, darting around the gaze of their red eyes. On the old man's skull, with his white hair, which flowered in disorderly masses, a crow had built its nest and remained perched there, unmoving. With its head to the right and its wings hanging down, it was reminiscent of the plume of a helmet. The old man's beard, thick and inordinately long, projected forwards, winding around the foot of the clock.

Sardal leaned over in order to look the old man in the face. And the old man's face seemed even more extraordinarily old than everything that surrounded him. He seemed to be made of a perpetual stone, older and more durable than time. His muscles, like metal cords, were immobile beneath the immobile mask. His mouth seemed definitively closed.

Finally, the visitor's eyes met those of the old man. Surrounded by snowy lashes, the irises had the color and glare of the full moon; they emitted a luminous fluid that was reflected on the polished steel of the needle whose progress around the dial of the clock they were contemplating passionately.

And now, as he looked into those eyes, the spirit of curiosity and bravery that was guiding the visitor was suddenly snatched away from him at a stroke, and terror, the intolerable anguish of hideous terror, saturated his soul instantaneously.

At the same instant, the silence was torn apart. The prelude was the voice of the clock sounding midnight. The sound was abnormal and deafening, and seemed to be a phenomenon so horrible that the visitor felt his heart twist and his head spin.

Then an atrocious racket burst forth. There were clashes of épées and cries of death, moans of love and groans of torture, noises of breaking glass and the grating of doors. Curses mingled with croaks, resounding blows and the roar of a cataract. The owls hooted. The crow flapped its wings and cawed.

Above everything else, Sardal heard the explosion of an insensate joy, the inordinate howling of triumph and deliverance proffered by a being standing a few paces away.

He perceived him, and recognized himself. He recognized his corporeal *persona* standing a few paces away from him. And he, Sardal, found himself in the immemorial form of the old man. He felt his eyes become those of the old man, and fix upon the clock....

Riveted to his stone seat, with the motionless crow that resembled the plume of a helmet on his head, he caught one last glimpse of the person who had taken his human appearance and who was fleeing the place, liberated.

He glimpsed him, but he did not hear him, for the noise had passed with the climes of midnight.

Silence was god once again upon the platform of the château, absorbing the voice of time itself, reigning over the voice of the clock, the progress of whose steel needle, in which his eyes were reflected, the old man was passionately watching.

The Old Man remained alone....

FAX-AGELIA,
PRINCE OF BELSÉDÈNE

The third comes back; it is always the first,
And always alone.................................
It is Death, or Lady Death! O delight, O torment!
The rose that she takes—is the rose-mallow.....
                                        —Gérard de Nerval

In his twentieth year, Fax-Agelia, Prince of Belsédène,[5] lived the adventure the dominated his destiny.

At the end of a day inflamed by the summer solstice, Fax-Agelia was walking through the immense park of his hereditary domain. Proud of his glorious name and his patrimony, confident in his youth, his strength and his beauty, he fondly imagined the days of his future, exalted with glory and love.

The park had a majestic serenity. Old sycamores formed the profound forests, with oaks and firs. The layout of the pathways was geometric. Statues stood at the intersections. In blue-tinted marbles, waters slept in which the furtive scales of tench gleamed, or on which black swans floated; and peacocks deployed their glittering glory on the rims of the basins.

Fax-Agelia drew away from the manor and roamed the

---

5. Belsédène is a village in the ancient region of the Île-de-France. The name Agelia does exist in Greek but might in this instance be a corruption of Angelia, just as Fax is presumably a corruption of faux; that would allow the name to be construed as "false message," Angelia being a daughter of Hermes, from whose name the word "angel" is derived.

wildest places. He reached the river, a green and sinuous line through the domain. In a boat, whose mooring-rope he untied, he allowed himself to be carried away by the rapid current.

Dusk vaporized the air. Translucent veils were oscillating over the water and drowning the odorant thickets that surmounted on the banks. A light breeze brushed the leaves and swayed the profound bells of distant flowers. The sky became starry.

Fax-Agelia was lying in his boat, contemplating the luminous constellations. The gentleness of the night intoxicated him with the perfumes that floated over the coolness of the waves, cradling his indolence, and he no longer knew to which remote part of his domain he had been drawn.

The boat slowed down as it approached the entrance to a broad pool whose contours were indefinable, for the water disappeared entirely beneath a prodigious paludal vegetation, dominated by reeds in profound masses, great starry water-lilies and white rushes. Climbing lilies, bracken and water-weed elongated their interlaced leaves and pale flowers everywhere. Thick mosses were floating in the interstices, and the water was no visible anywhere.

In front of the boat a narrow channel formed, which guided it toward an islet.

Allowing his boat to plough into the roots on the bank, Fax-Agelia set foot on land. He was confronted by an impenetrable mass of bushes and small trees. As in the vegetation of the pool, a route opened up, and he followed it in the gloom. After numerous detours he found himself in a clearing bathed by a pale golden light.

The shallow slope of the ground was covered by an extremely thick flowery mass strewn with rose petals. A profound curtain of myrtles limited the space, gripped by dense plants that interlaced six feet from the ground to form a tightly-knit vault with their dark fleshy red-edged leaves, through which the sky could hardly be glimpsed. Here and there, on these plants, vast unknown flowers bloomed, whose heart, seemingly golden at the center of a translucent corolla, emitted a nebulous light.

Other flowers, similarly luminous, lived at the foot of squat trees, among lilies and tuberoses. An exhausting and perfumed languor weighed upon the immobility of the evening.

On the mossy ground, a woman was harmoniously extending her beauty on silken cushions, naked and marvelous; and she appeared, in the strange charm of the place, more divinely seductive than any form that the chimeras of the man kneeling beside her, summoned by the caress of her luminous eyes and the smile of her lips, could ever have imagined.

In her arms he savored a sublime sensuality. In those kisses, those embraces, those oaths of love, he found the infinity of his dreams; and the hours of that night bound them together with all-powerful bonds.

Before the dawn of the morning, the woman relaxed her embrace. She placed her hand on her lover's shoulder and plunged her gaze passionately into his eyes.

"Listen to me," she said. "You must listen to me and obey me. The hours of our amour have passed now. The stars descending toward the horizon of the sky mark their final minutes. The doors of happiness close with the daylight, and I do not have the keys.

"Don't look at me like that. It's necessary for us to part forever. Your boat will go, far from me, to draw your destiny toward the world, toward human agitation, the vanity of passions and desires, the illusory emotions of the things of the earth.

"That will be, for that must be, and we cannot prevent it....

"We have loved one another well, have we not, on this islet, which no one before you has ever visited, and which no one after you ever will visit?

"I, who was virginal for your kiss, will remain virginal after your kiss. There will be no other embrace to soil your embrace within me; my lips will be closed to all lips; no gaze shall see my beauty, and the transports of my soul will not be born for any soul. I am yours—I shall never belong to another, and I shall have known love for this one night alone....

"No, don't despair; don't say anything. Listen: I leave you

my memory. I leave our mysterious joys in your memory, like an immortal perfume in the heart of a sealed bottle. I want to enchant the hours of your life, ever beautiful and every loving. I want to be the consoler, whose hands hold the flowers of dream, seated in the gardens of your soul.

"Adieu! Contemplate my mortal form one last time. Contemplate my eyes, which are my gift...kiss my lips once more...penetrate your heart with what will be its eternal light and abandon it without return, for it must be abandoned.

"Depart, go away, and above all—oh, above all!—never come back; that would be death, frightful death...."

He swore a solemn oath, subjugated by her voice. He dared not resist, he dared not interrogate. He left, bewildered.

In his boat, he allowed himself to be drawn along by the rapid current, in an unconscious intoxication of lassitude and floor, unable to collect his thoughts....

That man, returned to the rooms of his manor, plunged thereafter into profound meditation, struggling to calm the tumult of his soul. He found himself utterly changed. The former realities that inhabited his thoughts, his former reasons for living, disappeared, and nothing existed for him outside the delirious passion that enfevered him for his mysterious mistress, for the woman who had cast an invincible spell upon his life.

He recognized, in his immense affliction, in the intensity of his love, that if he stayed in the manor he would not be able to prevent himself from seeing her again, and he left that same evening for the distant court of his king.

He left in order never to betray his oath, and he hoped to find in real life sensations as strong and as delicious as the sensations he had savored on that islet, an unforgettable lost paradise.

When Fax-Agelia was in society, at that sumptuous noble court where he could compete with the greatest, he plunged into the ardent quest for honors and love.

He obtained, without great difficulty, the various triumphs that he desired, but no realized ambition could inspire joy in him, no woman, however graceful she might be, could create a real love in him. Indifference accompanied every event in his life and cruel and divine desire drove more deeply into his heart the mortal sadness of hopeless regret.

He attempted to forget in debauchery and combat. It was in vain that he plunged into the fever of danger and violence, it was in vain that he wallowed in lust and drunkenness. He was able to exhaust his body, and he was able to overwhelm his senses, but the memory did not die within his soul—and his soul, rendered desperate by the realities of the world, crushed by bitterness and disgust, hurled itself back, with a crazed vehemence of regret for his vanished love, enmeshing itself ever more profoundly in the memory of the past, drawing new strength and new dolors therefrom, to abandon itself, with reckless fury and savage violence, to the immense passion that burned him with eternal ardor.

Now, Fax-Agelia understood the full force of his adoration. Time, distance and comparison showed him that the woman had taken possession of him, entirely and forever.

Only the words that she had pronounced, forbidding him to return, which haunted his soul incessantly, prevented him from returning to his manor and proximity to her.

The time came when even that no longer stopped him. He rebelled against the persistent power of the woman who was the goal of his life and he shrugged off the yoke of her will. Nothing any longer subsisted in him then but the desire to see her again, and to die afterwards, if he had to die.

Thus, one evening, Fax-Agelia, understanding that the moment had come, regretting having delayed for so long, departed alone, riding toward his ideal.

He traveled relentlessly until he reached his goal. Dusk was falling when he reached his manor, the river and the boat. As before, he allowed himself to be borne away by the current.

It was a night at the end of autumn. The leafless trees seemed to be cursing the sky. The bushes were bristling with thorns. The raucous calls of night-birds rent the wind, and the rapid water agitated the boat.

When he reached the pool, he recognized that the landscape had become more sinister now, when it had been nothing but delightful before. Over the troubled water the denuded stems had the aspect of dead serpents. A cold wind was howling, and in the sky the full moon emitted a sickly light that the blanched clouds absorbed as they fled.

The traveler reached the island. Through the midst of the hostile thickets he passed, carried by his blind desire, tearing himself on the brambles.

He saw the empty space between the myrtles, which were no more than black skeletons linked together by slender cords of climbing plants. The earth was covered with decomposing leaves. A phosphoric light dragged a mortuary odor toward the soil.

Now a crouching form moved, of a hideous emaciated old woman clad in meager rags. She writhed, livid in the moonlight, sniggered with drooling gums, opened her bloodshot eyes toward the newcomer and suddenly leapt up, howling desperately.

"You!" she cried. "It's you!"

She ran toward the deep water. There was the dull sound of a body plunging in.

Then nothing more.

Thus the life of the Prince of Belsédène came to an end.

THE CLEMENT SHADES

"For us, if there is a Heaven and if there is a Hell,
The second is too far, and the first too dear...."

The decomposed splendor of a stormy dusk sends warm and enervating gleams through a window-pane trellised by ivy and vines. That light, in the bedroom, mingles with the flickering radiation issuing from the bronze lamp suspended by a long chain from the black vault of the ceiling. Thus the room is glimpsed, which is sumptuous, strange, dilapidated. No hangings veil the walls, where the wooden panels are the frames of ancient frescoes representing, in a naïve and scrupulous manner, scenes of torture and lubricity, which acquire, by virtue of the variable light, a fantastic animation.

Rare items of furniture establish their ebony solemnity in the corners. A clock raises its musical voice. Furs muffle the parquet. In a bronze vase, marvelous red roses spring forth and lean over, evaporating the languorous intoxication of their dying beauty.

Facing the window, between a divan and a door, an ebony bed thrusts up its canopy, half-buried beneath the dilapidated magnificence of ragged crimson gold-fringed velvet. The curtains are raised, and asleep in the bed is a woman, Sara d'Hellémone, who is a prostitute because her father, who is rich, permits her to be approached by rich and powerful men whom the unequaled seduction of her beauty has gripped in its enchantment, and who is a virgin since her father poisons her lips with the Black Poison that he alone knows, making her mouth the cup where all those drink death who, loving her in any manner whatsoever, desire to know her kiss.

Now, the woman who is in that bed is prey to a pernicious malady, and it is apparent that her death is near. That is obvious to everyone, save for her father, the old man, who does not want to see that she is dying and does not want to believe that she can ever die, for he opposes his profound material science, in which he has faith, to the force of the tomb.

The darkness progressively takes hold. The hour chimes. The sleeping woman emerges from her slumber and, parading her eyes over things as if her mind is elsewhere, contemplating the lamp with the mobile radiation, the frightful paintings on the walls, the great phantoms of the black furniture—contemplating in particular, through the widow trellised by ivy and vines, the copper- and violet-tinted tumult that the vanished sun is decomposing—breathing in dolorously the warm sensuality of the agonizing roses, she wrings her hands in anguish, sighs wearily, and speaks, in a halting voice.

SARA

The sun...the sun is dead! And I haven't contemplated its splendor! And I shall never contemplate it again! I've slept too long! I'm going to die now....

O Lord, what has become of the sun? A storm is menacing the sky...it took possession of my soul a long time ago.... Oh, I'm afraid of death. The phantoms of the dead are already visiting my dreams. They'll torment my slumber far better in the tomb...but at least the old man will no longer be there!

Have I no regret for life? Does the liberated slave experience nostalgia or his fetters? Oh, I've dreamed such beautiful things! Illusion has liberated me from everything that is myself. I have loved everything that I have not known. Who will voice my desires, my dreams and my hopes? Who will voice the delights, the luxuries and the glories that I have imagined? For sure, it will not be Sara d'Hellémone for everything spoken loses the most delicious of its seductions—that of secrecy. But no…no…I'm lying! I've desired nothing, hoped for nothing, dreamed nothing! I've lived, body and soul, in the ambiguity of my prostitution.

I sense my spirit fluttering like the wing of a bird ready to take flight, like the sail of a ship surrendering itself to powerful winds in order to set sail for unknown lands, toward the lands full of enchantment that are countries of the earth, which I have never seen—and which I shall never see! O dolor! O regret! I'm dying now, and there are landscapes I don't know, cities I don't suspect, peoples whose very names I don't know!

My life is decreasing, and yet here comes the twinkling of the stars, the souls of the great heavens. They shine, torches of hope or despair…mysterious beacons! But the blood-colored clouds are oppressing their light. They're going out in the storm…to be reborn more beautiful. My life will be extinguished, but won't be reborn. I shall die in the lightning, in the gusts of wind, in the tempest, in the battle of blind forces! My soul will let go of my flesh.…

My soul? The old man would laugh. My soul? He would laugh! And his accursed spirit has insinuated itself into me, since I'm laughing myself, very quietly, fearfully…

I've struggled, alas! The Spirit of Evil was the stronger. Should I not have been able to resist, though? Oh, I don't know! Why am I not better? Why is my soul so vain and feeble? The old man crushes me with his will, terrifies me with his threats and pleas…but then again, I like jewels, as he likes gold.…

And then again, I shall never have surrendered my body to vile embraces. My body is my own, in its beauty and its virginity, and no one has enjoyed it, in spite of the lascivious caresses that have soiled me, which have stirred me—in spite of the monstrous desire of the jealous old man who believes in my chastity.

My chastity! What has that become? I have found enjoyment in my crime. Am I truly innocent? In truth, if there is a God, he will judge me in his equity.… I'm incapable of seeing into the depths of my conscience!

Silently, a door opens near the bed and an old man shows his face. Beneath his white hair, his face is blanched. The black velvet of a long robe hides the thinness of his stature. He comes in, carrying a silver phial.

THE OLD MAN

My daughter, I have fought victoriously for your life, against the malice and the mystery of the eternal elements. My recompense will be the new flowering of your youth. Take this elixir; it will cure your illness.…

SARA

Everything is futile. I shan't drink. You'll no longer torment your slave. I'm liberated from you.…

THE OLD MAN

My slave, liberated from me? What are you saying? What work have I imposed on you, then, that you have not accomplished voluntarily?

But it's the fever troubling your thoughts. This is the cure that I've brought you.…

SARA

Go away! The death that is coming will put a barrier between us, which you will never overcome. The time has come when I shall be alone. The brief hours of my life belong to my soul.…

THE OLD MAN

What are you saying? Calm your delirium. I've brought you life....

SARA

Life is no longer for me. You know that full well, Father. There is no remedy against the Black Poison....

THE OLD MAN

The Black Poison?

SARA

Oh, there are so many who have died of it—all my lovers— there are so many who have died of it, before my eyes, that I know very well how to recognize the symptoms of the sublime Poison. I am dying of it in my turn, surely. Is that not just? I am dying, a victim of my frivolity, a victim of gold, a victim of Old Man Hellémone, who is my father. That is the way it is. And yet, with what patience, with what care, have I not accustomed myself to the Poison? Must I not have taken too much in a moment of disgust? I'm twenty years old, I'm a virgin, I'm dying....

THE OLD MAN

The poison! The poison! Horror! She's dying because of me, and I adore her more than my life, more than my science! But perhaps there's a remedy. It's necessary to fight...! But what point is there? It's invincible, it's the certainty of the absolute, the masterpiece of my genius! Was I not proud of it?

SARA

I can see, far, far away the specters of my lovers struggling in the tempest to conquer my soul!

Old man, your science is false, the mortal body is not God's! The soul exists and expiates! O terror...!

The darkness is upon me! The lamps of the evening are shining in the vault and all the voices are celebrating death. My soul is floating, suspended and softly swayed like a summer fog saturated with rain and scents. The tricks of the shadow are masters of the woods, the breeze is rocking the clouds and dreams in the sky, the bells of flowers are tolling, for the harmony of the evening, the languorous perfumes of its urns....

Life is a mobile and multiple mask, which inhabits the constant visage of death....

The darkness is almost complete. The oscillating glimmer of the lamp scarcely illuminates the bedroom, where the rapid dazzle of lightning-flashes vibrates. The storm, very near, rips the darkness and weighs over the extent like a suffocation.

SARA

I'm stifling! Oh, the light of the lightning, brief and pro-found, shows me the depths of my heart. My thoughts are like images before my eyes. I can see them, prostituted to base and cowardly desires. Will death be able to purify my life?

THE OLD MAN

My child, my child, cast your eyes upon your father...you don't know how much I love you....

SARA

Yes, I know....

THE OLD MAN

I love you so much I could die of it. I love you as one loves one's God.

SARA

Your god is named Gold.

THE OLD MAN

Gold? I would give all my gold for one hour of your life! You can't know what I suffered when I was torn between my passion for gold and my passion for you. What tortures have I not known? I wanted, and then I no longer wanted, and cupidity always got the upper hand over jealousy within me. For I was jealous of your lovers, even though they possessed nothing of you except your lips—jealous enough to die of it, jealous enough to be exultant when my artifice murdered them! Their death satisfied both my avarice and my hatred!

SARA

Gold! Sovereign God, such is the name that at Evil has taken! Yes, my lovers were rich. All my lovers, now lying underground—all my lovers, none of whom possessed me...for I'm a virgin; no wedding day has some for me, and my fiancés have betrayed me for the tomb! I've given them joys though; they have no reason to complain!

Where are you, you who loved me so much, and have paid so dearly for me? I've given you my mouth—my mouth, with the heady breath of my bosom, with the nip of my teeth, with my silken lips, with the maddening sensuality of my tongue…with all the satisfaction of my poisoned mouth. I watched you die in the anguish of unknown sufferings, to which I shall be subjected in my turn. I followed your vertigo, your disturbance and your pain, and I was full of pity. Nevertheless, I adorned myself with your jewels and I saw, not without horror, the old man counting his gold in the triumph of his cupidity, for a woman's soul is feeble, unconscious and vain.

Where are you, O my lovers? I'm appealing to you in the darkness into which your shades have dispersed! Rise up at my voice. Come to me, all of you! It's your lover, Sara d'Hellémone, who is calling to you from her death-bed! Rise from the darkness and yield your faces to the gaze of her eyes, before they are closed by the vision of the supreme Face!

THE OLD MAN

So the passion named Avarice has dragged me down into Hell! What can I do now? Where can my despair flee?

Already, in the past, the enjoyment that gold gave me was nothing by comparison with the tortures that its conquest imposed on me. No dolor, no rage, could surpass the dolor and rage that tortured me when Sara was alone with the man who had just paid me, whose gold filled my coffers. I stood behind the door and tried to hear, and I foamed with rage, without going in, held back by the thirst for gold. I knew great joys when those men died in torment and terror.…

No love can equal the love that I have for her. With a perfect devotion I adore the exquisite marvel that is her charming face. I enter into a voluptuous folly in thinking about her young body, which I've glimpsed during her slumber, when the lace and the silks partly uncovered, with reserve and perversity, the florid curve of her adorable breasts, the tapering line of her leg, or the undulation of her hip, and sometimes…sometimes her sex itself! Oh, I've moved around your couch like a beast in rut! My furious desire, permanently unslaked, has choked on the perfume of your moist flesh; my eyes have burned in contemplating your body....

SARA

Yes, I've seen you....

THE OLD MAN

There have been times when I wanted to tear you in my lust... there have been times when, before the irredeemable horror of my being and my fate, I have sobbed like a coward, without reliving my heart, saturated with dolor, love and disgust.

SARA

Now the sun is dead. The blood of the evening has drained into the sea, beyond the horizon, and night has dressed the sky's wound.

The storm is robbing the night of its suffering and its tears. The lightning is spitting and glittering in the frenetic voluptuousness of its tearing spasms. But listen! The rain is falling; the thunder has fallen silent; the storm has passed. It's morning— why hasn't the rainbow visited the aurora; why hasn't the sign of forgiveness deployed its ineffable wings? Alas, it will never console the souls buried in the darkness of murder, and the morning light will no longer shine for them....

....

THE OLD MAN

Death! Death! Is it possible that she's dying?

SARA

The darkness is terrifying. Sad gleams dress phantoms there. The shades of victims are haunting it, full of the bitter regrets of those who have died young and without having known what they ought to have known. Their severed destinies are appealing for vengeance. What will the torments of reprisal be? God! I am one of those who must expiate!

THE OLD MAN

Can the force of the tomb be bent by gold? Could I become its master by paying it? Does its avarice render it similar to the human souls that offer it the most?

Oh, I can give the ransom of a kingdom!

He runs to open a small cupboard hidden in the wall. He seizes a bag full of gold. A casket falls on to the bed and jewels spill out. The old man runs to the window and, abruptly, opens it wide. A gust of wind causes the flame of the lamp to vacillate. The night is dark, cut by the fulgurant flashes of lightning. A suffocating warmth comes in with the odor of the storm. The old man leans into the darkness and, seizing fistfuls of gold, throws them furiously into the darkness, shouting with savage violence.

THE OLD MAN

For you, darkness of horror and fear, soul of the lightning, force of the wind! For you, accursed and multiple powers of shadow! For you, evil thoughts, maleficent dreams, criminal hopes! For all of you, perverse energies resorbed in the unknown potency of darkness, here's gold, here's gold, here's gold!

Meanwhile, Sara, seeing the jewels spilled out of the casket, has lifted herself up and seized them. She contemplates them and makes them sparkle. She speaks in a whisper, and then more loudly:

SARA

This is what I loved on earth. Look at these divine adornments. Look at this lace-work of fragmented gold, more delicate than the trees of ice that winter frosts on window-panes. Look at the radiant eyes of stones the color of blood, the color of the sea, the color of the sky, glittering on the flesh, languorous and lascivious Oh, I adore you, exquisite jewels, marvelous baubles! You are the stars of subterranean regions, which can be collected without fading; you are the eternal soul of beauty in the sumptuous luminosity of your hues and the subtle artistry of your setting!

She casts aside her black silk tunic and puts on a necklace, whose pearls and diamonds hang down all the way to her breasts. She buckles a golden girdle constellated with gems around her waist; she puts on bracelets and covers her pale hands with rings. She is sitting up, and thus, beneath her scattered hair, her beauty scintillates in the alternating gleams of the lightning and the lamp.

SARA

All the jewels are for me! No lust, no splendor, is worthy of my beauty. My first lover said that. He was young and handsome, and I loved him. Yes, I loved him! I loved them all madly; that's why they took my poisoned mouth! I was innocent, sovereign Judge! It's the old man who did everything! A woman isn't capable of making a man she loves drink death from her lips. It's the old man who has damned me! The old man, who is showing himself to me now with his hands full of gold....

Who are you? What do you want? Is it me? I'm for sale. I'll deliver myself for your ornaments. Give me your gold too, so that my father will let you in....

And all the jewels are for me. Is that too much? I'm young, beautiful and virginal...would you like to see my beauty and possess it? Your jewels have conquered my desire; it is only just that I satisfy yours. Look at my body, which no man has enjoyed—I swear it to you on the darkness of my tomb!

(She throws back the bedclothes are, ripping apart her night-dress, the golden belt of which still retains it at the waist, she appears in the nude.)

See, the flower of my breasts, the flower of my mouth, the flower of my body, my virgin embrace, for your jewels...don't you want me? Am I not beautiful enough? No, you daren't... are you afraid of me? What's said about me is a lie. None of my lovers have died. Then again, what does death matter if it's voluptuousness that delivers it? Come on—you don't know; I know kisses that will make you choke with dolor and joy, caresses that are stronger than any power, which weaken everything. No courtesan is cleverer...I've had so many lovers....

THE OLD MAN

Cover yourself up! Cover yourself up! The sight of your body drives me crazy!

SARA

Help! The gold is burning me! It's the blood of all my lovers. It's the blood of the dead, who are emerging from the tomb, thirsty for vengeance...oh, what anguish! I've evoked them; they're rising from the depths of the sepulcher, from the depths of mystery, full of hatred!

....

A livid light has spread through the room, emanating from low phosphoric clouds. The flashes of lightning have almost died away, but a vaguely luminous shroud seems to be covering everything. A few raindrops are falling, awkwardly. The old man is kneeling, contemplating his naked, dying daughter, who is struggling in the final anguish, choking in the supreme torment, offering to the gaze her most secret beauty. And shades emerge from the shadows to surround the bed, menacing specters.

THE SPECTERS

Sara, Sara, where are your oaths of love? Do you recognize the fiancés of your life, your poisoned lovers? You're ours now!

SARA

Have pity, I'm dying. I loved you all, and I was your beloved. You've had my caresses, you died of your voluptuousness. Will you never forgive me?

FIRST SHADE

How beautiful she is! Oh, I remember the day when I caressed her marvelous throat for the first time…in her hair and on her breasts, I tasted the slumber of ecstasy!

SECOND SHADE

Sara, I never loved anyone but you. Your eyes were the stars of my life; they are the eternal lamps that enchant my tomb!

THIRD SHADE

Your mouth poured forth an infinite languor, stronger than life. I adored your mouth…I died too soon.…

FOURTH SHADE

Do you remember me? I was the child who placed his head on your knees and his lips on your hand. You were my friend and my sister; the day when I knew evil desire I died, which is just....

ANOTHER

I have no regrets. When I saw you naked, it was like an opium dream to me. When I kissed your lips, I knew that such delights would cut short the hours of my life....

ANOTHER

I adore you, and I adore the memory that I have of our hours of love. You were marvelous in sensuousness. You seemed crazy and attentive; profound groans rose from your heart to your lips; your pallor was divine. You swooned beneath my caress, and in your flesh, the emotion of the supreme joy quivered beneath my mouth, intoxicating me. My folly was to seek other kisses....

ALL THE SHADES

O beloved, you are beautiful, we adore you! Come to us!

THE OLD MAN

Get out! Get out, accursed phantoms, thieves of love! Go away! She has betrayed me, but now she's mine, dead or alive!

SARA

Back, old man! You won't be my lover! He's before me, the one who will be the last! I can see him, crawling out of the darkness of the abyss. He's coming, the man who shall have me, body and soul, who will enjoy my proud beauty completely… he's my master. His powerful rut will putrefy my flesh! He's the grave-worm! I feel him penetrating my life, fiber by fiber; my skin is already moistened by his kiss, and my eyes are melting in my head!

Can you not help me, you who have loved me so much? Is there no salvation? I'm going to him! I'm dying.…

She falls backwards. The old man launches himself toward the fatal beauty of the woman who was his daughter, but the shades have already seized Sara and vanished, taking away the one they loved so much, body and soul, far from terrestrial corruption, into the purifying fire, toward the great clement darkness.…

Now the rain is descending in floods in the darkness, with a grave and harmonious whisper, a sharp and vibrant perfume. The old man experiences pleasure. Fate has thus allowed him to taste, for a moment, an overwhelming unconsciousness; but the respite is brief, for now, born of that which is irremediable, born from dolor, crime and death, born of the mystery of future expiation, a powerful phantom is the old man's master.

And upon the old man descends the power of the Eternal Shadow; and the entire sum of misfortune and torture cannot equal the horror of his fate, for the phantom is Fear.

THE VALLEY
NAMED SOLITUDE

I shall give you
The magic opal and the gold ring
And what is worth more than glory or fortune,
My robe woven with moonlight.

Leconte de Lisle, "The Elves"

A summer night, warm and moonlit.

The valley is slumbering in Solitude. And in the primitive majesty, the hills, covered with woods, hold up their immemorial peaks to the heavens.

To the west, a torrent surges from an elevated gorge, tumbling down the mountain-side. Framed by hanging draperies of ivy, singing with its harmonious voice, the stream runs over the shiny rocks and rebounds in crystal spray and vaporous foam. Masses of vegetation emerge and, seemingly floating in the middle of the water, mingle there in long filaments, which descend all the way to the lake bathing the foot of the hill.

The lake is sparkling with silver, thanks to the indolent waves softly agitating the rushes and water-lilies girdling the water. Toward the middle, pale lacustrian plants extend their corollas, in soft or violent hues, and their fleshy leaves. The banks are fresh grass speckled with asphodels. Large trees shade the base if the mountain,

The most beautiful flowers grow in multitudes in the valley, where woods of myrtle and ebony mingle with holm-oaks, whose old mossy trunks welcome virgin vines, honeysuckle, jasmine and wild roses. Great white rocks loom up in the clearings, along with grass banks that are reminiscent of altars or tombs. No animate being appears to inhabit the valley.

The full moon, bathing the valley with its magical light, adds a romantic prestige to everything. On their obscure slopes, the high hills conceal mysteries and apparitions; white vapors visit the profound and woods and linger in the shadows cut out on the water; at a distance, the flowers seem as far away as the nebulous stars, swaying the harmony of their embalmed heads; the reeds stirring in the silvery undulation of the lake seem to be listening to distant voices responding to the voice of the cascade, which is expanding into the silence and vibrating languorously.

And in the enchanted purity, Night reigns over the Solitude.

Now, two human creatures appear, emerging from the wood: a man and a woman. They are young, walking side by side, wearing cotton tunics.

Beneath her black hair, covered by a white veil, the woman's face seems possessed of a passionate, troubling and triumphant beauty. With her large blue eyes she contemplates the valley, and sometimes glances at her companion, who remains taciturn.

Both move toward the lake. They stop by the cascade, on the grassy bank where the waves die indolently at their feet.

After a moment, the man, extending his arm, calls three times to the Enchantress whose name is Solitude, or Chimera, but whom no one knows.

And the face of the Enchantress rises from the lake. She looms up in the midst of the flowers, in the middle of the waters, which seem to form transparent draperies, as light as rays of moonlight, streaming with iridescent pearls, dressing her with long pleats. Heavy tresses, glaucous and amber, fall over her shoulders. Her eyes, luminous and changing, are like the sky or the sea. Her smiling mouth is melancholy. Above her forehead, large droplets form a crown, scintillating like diamonds, while others form a necklace at her throat and bracelets round her bare arms. And the beauty of the Enchantress spreads invincible charms, and there seems to be an indefinable allusion within her to the beauty of the young woman who is contemplating her, standing on the banks where asphodels flower.

The man's eyes are lowered, and he stands there silent and tremulous. Finally, his voice rises up, hesitantly, in the harmonious music of the cascade.

"Solitude," he says, "Chimera, Unreality, whatever your name is, whom I have loved uniquely in the past, I am abandoning you because I want to give myself, with no return, to the woman beside me—to this woman, love for whom has arisen before my disgust for the real world to make me adore everything real in her person. She has entrapped me with light bonds stronger than any chain. He smile is now my life, her body is my universe, and I am the slave of her eyes.

"Adieu, you who are the multiple, adorable and deceitful soul of the valley named Solitude! Adieu. My hours will no longer be your hours. Charms stronger than yours have enchanted me, for living lips have educated me in love...."

He falls silent.

The Enchantress cries: "You want to leave me, then, for a woman! Have you lost the memory of dreams in which I have cradled you for so many nights, the immense joys that you have known in me and the marvels I have created for your pleasure? With me, you have possessed all things by means of thought, and is that not the true possession? Have I not given you all splendors and all voluptuousness? We have built magical palaces in the sumptuous domains of our caprice. In the gardens of our fantasies we have extended rivers and lakes beneath the setting sun, magic mirrors through which our visions have passed. We have made the most beautiful flowers grow, more perfumed than the flowers of the earth, and the breeze has engendered heady religious effluvia and unforgettable harmonies in the embalmed branches.

"Our dreams have sailed over seas of amethyst, emerald and topaz, beneath skies of unknown purity, beneath clouds as pompous as fêtes. We have, for ourselves alone, brought all centuries, all civilizations and all barbarisms to life again. Every city and every nation of times past and present has offered itself to us, without ever causing us to know disillusionment, since its decor reproduces our very dreams.

"You have known all glories and all triumphs. You have been an invincible conqueror, made peoples tremble with the hoof-beats of your horse. You have been a philosopher and a scholar; masters of science throughout the world have bowed down before your genius. You have been an artist whose divine works were adored by generations. You have possessed perfect beauty allied with irresistible force and universal intelligence!

What women have I refused you? Empresses celebrated for their charm, the priestesses of every cult, the most famous courtesans, all women, in their various beauty, have been delivered in turn to you with passion, with terror and with pride, in accordance with your caprice. You have descended the tenebrous roads of vice, horror and blood. You have known corruption, theft, murder and sacrilege. You have known the proud abasement of supreme debauches and the delights of cowardly ferocities. You have enjoyed tears that you have caused to flow. You have enjoyed supplications and impotent rages, broken by your will!

"Have you not lived all lives, savored the bitterness and charm of all joys and all misfortunes, all strengths and all weaknesses? Have you not possessed all human things completely, and have you not raised your proud desire toward things that are not of the earth, toward unknown paradises, supreme delights?

"Come back—you do not know what earthly loves are, in which sensuality engenders dolor and death!

"Come back, come back—I have the secret of every dream, the key to every door, and my kiss is immortal...."

Thus speaks the Enchantress—but the rival voice of the living woman rises up and replies to her: "No, you're not immortal, and you're not anything at all. In you there's nothing true, and the joys you invoke are not your own. You see them in the distance and cannot attain them...as water flees the thirst of the damned. In vain you try to entice them, in vain you strive in exhausting struggle; your imposture cannot deceive entirely, and your voice is false, to which you provide the reply yourself....

"A man cannot believe you, he cannot love you; you have prostituted, in your impotence, the very identity of his desire, to which you have given birth without satisfying it, of which you are the reflection without ever being the image.

"You are within him, and too much within him. He lacks in you the unforeseen that is present in others, which is the personal soul of a living creature whose will, taste and desire, acting out of free choice, gives the pride and joy of having been chosen.

"You are an automatic figure, whose mechanism always acts in the same way. Like the actor of an overly familiar play, you know the intrigue before it is knotted, and the vain simulacrum of the anticipated denouement, only suggesting the joy that it would give if everything were sincere. And your kisses give themselves to the void, and your arms open to embrace a fugitive shadow....

"That is the Paradise you promise to your lovers. It is by means of that bait of lies that you want to vanquish me, who is soul and flesh—who possesses, for the enjoyment of pensive tenderness, the enigmatic profundity of my eyes, the mysterious softness of my passionate words and the expression of love that extends over my beauty, like the caress of a spring evening over a garden; who possesses, for sensual pleasure, the irresistible attractions of my naked flesh, the transport of my embrace and the intoxication of my kiss....

"I am the dream and the reality; I am the divine flower that is uniquely capable of intoxicating the body and the mind! I am the One who is stronger than the World! And all joys without me are nothing, and all misfortunes with me are nothing. A single one of my loving glances can send the bitterest dolor to sleep, and render all pride and enjoyment to my lover, in disdain for those who are not loved.

"When a man drowns his eyes in mine, he forgets earth and heaven; when my lips are on his lips, he faints, scorning everything else; when voluptuousness turns him upside-down on my quivering breast, from which perfumes of love rise, I am his triumph and his God!

"Don't try to fight me; I abandon to you those of whom cruel destiny has made objects of horror, disgust and pity, and who only have your exaltations to deceive the desires of their flesh that real kisses will never calm. They are granted to you in advance and no one will compete with you for them, but my lover, in his youth and beauty, is not destined to that puerile pursuit of an ungraspable mirage. He was created for sincere embraces, for living caresses, for all the seductions of human passion! I love him and he loves me, and for our marvelous amours the days and nights unfurl their enchanted future...."

She has seized her lover's hand, and gazes proudly at the Enchantress named Solitude or Chimera, but who is unknown. Now the poignant voice of the enchantress rises up again, to the accompaniment of the rhythmic resonance of the water.

"Oh," she said, "your reproach is unjust! The soul of a man cannot be content with the world; it always seeks the impossible here. Borne by my wings, with me, the Chimera, it launches toward the great sky, where its dreams search madly for their incarnation....

"A man soars into the sky with me, his Chimera...and if he is able to give himself to me completely, I envelop him with unparalleled joys. If he does not ask himself whether he is dreaming or not, the dream will not deceive him and will give his mind unequaled voluptuousness, and even give him voluptuousness in the flesh. However, the majority cannot; they want to attach me to the earth and search around them for the realization of that which cannot be realized.

"It is the cruel dementia of this man that wants to abandon me; that is his damnation, for what he loves in you, poor creature whose attractions will wither tomorrow, what he loves unconsciously in you, is me: the Enchantress named Chimera. With his dreams, his hopes and his sense of beauty he has woven a magical cloak of seduction and harmony, which he has thrown over you. As he has made up the appearances of your body cosmetically, with his illusions, he has fashioned another soul for you, a companion of his own soul. He has created you in the image of his desire, and has so much desire that you should be thus that he truly believes that you are....

"What he loves in you is the reflection of his dreams of me! You are the road guiding him toward the goal, you are the opium that procures intoxication, but you are not the goal and you are not the intoxication; you are merely the mask of the phantom he adores, which he embraces recklessly upon your lips, to which he addresses his passionate plaints and all the delirious ardors of his soul: the redoubtable phantom that makes you shiver when you see its shadow passing in your lover's eyes; the phantom that, on earth, is known as the Ideal.

"O Ideal, eternal enemy, eternal benefactor, it is for you that the prodigious efforts are accomplished of solitary martyrs, the destined suffers of torment whose Hell and redemption you are. It is because of you that the happiness attained is poisoned by disillusionment and the worst dolors are soothed. It is because of you that there are supplicant triumphs and agonies full of ecstasy, for you are glory and misfortune, and the true God!

"Be careful, O Daughter of Men, for I tell you this: it is the Ideal that your lover always thinks that he has found in you, and will find until the moment he sees you for what you are: an imperfect human creature a thousand times inferior to his dream. Then he will weep all the tears of dolor and shame, and you will suffer a distress more atrocious than any other, for he will scorn you, and that will be unjust....

"And in the reality that you possess, the horizons of the dream will be effaced forever, definitively, and you will be condemned to veritable life, to the horror of monotonous days of bitterness and hatred, to the intolerable unhappiness of having lost faith in the Chimera...and that is the unavoidable Future."

The young woman, leaning toward her lover, smiles, and,

plunging her eyes into his, intoxicates him with her breath, which has the scent of jasmine, murmurs: "Come, my love, it's the nuptial hour; the night is enchanted and I'm mad with love. Come—our first kiss will give us the Ideal.

They both quit the bank where the waves die near the asphodels, going toward the woods of flowering myrtles, toward voluptuousness, toward real life…

They walk, enlaced together, madly in love, without seeing the tenacious shadows that attach themselves to their heels: the shadows named Disillusionment, Lassitude and Disgust; those named Jealousy, Deception and Hatred; and without seeing, in front of them, seizing each of their seconds in order to make it the prey of the past, the hideous Old Age that oppresses, ever more cruelly, and the fear of Death.

And the Enchantress named Solitude, named Chimera, but who is unknown, remains in the middle of the waters, weeping crystal tears, raising her bare, writhing arms toward the heavens, as if to implore or curse the enchanted Moon.

LIKE CHILDREN WHO
RUN AFTER A MASK

*There are men for whom illusions are as
necessary as life.... When they approach the
truth they draw away very quickly, like
children who run after a mask, but flee if
the mask turns round....*

Nicolas Chamfort

Yes, said the old man, it was somewhere near here. As I came around the great rocks that form the summit of the hill, on my way back from the Orient, the sunset was red and dusk was emerging slowly from the gorges, the idle precursor of night. When I reached the western slope, darkness already had its empire.

I descended through the darkness of a sycamore wood and halted on the edge of a plateau overlooking the valley. The moon's disk emerged from the profound horizon and rose into the back sky. Its green light bathed the jagged chain of the mountains and the plain at their feet.

Something was happening in the plain at the feet of the mountains.

Emerging from a narrow defile, a cortege was advancing slowly. First I saw a troop of halberdiers with shiny helmets. After them, came men in robes on horses under strict control, and then priests clad in black or white. Among them, preceded by a cleric holding up a silver crucifix, was a bishop with his mantle, crosier and miter. Then I saw two men who were isolated in the middle of the soldiers. One was the executioner and the other, bare-headed, gagged and chained, was the condemned man. They were walking side by side. More soldiers came next, in considerable numbers. Then there was a large crowd of people, sometimes silent, sometimes uttering deathly cries.

The goal of the procession was at the foot of the hill where I was standing. There was a gibbet waiting for them, with the gesture of its stiff arm.

Then, because such things interest me, I went down very rapidly, much lower, in order to get a better view.

The company had formed up around the machine of death, the priests in front with the judges, and then the soldiers and the common people.

The condemned man was brought to the foot of the ladder. The bishops approached with his crucifix, but the man turned his head away and I saw his pale forehead and the gleam of his eyes, although I was a long way away. Meanwhile, cries of anathema rose from the crowd. The condemned man climbed the steps toward death. The rope was placed around his neck, but then, raising his bowed head, he extended his bound arms toward the crowd, the soldiers, the judges and the priests, as if to bless and forgive them....

Already, without the executioner having touched him, he had abandoned the ladder and was hanging there, motionless—dead.

Now, all of those who were there looked at him for a moment, and then looked at one another, in silence; and it seemed that they were gripped by a great fear, for they fled in bewilderment. They bumped into one another, were knocked down and trampled, and got up in order to flee more rapidly, without looking back. The soldiers dropped their weapons, the priests tore off their robes and the judges whipped their mounts, pitilessly bowling over any obstacle.

They disappeared pell-mell, and nothing remained but the hanged man and his scaffold, in the greenish glimmer of the moonlight.

I went down the steep slope, reached the plain and then the gibbet. I leaned toward the ground and I recognized, amid the dark grass, the presence of the magical plant known as the mandrake.

Turning toward the brilliant moon, the mother of incantations, I dismounted, knelt down, and, pronouncing the magical words, I tore the marvelous root from the ground, fearfully. A few drops of bloody sap sprang from my hand. I was not burned by it, and knew that was a beneficent augury.

I climbed the ladder that was still below the scaffold, seized the hanged man and lifted him up to the arm of the gibbet, which was a broad and sturdy beam.

I sat down with the body beside me. I untied the rope, removed the gag and freed the hands. Then I shouted loudly, toward the stars, the invocation of life that is found in the Book that comes from Nineveh[6] and nowhere else—a book more profound than any other. I shouted the invocation at the stars and I put the salutary root into the dead man's mouth.

The dead man's eyes opened, and the dead man sat up beside me under the gibbet. Then, casting the plant with the human form over his left shoulder he said: "That which had to be accomplished has been accomplished." And he added: "Why intervene in my destiny?"

"I saw you dead," I said, "and then I saw the fear of the executioners and their disorder. That told me that you were beyond ordinary human beings, and that there had been iniquity in your execution. Then I desired to know the cause of your martyrdom, and the measure of their injustice. I desired to know too, if you can tell me, what land you have traversed

---

6. Fragments of the *Enuma Elish*, containing the Babylonian Creation myth, allegedly the oldest book in the world, were found by Austen Layard in the ruins of Nineveh in 1849; a version was published by George Smith in 1876. The text acquired a reputation among nineteenth-century occultists as a repository of Hermetic secrets—supposedly contained, of course, in the bits that Layard did not find.

in going toward the Shadow. And that is why I dared to make use, on this propitious night, beneath the incantational moon, of the science that I acquired at the price of my very soul in the arcana of the profound Book of the Divines of Nineveh—the book more profound than any other. I beg you, if I have done wrong, to absolve me...."

"Yes," he said. "There are causes that you have been able to know, but another cause, coming from the Unknown, has engendered them, which is this: the things that must be accomplished, are accomplished. Now, that was engraved on the page of Time.

"For you, for as long as I can, I shall continue to speak. I shall tell you what I know about my terrestrial existence. About death, I shall tell you nothing, for it is not permitted that humans should see beyond, nor prior to, their momentary existence. But that country is not a country of shadows....

"I do not know my beginning. Always I have been similar. I have lived for many centuries and I have seen, as in a dream, things changing around me. I did not pay much attention to them, for I looked into my soul, preferably the soul of dead time. I have lived in the lands where the ancient sages lived. I understand all languages, I have read all books. I have plunged into the mystery of all religions, but Doubt remained my companion, with the cold light of its clairvoyance. It has never left me, and that was the burden of my hours....

"But I have thought so much, in silence and meditation— sometimes on the precept of the god engendered by the waters, with the fakirs that guard the pagodas on the Ganges; sometimes on the tenebrous hieroglyphics at the feet of sphinxes in the Egyptian deserts; sometimes on the books of sacred morality in the monasteries of the Middle Kingdom; sometimes inspiring myself with the belief of the Prophet in the shadow of a mosque; and finally in the solemn meditation of abbeys where the monks seem to be shadows exalting the maxims of the crucified Nazarene—I have thought so much that my mind has surpassed the ordinary limits of human understanding.

"With the aid of philosophers of all times I have acquired a perfect knowledge of the human heart, and I have also penetrated the arcana of the Rose-Cross, and fathomed the unique book of Hermes Trismegistus. I know all the secrets of Solomon and the science of the heavenly bodies, the recorders of terrestrial destinies....

"Now, as I found myself in the desert where Babylon was one night when I was dreaming, the cause of human evil was revealed to my soul; it was revealed to me in its entirety, at a stroke, and I learned at the same time, that which it was good to know, and the method of knowing it.

"Yes, I knew then, by virtue of a manifestation of eternal powers, that all the misery of life stems from this alone: that human beings are unaware of their duration. I also knew by what mathematics it was possible to calculate the number of days allocated to the existence of every human being.

"I began by calculating the end of my terrestrial destinies. The presages indicated the evening that is upon us. The presages also indicated that immediately afterwards, I would be resuscitated with a being torn from the earth.

"However, when I possessed the secret, I was aware that it was necessary for me to spread it through the world. I quit the solitudes and the society of the dead. I thought that I ought to choose an isolated city, create disciples and send them abroad bearing word of the Truth. After much research, I believed that the city behind those hills ought to be chosen among them all. I stopped there, and began work.

"I spoke in the streets, at the crossroads, in the schools and in the assemblies to announce what it was possible for me to teach humans. I spoke about the power I had. I represented the immense security in study and in action, in pleasures and in enterprises, that would emerge from knowledge. I spoke about the marvelous and tranquil certainty that would arise, with wisdom, in initiated hearts, permitting them, whatever their beliefs might be, to prepare for the inevitable end....

"I expressed these things, and as I know the words that

induce complete conviction and the words that no one can doubt, everyone had faith in me. They were gripped by invincible curiosity and begged me to extract them from ignorance of the number of days that still lay before them, to unveil the hour and the instant when that which cannot be avoided or corrupted would extend its irresistible power over their destinies.

"They begged me, with the most forceful supplications, and I was obedient to their desire. They knew, with no possible illusion, and all of them were immediately plunged into despair. They lamented, struck their breasts, cursing me and deploring their misfortune, that of now knowing how little time they had to live—however long the indicated time might be. Their anguish increased by the minute; they were more unfortunate than they could say. I was astonished, but I thought that it was only the manifestation of human weakness before anything unknown, and that they would recover their spirits before long.

"Meanwhile, those who did not yet know fled from me in terror, in order not to know—but the power of curiosity brought them back. They interrogated me with a feverish hesitation. They emerged from doubt and, falling down in fright, called upon the deadliest spirits of the earth, the air and the sea to assail me. Far from thinking of distributing sagely the days that remained to them, they thought of nothing but pleasure, in order to stifle the voice of time in their hearts. Scholars abandoned their work, merchants their business, and all of them, in terror, rushed in cowardly fashion toward lust and intoxication, in which they sought oblivion, sobbing with horror. And unhappiness, shame and fear dominated the city.

"The judges assembled and the crowd came to denounce me. Soldiers were sent to bind me and to take me before the tribunal. The oldest of the judges, whose long white beard covered his breast, said to me: 'Listen to me, Man, we have examined your work in its causes and its results; we have examined it impartially and we have found it detestable. You say that you are a benefactor of humanity, when you are the worst of torturers. You said that if we knew the hour at which the supremely redoubtable one will extends its power over us, we would be able to await it with tranquility, and would be able, with wisdom, to prepare ourselves to receive it. That is false.

"'Look at what has become of those whom curiosity has gripped under the influence of your fallacious word. See their anguish and their torment, and recognize the fruits of your revelation. As they have found it, so will all those for whom the veil of fear is lifted find it. Now, we wish this to cease. We want to remain in salutary ignorance, in unconsciousness and indecision. Tomorrow frightens us and we adore the mystery that permits us still to believe in life. We are confined in hope, and we close our eyes, block our ears. However, the anxiety survives and no one can kill it completely.

"'What would happen, then, if we knew the law of our destinies, if we had to count every hour, every minute, every rapid temporary second, fleeing irrevocably? What torture could equal that of being able to say, with certainty: now, so many days, then so many, then so many…now it is in three days, now it is tomorrow…it is today, already, and what fate awaits us? That is the true mystery that we do not know, in spite of our religions and our priests. That alone is what it is important for us to know, and which you do not tell us. You destroy what is good in our doubt and you leave horror to subsist.

"'And after all, what need to humans have to know anything whatsoever? We do not want any certainty that shackles our pleasures. We have bodies, and those bodies want to kill their soul in order to live in tranquility. It is necessary to abolish all looking forward. The future is troubled. We only want to see the present and to deny death even when it touches us with its terrible hand. We refuse to fathom anything. We want to enjoy possible enjoyments in peace. Spiritual science is the mother of unslaked desires, dolorous meditations and scorn for the sensuality that is the only thing that matters.

"'Ignorance, with its indifference, its idleness and its vices, is the best companion of human beings for their ambiguous destinies. We want to conserve it, and you shall die, you who want to extract us from it. You shall die. You shall be hanged. Don't try to respond; our ears are blocked with wax, for your voice is more dangerous than that of the sirens, and will infuse us with accursed curiosity. Tomorrow, you will be hanged. You will be declared an impostor and guilty of sacrilege, and everyone will believe it, in the joy that your predictions are belied.

"'Tomorrow, your science and your strength will be destroyed. That must be, for the happiness of human beings is not to know....'

"The judge fell silent, and I saw that I did not know the human soul very well, and that, for the science in question, humankind is the only book, and not books, of which I had not read enough....

"Thus, this evening, I was brought here and hanged, amid the howls of the multitude.

"Adieu. You know what you desired to know. The moon is high in the sky. This is the hour when I must return whence I came. My secret will go with me, for that is also written on the page of Time...."

He let himself slip from the arm of the scaffold and remained hanged at the end of his rope.

As for me, I took the ladder away, and then I left the plain forever, leaving the gibbet, its hanged man and the incantatory light of the green moon.

Ever since that time, however, which is very distant, my mind has been stubbornly tormented by a problem that I cannot resolve: that of knowing whose situation is worse—the situation of the hanged man, or the situation of those who hanged him.

THE REFUGE

Then, everything would blaze with a
chaste festival of light and from
subterranean auroras, between the
stones, inflexible lilies would grow....

Henri de Régnier, "Hertulie"

Covering a prodigious area, the immemorial Forest supports the passage of centuries.

The power of winter has ensorcelled the Forest. Snow reigns there; it resides in the clouds that the sun never penetrates, descends therefrom to bury the ground that is already buried and load the branches of trees, and, by virtue of the accumulation of its flakes, the sorrowful giants reveal their black nudity, which leaves have never reclad, and the solemn tranquility of their meditation is untroubled.

The snow resides in the clouds, covers the ground and loads the trees; its perpetual domination establishes the triumph of silence, immobility and mystery. There is no night or day there, but a vague light bathes everything with a vaporous shroud.

In the Forest, no human being can live, but naked maidens, daughters of the snow, haunt the roads and the crossroads, swinging from the branches of trees without causing them to bend, whirling around in the clearings and raising their persuasive voices, which sing of desire, repose and death—which sing of the joy of the slumber without awakening, drowning all lassitude in the icy layer to contemplate forever the supreme mask of one's dream.

They are seductive; their bodies are supple and their skin is cold. Their victims lie beneath the snow, in the embrace of the funerary cloak, their limbs stiff, their faces blue, their frozen tears attached to the lashes, their lips drawn back from the teeth in order still to smile, to smile definitively, with ecstasy, at the murderous and divine faces of the maidens, the daughters of the snow, the daughters of death.

To the north, the Forest comes to an end at a wall of rocks that bars the extent, vertiginous and covered in ice. There is a door, which is made of bronze. Its thickness forms, on a pedestal, the seated figure of an old man, inclining his attentive visage toward the woods. An identical statue is back to back with that one, and makes up the other face of the batten. The two figures are prophetic. No human power can violate that door, for it was established by dwarf blacksmiths, and it closes the exit from the place where the Chief resides who reigns over the ensorcelled Forest, over the polar regions and the subterranean expanses, who is the sovereign of beings that humans sense but do not know, who holds in his hands the keys of silence, darkness and winter, who is the monarch of mysterious forces....

Closed by the door, the grotto develops its immensity, toward which the metallic face directs the gravity of its surveillance. The grotto is extracted from darkness by a hundred torches fixed to the walls. The walls are marble; the ground is covered in sand. The area is striped by a curtain of icy trees, whose translucent frosted branches overlap, reflecting the torchlight and allowing glimpses of the forges burning in the background, perpetually, in a vast gallery. Sometimes, the shadows of dwarf blacksmiths pass by, and their songs rise up, cadenced by the resounding noise of hammers.

The Chief is in the grotto. He walks, holding his giant stature rigid. His eyes are hollow; his beard is white. His robe and bonnet are made of chain mail, his blue steel belt bears engraved charms and supports his blade. Under the Chief's eyelid, his first tear, which has never flowed, remains frozen by the bitter

pride of power and solitude. And yet his soul burns with reck-
less ardors and passionate torments, and all the desires of the
earth assail him and tear him. The Chief walks from one wall to
the other, grave and strong—and full of anguish, for he senses
the hour approaching when his fate will be decided.

Against a wall a maiden is chained, the daughter of a distant
king, abducted by magic from the beautiful land where her
father reigns, where the young woman lived adorable years in
the luxury of palaces, in the mild shade and sunlight of gardens
of flowers and streams, surrounded by the primitive charm of
woods, in pleasures, fêtes and fantasy, in the intoxication of the
glimpsed charm of love. The maiden is held by a golden chain;
she is naked beneath a white fur that leaves her breast uncov-
ered. Her beauty is striking and delicate. Her head inclines the
gilded shadow of her hair over her bosom, and her blue eyes
follow the internal evocation of happy memories, which domi-
nate and are mingled with the astonishment of her adventure,
and, above all, the anxious ignorance of her fate. In her right
hand she has conserved a myrtle branch whose flowers have
withered.

Thus, the dwarfs sing in the silence.[7]

THE DWARFS

We are the children of the bowels of the earth! We are the
blacksmiths whose work is incomparable! We are the patient
miners who have never seen the sun!

Black, ugly and robust, we increase the curvature of our
spines by leaning over our anvils; our muscular arms brandish
the hammer and out hands make the fire spring forth! We have

---

7. Although the headquote is from Henri de Régnier, this scenario is
clearly derived from Anatole France's extended fairy tale "Abeille" (1882;
tr. as "Honey-Bee" and "The Kingdom of the Dwarfs"), in which a princess
is abducted by the King of the Dwarfs, from whose subterranean kingdom
her fiancé Georges sets out to rescue her. Boutet's story might be considered
an ideological reply made on behalf of a nocturnal *homme sauvage*.

been working thus, without fatigue, relentlessly and joylessly, forever, for we are very old....

Sad and repulsive, we create marvels, and our disgrace inhabits splendors that we alone contemplate. Ah, we would be rich and well-adorned if we wanted to be! And all women would sell themselves to us, if we were not so hideous, if we could approach them!

We know the mines where all the riches of the world slumber. We dig out all the seams of virgin gold and fine silver. We unearth diamonds, rubies, amethysts, sapphires, topazes, emeralds, heliotropes and hyacinths. We discover beryls, sardonyxes, thallites, tourmalines, chrysoprases, sanguines and amphobolites. We fish for pearls in subterranean seas. We sculpt crystal. We have found gems fallen from the moon, and the tears of stars, and we have hidden the fabulous jewels named Carbuncles, which no human has seen and for which the Wyvern, now blind, seeks indefinitely.

Perennially burned by the ardent flames, always bent over by labor, always imprisoned in subterranean locales, we are unfortunate. Our destiny is odious; it is even more odious because we know that there are enjoyments on the earth, and that we shall never possess them! We know that the sun exists in the great chimerical and divine sky, that the moon rises in the vapors of evening, above troubled seas and somber forests. We know that there are flowery gardens, harmonious and aromatic marine strands, women more beautiful than landscapes, more voluptuous than the caress of spring....

We are aware, vaguely but surely, all the joys that are not for us, all the beauties that scorn our ugliness, and we are thirsty for tenderness and idleness, for lust and dreams, and there are furious desires within us that will never be appeased.

Relentlessly, for the master who suffers our dolors, we blacksmith dwarfs, sons of inert matter, have always forged the hard metals, shaped the scintillating stones, hollowed out the eternal masses of the round Earth. We do not complain, but are devoid of hope. We now full well that our destinies will never be modified, and the songs of our hoarse voices have no other effect, no other purpose, than to measure out on the polished anvil the beats of the sonorous hammer!

And the chained maiden murmurs the plaint of her dolor and her fear.

THE MAIDEN

Oh my Lord, help me in my distress! What has become of me? What power has taken possession of me? To what place have I been taken? I'm full of shame at being naked, under the horrible gazes of supernatural statues. I'm frightened by these wild clamors. I regret everything that I have lost; I fear everything that surrounds me. I'm afraid! Oh, I'm afraid of that redoubtable Chief, who is the master here, marching from one wall to the other in his limitless strength. Am I not to be rescued? Where is the power of my father the king, and his faithful guards and armies without number? Will the man I love and who loves me not attempt anything for me, or has he already been vanquished by the strength of which I am the slave? Is there no more hope for me save for death?

The iron form, who is extending his attentive face toward the grotto, of which it is the inviolable door, causes his voice to resound:

THE PROPHETIC VOICE

Chief, the adversary is approaching! My exterior face, turned toward the horizon of the world, can see him. He is crossing the wilderness at a gallop. His breastplate is silver, his helmet bears an eagle and his face is as handsome as the visage of a god!

He is galloping, galloping, galloping! And his horse in marking the primitive snow with the iron of its shoes, and his black hair is whistling in the icy wind, and it's in vain that the deceptive maidens whisper their prayers and seductions in his ears. He is galloping, and his horse is moving more swiftly than the wind, and before him bound passions, hatred and love!

He is galloping; he is here now, and is voice is going to demand entry, and my exterior face, turned toward the horizon of the world, will be able to respond to his prayers and threats... but the door will open for him, O Chief of Solitudes, for the passions that are agitating in him and carrying him away cannot be vanquished by any other force than themselves!

Outside, in the snow, muffling the hoofbeats of a horse, a human voice is heard in the solemn silence of the solitudes.

THE VOICE OF THE KNIGHT

Statue, turn on your hinges and let me pass!

THE EXTERIOR FACE OF THE STATUE

Knight, return whence you came!

THE KNIGHT

I shall enter! I shall see the accursed Chief and I shall recover what he has stolen from me!

THE STATUE

Knight, there is no strength to master my strength.

THE KNIGHT

Let me pass. I come in the name of a powerful king who reigns over the countries of the center. If his daughter is not released, his invincible army will march here, burning the forest before it; his vengeance will be pitiless.

THE STATUE

Knight, your threats are vain. Either you are speaking without thinking, or your lost love is absorbing you to the point at which it is allowing you to ignore your surroundings.

How dare you speak of an army after having traversed the Forest? Have you not realized that a force superior to human forces defends its integrity? Have you not understood that the primitive snow could, in the space of an evening, bury thousands of men in its moving tomb? Have you not understood that the mirage of deceitful fogs can lead entire populations astray in the mortal paths of despair and hunger? Have you not recognized the existence of abysms that bar the route with their hidden maws, capable of swallowing hosts as numerous as the stars? Do you remember the fits of dull anguish that came to assail you, the superhuman specters flying through the clouds and augural voices heard in the clearings? I tell you this: there are material perils in the forest as well as supernatural perils, and only the protection of the Chief has preserved you from his somber guardians, Terror and death!

THE KNIGHT

I sense that you are telling the truth. I remember strange perils glimpsed in the Forest; I remember the temptation that sang in my ears. But if I am thus protected, it is with some objective in mind. Will gold satisfy you?

THE STATUE

Are you insane, Knight? Do you not know that we are masters of inexhaustible mines where there are gold, silver and precious stones. Your riches come from us, and you only possess what it pleases us to abandon to you.

THE KNIGHT

What do you want, then? Speak? Are you toying with me?

THE STATUE

Knight, your anger is vain, Return whence you came.

THE KNIGHT

Let me pass, let me pass! She is my life. I want to see her!

THE STATUE

Knight, are you sure that she loves you and that you love her?

THE KNIGHT

Her soul reflects my soul; I have read in her eyes what I read in my heart: we love one another.

THE STATUE

Long ordeals fortify love…or extinguish it!

THE KNIGHT

I love her! I adore her! I implore you, let me see her!"

THE STATUE

Knight, the masks of shadow are the form of our will and we model in the clouds the resemblances that we please…but the shadow is not the face, and the clouds and wind are deceptive.

THE KNIGHT

Ah! I shall enter or I shall die fighting hand to hand with you, ironic Figure who laughs at my dolor!

THE STATUE

I do not have a perishable body.

The knight leaps down from his horse. He draws his sword and precipitates himself toward the face of the door—but he is stopped by an enchantment. In vain he struggles and agitates his blade; his strength can do nothing, and he stops, exhausted. Then, despairingly, he wrings his arms, kneels down on the ground, and prays.

THE KNIGHT

God, creator of the world, master of all things, have pity, in the name of Justice and in the name of Love.

THE STATUE

You shall enter, then. You have finally said the words that you had to say. You shall enter, for that must be, and, for you or your adversary, the coming hour will be fatal. Pass, Knight! Go to your destiny. What shall be accomplished, shall be accomplished!

With a loud sob, the door turns on its hinges and grants passage. The knight goes in and the metallic mass closes again behind him. He sees the entire grotto; he sees the Chief; he sees the maiden. He wants to run forward, but enchantment binds him. The maiden reaches imploring arms toward him. The dwarfs stop singing. The Chief of the Solitudes is standing against a wall, motionless.

THE KNIGHT

Chief, I come to you with no offers and no threats. With me, there are justice and love. Surrender the woman you have abducted unjustly. I have come in search of her, for we love one another, and no force cam combat Love.

Chief, release the maiden, break your enchantments. The time of ordeals is over and I want to carry her away on my horse in the intoxication of passion and liberty.

THE CHIEF

Your words are true. Love is free, and master of the world. That is what guides me. The ordeal must be concluded.

Speak, O Knight! Tell the one you love what joys you promise her. Describe all the happiness and all the attractions of your country, of her country: its charms, its fêtes, its sensualities. Find the words that move the soul; seduce her once again by means of that which has seduced her before, by means of that which is her very life. I shall speak thereafter, and she will chose her fate freely.

THE KNIGHT

Are you jesting, O Chief? Is not your clemency mere derision? Is it not evident that, without hesitation, whatever words are pronounced, the released Maiden will come into my arms to flee toward the land of liberty, sunlight and love?

THE CHIEF

What I have said will be.

THE KNIGHT

Well then, I shall speak. What does it matter to me, after all, if I torture your soul with the evocation of joys that you will never possess? What does your very presence matter? I shall sing the divine poetry of nature and love to charm my beloved.

I celebrate the glory of happy lands that light and warmth bathe with their vibrant caresses. I evoke the sun of spring streaming over the sea of amethyst, emerald and topaz, sailing, a god of flame, in the immense expansive sky where the clouds are draped, in love with the day, swaying and vanishing. I invoke the splendor of midday in summer, over the vast fields of ripe wheat, gilded like the hair of the women of our country.

I evoke the profound languor of stormy sunsets. Glory of autumn! Ruderal charm! Melancholy glamour! Aromas linger in the evening air, the dying sun bloodies the clouds and, already, the crepuscular mists mysteriously invest the lakes and valleys.

Darkness is falling. The moon is pouring the vaporous magic of its silvery rays over the sea and the woods. The marine strands are full of the acrid perfume of spindrift; magical gleams sparkle in the foam; the rhythm of the waves dies at our feet on the sand and shingle.

Let us go into the forests, let us penetrate the august and familiar peace of the great trees. The moist grass yields beneath our feet in the clearings. In the cool aromatic thickets the rain has calmed the expectation of thirsty leaves. A wild perfume floats around us and the soul of the woods quivers in the religious shadow....

Let us visit the gardens: here are harmonious fountains; here are basins with pure waves within marble rims. Plants are bathing here, golden fish are gleaming furtively here; swans are resident here; marvelous flowers mirror their dreaming corollas. Let us walk softly; the laurels and myrtles brush our hair....

Here is the terrace, bathing its polished feet in the lake... come, the night is profound; the scintillating dream of the stars reflects its golden fires in the velvet of the waters where the shadows transfigure familiar sights, where visions pass and die. The nightingale sings to your beauty. The emotion of the evening becomes nonchalant, our senses languid; the flowers swoon and intoxicate us....

O charm, here is silence! The darkness dreams within us. Like a spreading perfume, our transported soul expands, exalted in the sublime poetry of ineffable nature!

Oh, I love you! Let me plunge my gaze into your large eyes, as profound as your heart. I love you, O my soul! For me you are the universal beauty, the supreme seduction in which all the charms of land, sky and sea blossom! The sound of your voice is my delight; beneath your blonde hair, your fresh pallor is that of a young, newly-opened rose; your mouth is a dream of love and the flexible grace of your body inclining on my arm intoxicates me with a ravishing bewilderment....

O my bride, allow the enchanted softness of the night, perfumes and silence to palpitate within you, and you shall know what you are to me!

I belong to you; I admire you; I adore you. In you exists my strength, and my pride; to you aspire all my desires; for you, all my emotions are born and die. I no longer know anything that is not you, and you are the source and objective of my life.

Let us love one another! The hours are gentle. The ardor of youth is singing its divine song in our hearts. The voluptuousness of our love frightens my dream like a sacrilege and, for me, the enjoyment of God will be the kiss of your mouth....

The illusion of the silence is reborn. The Maiden is still listening to the voice that delights her. A bitter pain wrings the heart of those who are alone. Already, for some time, the vibration of the final echo has died away, cradled and abated between the marble walls.

THE CHIEF

Few words will be said now....

Something exists beyond that which you have celebrated, O living man! Night charms as daylight does, winter seduces as spring does, and what is known is very little by comparison with what is unknown. Insouciant and ignorant pleasure does not destroy the eternal anxiety, full of bitter joys, that is the consciousness of the immortal secret.

Maiden, lean over my soul. It is full of the shadow unknown to humans. In me reside all enigmas; I have penetrated the secrets of the potent earth; I hold the keys to mysterious doors; I know the magic words. Within me are miracles, cataclysms, prodigies. The aurora borealis is my torch; the darkness of the pole covers my slumbers; the terrestrial depths conceal my treasures. What humans do not know has been revealed to me. I have fathomed the things of the night. I know the mysteries of Time, Space and Number.

Oh, I suffer too! I am fully laden with power, but fully laden with misfortune! Solitude weighs upon my soul like a stone upon a sepulcher. Believe me, my destiny is superhuman; all pride intoxicates me; all regret strangles me. Sometimes I feel that I am God; sometimes I envy the shepherd who bathes his feet in the river and kisses his wife on the mouth. Enigma is within me like a splendor and a torture. I suffer because I know!

O Maiden, I offer you the dolorous grandeur of my fate, the terrible enchantments of the dark. In my arms you shall understand everything; you shall know what I know.

I shall not speak to you about the strength of my love; know only that for me, you are what God is to the elect. Into my destiny you would come as the angel of tenderness and poetry. For me you would be the sky, the stars and the sun, and the perfume of flowers and the shores of the sea, and the purity of springs, and the peace of the great woods.

You would give me the caresses of spring, the fresh softness of the morning breeze, the seductive languor of blossoming nature. I would drink delight and innocence from your lips, my forehead would be rejuvenated by your breath and my obscure consciousness and my heart torn by unslaked ardors, would finally be able to quiver with love....

O my child, O my queen, you alone will decide my fate. Your flight will plunge me into the abyss forever; you are the only woman I shall ever see; you are the beauty of my dream; you are the star in my darkness!

Stay or go...you are free.

The golden chain falls at the Maiden's feet, and again, there is silence. And claws of anguish tear every heart.

THE MAIDEN

Knight, return whence you came! I shall not go with you; I no longer know you. Tell those who are waiting for me that I am dead to them. Tell them that I am irredeemably wed, in the full determination of my youth, my beauty and my liberty, to the somber Spirit that has taken possession of me. Tell them that Shadow has become my homeland.

Oh, I know now what passion is! I am bound by the attraction beyond dolor; I am intoxicated by the joy of voluntary sacrifice; I am possessed by the irresistible desire to know what the living do not know.

I love you, O Chief! I recognize in you my master and my husband! I surrender myself to you forever, body and soul. You are the supreme power; you are the unmatchable love; you are strength and splendor, but above all, you are the Unknown and you are Misfortune!

With a passionate gesture, the daughter of kings hurls herself upon the bosom of the mysterious Chief, whose arms fold around her. An immense delight fills the grotto. The torches shine like the sun; the icy trees agitate their frosty foliage like gren branches rocked by the wind.

The dwarfs are prostrate in silent veneration, adoring their new divinity.

Miraculously, the withered myrtle branch in the Maiden's

hand flowers again, more beautifully, and emits indescribable perfumes. A breath of spring enchants the place, and the Chief's first tear, frozen in the corner of his eye, melts, as the dolor melts in his heart, to flow into the bosom of the one who has given herself to him.

The knight in silver armor knows the paroxysm of despair. He runs toward the door, which turns on its hinges and grants him passage without further tormenting his unhappiness. He mounts his horse and, followed by the attentive gaze of the man of bronze, who seals the grotto, he flees through the forest. He travels more rapidly than the wind.

Drunk on dolor and distance, he goes, but he will never see the sky of his homeland again, for his soul is open now to all temptations, and the pleas of the snow-maidens are persuasive, and their deceptive beauty charms the gaze that will never again see the face of his Ideal, and their voluptuous love offers the mirage of the eternal refuge to the sad heart that has lost everything, irredeemably: Oblivion in Death.

JOURNEY TO THE CITY OF THE DEAD

The goal of our career is death; it is the necessary
object of our aim; if it frightens us, how is it
possible to take a forward step without fever
It is certain that death awaits us; let us expect
it everywhere. It is necessary to remove
the masks from things as well as people....

Michel de Montagne

Since the moment when he had crossed the frontiers of the country ruled by Death, although twenty-four hours had gone by, he had not seen the light of day again. An immutable, incessant night had weighed upon him, and he would have been unable to find his way had an unknown influence not guided him.

Finally, as he emerged from a cypress wood occupying the summit of a hill, he saw down below the livid and bloody cloud established in the darkness over the city where Death was resident.

He stopped and sat down on a boulder. He was invaded by a profound emotion.

The man was a philosopher and had come there driven by ignorance. He knew all the secrets of the soul and human life, but not that of the tomb, and that mystery possessed him perpetually. The subject of his meditations was Death. He had delved into everything that had been written about it through the ages; he knew all religions and all human beliefs, but doubt was his eternal companion. He could not be persuaded, and that was an infinite suffering.

In vain, despairing of finding any certainty in books, he had studied death-throes in order to interrogate therein the final frissons and spasms. In vain he had invoked the souls of the dead, and the science of necromancy had been exhausted in vain for him. His thought rejected everything that could not be proven. He was devoid of conviction and, with the years of fruitless research, his desire to acquire it had developed immensely, had penetrated his life with an anxious passion that enfevered him with ever-more-forceful despotic torments.

That is why, toward the end of his prime, intolerably tortured by curiosity, courageously, he had undertaken, through multiple sufferings and great dangers, the prodigious journey to the city ruled by Death, to the very mystery he hated, all of whose secrets and defenses he was determined to vanquish, in order to tear away, with the same effort, the veil of the enigma and the uncertainty of his heart, to conquer repose in the revelation, in the pride of supreme knowledge.

For a long time, he was plunged in thought. Anguish inhabited his soul, and his approaching old age had not supported the ordeals of the journey well. His decision was firm, however, and although his goal filled him with fear now that it had appeared, nothing would have been able to make the man retreat.

He got to his feet and went down the slope toward the city. At the bottom of the hill he saw the enclosing wall, black, vertiginously high, and pierced by four gates at the four cardinal points.

From each of these gates to the center of the city a broad straight avenue ran. The areas between these avenues were divided by a large number of concentrically spiraling serpentine by-ways, doubling back on themselves and intersecting in an extensive labyrinth, formed by black walls similar to the exterior walls but not as high. There were no other buildings, but innumerable plazas were formed, enclosed on all sides and having four ever-open doorways orientated like those of the city.

Over the entire city hung a motionless cloud whose aspect

was fuliginous and pale, smudged with large bloody erosions.

The cloud supported its edges on the enclosing wall, thus oppressing the city, as deadly and perpetual as the lid of a sepulcher. Dismal gleams, stagnant and unhealthy, were engendered there, floating like paludal emanations. An insipid odor trailed through the unbearable humidity of the atmosphere. A fine, extremely cold rain fell relentlessly from the cloud. The traveler was inundated by it and recognized that it resembled blood. The hard brown earth absorbed the rain while remaining compact, and so glacial that a dolorous numbness gradually took possession of those who walked upon it.

Nevertheless, the traveler saw a great multitude of human beings around him. They were all similar in the lividity of their haggard faces and their expressions of alarmed anguish. They were all dressed in long black robes; their heads were bare and their hair or bald heads were streaming under the scarlet rain.

The majority were walking with desperate slowness or feverish agitation, many remaining motionless, plunged into mortal meditations that contacted their features. There were also some who were lying on the ground along the walls; others were sitting, as if felled by dejection. A few, seemingly afflicted by madness, were running back and forth abruptly.

In the faint and awkward light arms were seen writhing, faces convulsing, fists waving at the sky, bodies struggling and falling to the ground. The silence was troubled by the grinding of teeth, groans and sobs. And fear was resident there....

The traveler advanced in the midst of these beings, none of whom seemed to see him, and was invaded by terror, for he did not understand at all.

He went into one of the areas enclosed by walls the color of darkness. The walls were so high that they gave the impression of being at the bottom of a well. The center was occupied by a great iron tripod supporting, ten cubits from the ground, a vase of the same metal, from whose rim vomited a vigorous conical flame, spreading, without being obscured by the rain, a red radiation that mingled with the gleams falling from the sky.

On the ground in the vicinity there were a great number of the city's inhabitants. All of them seemed plunged in distress and fear—and their desolate voices were lamenting in a language that the philosopher did not know, but which he could nevertheless comprehend.

"She is coming," they were saying. "Here she is—here, there, everywhere...the cloud is bleeding anguish on our heads...will it never end? Is this eternity? No, she is coming and will possess us. We are her slaves, but who will tell us what she is? Her mystery tortures us, hr menace terrifies us. Who among us will she take? She, the ever-present...who will explain her unknown to us? Oh, what God shall we invoke? Is she not the only God?

"Expiation...alas, is that not the expiation of our sins, various and similar? Various according to our various natures, similar because we are all human! But what are we now? For the living, we are the dead, but we know full well that we are not dead, since She has not come, since we are merely in her domain, under her immediate power, subject to her fatal caprice, without being able to flee or seize her voluntarily....

"And the rain falls on us like doubt, the chill of fear in our bones, the permanent suffocation of the ambiguous odor....

"Whom can we implore, in truth, since we cannot implore? What can be done...what can be done to turn her back? Oh, any horror whatsoever, but not hers! Any torture, but not her torture...the one that one does not know!

"She's coming! Her breath is passing" Here, there and everywhere! Oh, over us...!"

They had risen to their feet and, without being able to quit the plaza, in an agony of supplicant horror, they ran in all directions, writhing desperately, tearing their faces and their breasts. They were crying and sobbing, and their tears were also blood.

The traveler considered an old man nearby, who was tugging at his beard with delirious gestures....

And suddenly, they become motionless. The rain stopped; the flame on the tripod disappeared; silence extended. An intolerable vertigo hung in the air. Mystery was manifest, doubt immutable....

The philosopher saw the old man beside him raise toward the sky a face in which there was no longer any human expression, solely dominated by the convulsions of a prodigious, unknown emotion...and then the old man disappeared....

And his black robe, vainly sloughed, collapsed on the ground....

And the flame sprang forth again more vigorously; the rain streamed, and the people, emerging from the influence that had paralyzed them, fled, crying:

"He knows! He knows now! She possesses him; he can look her in the face!

"Terror is within us, tearing us apart with the ever-menacing mystery of its abyss, by the fatal unknown whose apprehension twists our entrails!

"Should we hope for her coming in order finally to know? But no, the knowledge would be horror: she is horror itself!"

The visitor heard their voices fade away as he contemplated the old man's robe, which lay on the ground. He was dazed, agitated by a more immense curiosity—and now he saw a naked woman; the red rain was running over her body; with a lugubrious resignation she picked up the robe, put it on, and sat down. Through the four gates people came in, and formed groups. They remained there, lamenting, as the traveler walked into the by-ways.

He entered many open spaces, all similar to the first. He saw many faces shivering in terror, inundated by the bloody rain, illuminated by the lugubrious flames of tripods. The people in the by-ways were numerous, and their misery was limitless. Everywhere, the redoubtable advent extended her caprice over them, suddenly seizing one of them, multiplying their torments every time, maddening them ever-increasingly by decimating their ever-renewed host. They were jealous of the initiation of others, while they remained in ignorance, but were agonized by fear at the thought that they might be initiated themselves; they were in the madness of uncertainty, in the paroxysm of hopeless anguish—the tortured subjects of the City of the Dead.

Thus the traveler found the city. And he wandered through it for sixty hours, relentlessly, before reaching the center where Death resided.

The center was enclosed by a high circular wall of shiny black marble, pierced by four portals corresponding to the broad avenues. Inside that enclosure there was another, with only two passages, to the East and the West. Then a dome extended, displaying no opening.

The philosopher, driven by an irresistible force, went all the way around it and stopped. Then a gap was hollowed out in the stone, enabling him to enter.

He was under the vault, which was extremely high, and pierced at its summit by a round hole, through which the rain and the gleams of the sky passed. The bloody drops inundated a vast slab of livid metal.

And that was the center of the city.

When the traveler reached it, the slab slowly lifted over a stone stairway that plunged into obscurity.

The man went down the steps. Above him, with a mighty groan, the metallic mass fell back. Enveloped by darkness, he went down the spiral staircase for a long time, between walls that were not far apart.

Afterwards, there was a narrow tunnel carved in the stone, circling a gulf of unfathomable depth.

Eternal night dwelt there. The silence was crushing. A great chill rose up from the abyss.

Although his eyes could not distinguish anything, the traveler was conscious of the place in which he found himself. He was conscious, too, in a certain fashion, that this was his goal. He gathered his strength and leaned forward over the unknown of the Gulf of Death, in order to interrogate it

He saw nothing but the unknown Shadow....

Then a frantic fury exploded within him.

"Monster!" he cried. "Monster! Bearer of horror, torturer of everything that exists, you shall not toy with me any longer!

You are only mystery and shadow for earthly existence, and I shall vanquish your mystery by throwing myself into it. Now I am within you, and I prefer to die and to know!"

The man attempted to hurl himself into the Gulf of Death—but the gulf would not receive him. The darkness refused to open for him, and, in spite of the furious energy of his effort, he did not emerge from immobility.

His destiny then appeared to him—which was to remain on the narrow path skirting Death, without being able to die, eternally circling around the abyss, leaning over its Cimmerian darkness, howling at the unknown and the Shadow the vertiginous torments that were racking his soul with their contrary paroxysms, engendering devouring curiosity, perpetually multiplied…engendering hideous Fear.…

His constant destiny, for as long as Death.…

DIFFERENT MASKS

Well, that makes no difference.
Nothing matters to me....
> —Rudyard Kipling, "The Gate
> of the Hundred Thousand Sorrows"

*Darkness reigns. An October wind is blowing. On a plateau
in the midst of hills a man, feeling weary, has sat down.*

*The country is desolate in appearance. Peaks loom up against
the somber sky; woods, near and distant, are more obscure
than the night. Here and there, immense rocks protrude; dense
brushwood covers the foothills of the mountains. Amid the
vigorous grass boulders are scattered, and the man is sitting
on one of them, on the very edge of a steep slope that descends
toward a lake. Far below, the waters are stagnant; reeds grow
there in abundance; the mobile clouds mirror their indecisive
faces therein.*

*The man has fallen asleep, enveloped by the nocturnal gusts,
and, during his sleep, three companions have arrived. Like him,
they have the appearance of travelers; their humor is taciturn.*

*The man has woken up, and all four of them are talking
together, as men talk who have met, and do not know one
another.*

Now, one of the companions says:

We're tired. The autumn winds are drunk with melancholy, and their violence is a kind of sensuality. However, it's

dangerous to go to sleep here, and these hills seem perilous to those who confide themselves to it. Let's remain awake, telling stories. Everyone knows strange and true stories that he alone knows. Everyone suffers from not confiding them. We can talk between ourselves now.

THE MAN WHO HAS SLEPT

I'm tormented by one thing that happened to me. Before, I didn't know any stories. Now, I know mine. I know the adventure that has just happened to me.

I'm a simple man; I don't understand its significance. I'd like someone to explain it to me; I'd like it not to have happened to me. It's stranger than any other. I think about it incessantly. I dare not tell it....

THE COMPANION

There are many mysterious things. Beneath the heavens, many men have experienced troubled hours. They do not know why they have experienced them, and have not even been able to penetrate their equivocal symbolism. The ambiguous enigma of events is a constant and vaguely mocking threat that torments souls.

Let each of us speak. My voice will be the first. The tale I shall tell is singular, although it is not one of the most singular. Such as it is, I shall tell it.

I was a child raised in a convent by monks. The monks were good, their discipline was mild and salutary. In the peace of old stone cells I was initiated into the sciences, and in the liberty of the woods and the mountains my body was fortified. Later, I received profound lessons regarding the soul and philosophy and I learned the use of weapons and all corporeal exercises. Thus I acquired a complete strength. The man born within me recognized his power....

At the same time, I also understood my soul; my conscience

penetrated me and I decided to leave the convent. All the savage violence of the passions burned within me. The multiple energies of desire troubled me with despotic sensations. I wanted to live.…

On the last night that I was to be the monks' guest, some hours after sunset, I walked in the darkness beneath the low arches. The solemn darkness of the cloister oppressed the solitude; silence dressed my melancholy intimately. I was agitated by a complex emotion. What I was leaving behind was revealed to me; my determination hesitated in anxiety and regret…but then, my romantic desire imagined life; the unknown visage of love smiled upon my tenderness; glory enchanted my chimera.…

I turned the corner of a pillar, and it was then that destiny gripped me. In the shadows, the slenderness of a white apparition was passing along the high walls. I was not astonished. I stopped. I was trembling. A divine perfume bathed my soul. A new being quivered in my heart. She was walking…she was gliding over the flagstones liked the winged figure of my childish dreams.

Her vaporous veil brushed the pillars; a luminous seduction haloed her grace. A sovereign enchantment mastered me with the vehemence of its poignant softness. My delight died away in anguish. The rhythm of my blood was enfevered for her, and I sensed my life palpitating beneath her footfalls. Oh, I swear to you, no man has has known as I have the power and suddenness of passion. I cannot say what I experienced. Was it love? No matter! Whatever the name of the sentiment was, I then became its slave!

And without daring to implore her, without being able to catch up with her, or even to glimpse her face, I marched in a daze, enchained to her footsteps.…

Meanwhile, the places through which I was moving were strangely modified, for I now found myself in a vast sinuous corridor in which a faint light wandered along the stones amid moving shadows. And piles of gold and silver rose up and crumbled against the walls, with ingots and overflowing bags.

Precious bowls came next, full of fabulous stones, incomparable jewels, and it seemed that all the wealth in the world was gathered there.

Voices whispered in my ear: "Bend down, fill your pockets. Pause, then; it's all for you. You'll rule the world; gold is God.… Each of those coins represents a joy. Everything can be bought when one can pay the price.… But no, gold absorbs, its draws its enjoyment from itself, it's made to be conserved.… Pile it up; there's enough for you to bathe in it.… Look at that diamond, gleaming like the sun.… Look, here's my present; it's a unique jewel; seven generations have worked on it. The first six workers died very old, without having finished it; the seventh, having completed it, died of joy.… Come here, take this bag.…"

And my pockets filled. I was laden with enormous purses. The weight of gems and gold slowed me down. I threw them away and went on.

Suddenly, I was in a miserable and deserted street. The ruined houses were hideous, grass was growing between the damp cobbles. I stumbled over a body lying inert, with a wound in the throat. However, I had the inexplicable sensation of still being in the dark corridor, and still on the track of the woman who was my strength and my hope.…

I had to pause, but I knew that she was waiting for me. I don't know how I perceived that; it seemed that two men were within me. At each vision I had, it was the same, and between each of the visions, it seemed that years passed, with the result that the memory of each one was pale and distant in my mind when I was subject to the next.

A door opened in the street. A lamp lit a red room. I saw a woman sprawled on a low bed. Her plump flesh appeared beneath a scarlet velvet dress ripped to shreds, which dappled her white skin and russet down with bloody shadows. Her beauty was sensual and violent. She got to her feet, entirely naked as her garment fell away, and with the languor of a beast she came toward me.

"Come in," she said, "I'm expecting you. These are the hours when I become irritated, thinking of you, whom I love. Come, then, my kisses will give you a taste for corruption and the strength of a brute. We shall be the foremost of the antisocial workers who sleep by day and struggle by night, whose labors are bloody. We shall reign as masters in the drinking dens; we shall consume alcohols that render one frantic; we shall lean our elbows on greasy tables; you shall kiss my lips to excite jealous furies, and in the rage of merciless duels, you will fight for me against excessively ardent desires that will howl their covetousness and agony simultaneously. We shall be vile and ferocious; we shall murder our accomplices; we shall torture prisoners, finish off the wounded. We shall mingle the fevers of our brutal love with the fever of murders; the odor of my sweating flesh will fuse with the odor of blood, and the moans of our enjoyment will drown out the groans of the dying!"

Such were her words, and, I must say, the base temptation gripped me momentarily…but now I sensed myself becoming distant from the one who was my dream. I drew away from the den of vice and found myself in the magical corridor once again, enchanted by its ineffable seduction.…

I saw other things too. There was a rustic hall. At the back, in an immense fireplace, high flames were rising from entire tree-trunks, before which meat was roasting. Abundant provisions hung down from the beams of the ceiling. The walls were decorated with weapons and panoplies. In a corner, a confused heap of game was piled on a massive table. In the middle of the room there was another, even vaster table. Copper lamps illuminated the profusion of meat and bottles. Several men of rude appearance, frank and joyful, were gathered around it, wearing the leather garments of hunters, drinking frequent draughts from large goblets. Serving maids were hurrying back and forth; dogs were sleeping by the fire; venison was being carved with knives; succulent aromas were emanating from the dishes.

The oldest of the hunters got to his feet, His beard was gray and his forehead devoid of hair, but his robust limbs had the vigor of youth and his bright eyes shone with a vibrant fire. He offered me his cup full of fresh red wine and said:

"Take this cup, Companion, and let us drink together to the robust joys of the free man in nature. This wine will give you strength, skill, patience and audacity. This wine will fill you with disgust for everything that is not our life.

"With us you will spend days far from vain agitations, futile ambitions, mortal struggles for gold and power. We shall be your brothers, grave, loyal and strong. The call of our horns will bring us together in danger and in joy. Together we shall hunt red deer, bears and wild boar. On snowy nights we shall follow the tracks of large solitary wolves; on bright mornings we shall fire at flocks of migratory birds. To this old dwelling, which is our domain, we shall return every evening, weary and content; we shall sit down at this joyous table, we shall eat, we shall drink, we shall sleep peacefully! We shall only think in order to admire the work of God.

"Brother, share our lot. Far from the scorned tumult of civilization, far from intrigues, prejudices and weaknesses, we live without law and without fear. We live to live! Like the men of ancient times, we love strength, danger, fatigue, space! We love, with passion and respect, great Liberty, mother of the Strong! When the time comes to die, we lie down among our forefathers and we sleep on the hill, beneath the heather, in Nature!"

He fell silent. The perfume of the forests and the appeals of the horn floated around me. The joy of physical energy swelled in my breast, and I sensed the desire for vigorous effort in my muscles. I wanted the calm and powerful independence of those men; I wanted their perils and delights; I wanted to win their sincere friendship....

I drew away regardless, but I knew regret.

I was on the shore of the sea, in a busy harbor. A confused activity animated the mobile and multiple décor feverishly. Countless spectacles attracted my gazer. A tumult of various cries deafened me, and the scents of tar, mingled with the fresh and acrid gusts of spindrift, filled my nostrils. A great ship was making ready to set forth. The half-deployed sails were shivering as if impatient to espouse the marine breeze. The tide lifted the gilded prow where the face of a gorgon glittered. Boats were ferrying the last passengers. They were singing.

"Let's go! We can't live any longer on this overly familiar land. We need movement and change. Let's break all the old ties. Let's go elsewhere, always elsewhere. Let's live at the hazard of the winds and sail to the limits of the world.

"Curiosity is agitating us, desire is burning us. We want to know everything and possess everything. We want to grasp the immensity and drown our old dreams in the constellations of enchanted skies, to fill our memory with perils, sensual experiences and landscapes. We want to contemplate all spectacles, listen to all voices, breathe in all perfumes, enjoy all delights, live all lives!

"The unknown tempts us, distance fascinates us. What we don't know is unmatchable for us. Our chimera sparkles on the horizon; the sun is more beautiful out there than it is here; the stars form prophetic signs in the sky in which we can read our destiny. The glamour of danger excites our fever!

"Oh, we've had enough of our homeland! We're too familiar with its tedium, its horror and its vice; our hearts are still bleeding from the dolors that torture us here; misfortune and crime are eternal here, and their uniform baseness fills our souls with disgust. Let's go! Let's go throughout the world. Nothing will stop us but death!"

The boat was waiting for me. Should I not go too? I envied those happy voyagers with all my heart. Their words were the echo of the emotions of my soul, their fate seemed marvelous to me. I cursed my destiny bitterly, but I followed the one who possessed me, and was becoming dearer to me the more I sacrificed for her.

"Now I was on a hill, dazzled by a blazing sun. In the plain there was an innumerable army to the right, occupying the entire area that my gaze could cover. The other side of the horizon was occupied by an immense city. Sumptuously-armed officers surrounded me respectfully. A horse, magnificently harnessed, was brought for me. I was handed the staff of the supreme commander; a chamberlain lifted up the imperial crown; a red cloak was deployed. I heard these words:

"Dress yourself in red, mount your horse, take the scepter, wear the crown! We await your word, O magnificent Emperor, master of the world, ruler of kings!

"Your generals desire your orders, the least of your soldiers would die for you, your city quivers with joy in the expectation of our arrival; your people adore you; the world fears you. You are everything: day and night, joy and terror; liberty and servitude. A stream of blood flows beneath your footsteps; flowers are born of your passing; love and hate solicit your emotion, which does not deign to see them; life and death march beside you, holding you by the hand. Your shadow fills the horizon; your triumphs cannot be celebrated; victory is your maidservant! Emperor, I salute you in the apogee of your glory!"

Full of enthusiasm, all the officers waved their swords toward me, crying: "Glory and triumph! Long live the Emperor!" The soldiers rattled their weapons with a bellicose racket and repeated their powerful cry. "Glory and triumph! The Emperor is our God!"

I did not mount the horse; I disdained the scepter, and I drew away, rejecting the ambition of power that was laying siege to my soul.

And now, in my path, there was a great stone sphinx. As I passed by, a voice called to me: "Man, stop before the sphinx! Question me, look into my eyes and decipher the eternal mystery in their depths, listen to the words that my stone lips whisper in your ear. Open your mind, I am Thought. Through me, you can know all things....

"Come, interrogate the sphinx, listen to her voice, read what is in her eyes. In her, there is knowledge."

"Ah!" I said to her. "Even if you were to offer me the power to create Life, with the science of Good and Evil, I would not stop!"

Another vision: I was going through a garden at dusk. Tall

trees arched over long pathways; water lay dormant in marble bowls; flowers embalmed the lawns. At the intersections, statues were meditating. There were dead leaves on the gravel; their rustle accentuated the silence, their delicate and withered odor scented the softness of the evening. A misty robe dressed the distant woods. The fusion of the fiery sunset was attenuated by soft vapors. I was walking along a terrace, under old sycamores, toward a house.

It was dark when I got there. I climbed three steps and a door opened into a room in which nebulous lamps shed an amber light on to orange silks. I saw a woman. Her supple body was molded in a myrtle-green dress, ornamented to the corsage and the hem of the skirt with heavy enamel roses. An emerald girdle tightened the waist, and a similar collar drew a high turned-down collar around the neck. A narrow fissure left the cleavage between her breasts naked.

Nonchalantly, she put her arms on my shoulders. She looked up; her face was, for me, the supreme and unforgettable beauty. Her dark hair had solar glints; gems scintillated in its undulating waves, massed over the temples and the nape. A vague smile on her melancholy mouth only parted the delicacy of the exquisite lips very slightly. Her nostrils were translucent. Her brown eyes, specked with gold, long and velvet, were reminiscent of stars and flowers. Light make-up enlivened her grace. Invincible perfumes floated around her....

"Leave the garden," she said. "Pass over the threshold, enter my house. Dreams and love are everywhere here, and the happiness of this world exists within them. There are marvelous decors here, and strange adornments. The nebulous dusk of lamps languorously cradles the soul of flowers and scented sachets. The song of harps and the plaints of the harpsichord sharpen and caress my chimerical nostalgia to the point of tears. My voice, to which no music is perhaps comparable, pours out the poetry of nocturnal harmonies, and its passionate tones move my own heart. The perfume of my flesh is an enchantment, and my beauty in the mirrors dazzles my eyes...."

"O intoxication, what point is there in searching outside oneself for something that is within? What voyage can discover landscapes more beautiful than the imaginary landscapes in which my indolent thoughts dream? What earthly palace can equal the luxury of the palaces of dream in which my dreams hold their fêtes? What effort, what success, can surpass the visionary sloth in which one languishes with an exalted delight? What glory can match the glory of the man to whom my mouth will say: 'I love you!'

"Embrace me, you whom I desire so much. My figure yields in your arms; let me shiver against you, breathe your breath between my lips. Oh, I am made of love! Come, my bed is profound and perfumed, the skin is softer there, and love is stronger.... Come, let us separate ourselves from the world in voluptuousness! I will give you all caresses. I love you; take me! I love you!"

She held me against her, her figure braced in order to glue her side to mine; her adorable mouth parted...and her eyelids suddenly fluttered, and lowered over the drowned iris; her languid and ardent beauty became sublime with dazed emotion, and her perfume maddened me....

I learned over, drunkenly, toward her adorable face...but no! Already I had torn myself out of her arms and, my heart torn by love and regret, I launched myself in pursuit of the one who was drawing away, taking my soul with her....

Insensate! Thus I walked for a long time yet, without encountering anything more, save for the black phantoms of chagrin and discouragement! I marched, and, far from my eyes burned by tears, her divine form glided in the half-light. Now I implored her in a loud voice, calling out to her in my desire and my distress. I walked on, drunk with lassitude, despair and passion.

Suddenly—God, what a torrent of ineffable joy! Suddenly, I saw that she was immobile and thought that she was waiting for me. Ah! My dolors would no longer exist. I drew nearer. A slight mist floated before my eyes. I drew closer. She was there.

O delirium! I ran...and I reached the end of the corridor, and what I found there was revealed to me.

There was a large mirror there, and in its infinite grayness resided a white form, which was a reflection, which was the reflection of myself in my monk's robe....

And there was nothing else.....

I saw that reflection face to face, which was myself, and the image was that of an old man, a very old, decrepit and worn-out man, near the end of his life. I took wisps of my hair in my hand, in order to see them, and they were white, and I cast my eyes over my feeble limbs and my old, wrinkled hands. Thus I recognized that I really was the old man.

I was weary. I sat down on the ground. And I found that I was mortally sad.

Thus ends the first companion's story. The man who has been asleep spoke:

I don't understand. That story is astonishing. Can you explain it to me?

SECOND COMPANION

Nothing can be explained. This is what I can relate:

Blandine was sixteen years old when I knew her. I had then reached the sixth lustrum of my life. From the first moment, I experienced a love without limits for that child, She alone enabled me to savor the sublime emotion. Under her influence, all the sentiments that existed in my soul gradually weakened and paled until they were no more than decreasing shadows, effaced by the constant and irresistible fervor of my passion.

Her exquisite beauty was harmonious and melancholy. She seemed to remember some past bitterness; her smile had a divinely plaintive charm. That was singular in so young a person, but it was so tangible to me that sometimes, as I gazed at her silently and adoringly, I found myself penetrated by a sharp desire to enable her to forget, by force of tenderness, what she had suffered. They were, however, only fugitive sensations into which reality never entered, for I knew that calm happiness had always cradled the youth of the one I loved. She became my fiancée; I adored her, veritably, and I had reason to believe that she loved me too, for she told me so in an innocent voice, and her eyes seemed to be the mirror of her soul.…

O past time, how I regret your hours! Alas, nothing can be done to bring them back!

A strange folly caused me to defer our union. In order to acquire more wealth, in order to offer my spouse more beautiful adornments, I went to sea for a long voyage. My departure tore my soul; I suffered dolors that were out of proportion with a temporary absence. That should have enlightened me. Why does a man seek to challenge his destiny? Blandine begged me not to leave. I left.

The beginning of my voyage was fortunate. I succeeded in my endeavors and the result surpassed my hopes. Satisfied, I embarked on the return journey. The crossing soon became perilous. A tempest assailed us. Obstinate winds drove us far out of our course; the swell that followed broke our damaged vessel and ran us on to a reef. In the terrible impact I lost consciousness, believing that I would die.

I was picked up, however, alone of all my companions, by the crew of an unknown warship. The vessel was sailing in a direction that I was unable to discover, for none of the crewmen understood my language and theirs was completely foreign to me. In any case, they never attempted to communicate with me, and when we reached port, after seventeen days at sea, I knew absolutely nothing about them and not a word of their language. Before leaving them, I offered them some of the gems I had in my belt, saved in their totality, but they refused and, on the first morning after our arrival, having set me down in a safe place on the jetty of the vast harbor, they broke off all communication with me.

The city seemed to me to be immense; its aspect was that

of the commercial maritime cities of northern Europe. There too, after searching for several hours, it was impossible for me to find any individual who understood any of the languages I knew. My astonishment was boundless.

I was able to sell one of my gemstones. I received several gold coins stamped with an unknown effigy. I took a place in a small boat that went up a broad river, taking me into the heart of the city. It was night when I disembarked. Not far away, in a tavern, I obtained a meal by means of sign language. I went out and, not daring to venture into the streets, where I feared getting lost, I contended myself with following the quays. To the left, at the base of a high stone parapet, there was the obscurity of the river, where the lights of boats were gleaming. To the right, tall houses raised up their somber façades, in which no lights were shining. Beacons directed their glow here and there. Passers-by were scarce.

I walked for a long time. Gradually, the place became more wretched. The habitations were half in ruins, the ripped-up paving stones were lying in long grass. The lanterns spaced their flickering flames at increasing intervals. The shadows of nocturnal thieves were prowling along the walls. Prostitutes haunted the side-streets that opened on to the quay, and their offers took on a menacing tenacity....

Now an icy fog covered the waters of the river. I thought about going back, but curiosity pushed me further forward. As I turned the corner of a large abandoned house of solemn and dilapidated appearance, a young woman seized my arm. She was alone in that place. A thick cloak concealed her, but an indefinable attraction emanated from her person. The hazardous idea of going with her crossed my mind, and I stopped, hesitantly.

She took me by the hand and dragged me toward the solemn house that I had assumed to be abandoned, the massive door of which she opened, in order to plunge into the obscurity of its corridors with me. We walked in the calm of high walls and unfurnished rooms, and I was assailed by sentiments that were almost superstitious....

We finally stopped. My conductress pushed a hidden door. I went into a small, delicately decorated room. Mauve silks, beneath lace, draped the walls over white and lacquered panels; mirrors reflected the soft glow of a silver lamp; divans invited repose and amour; a large fire was burning beneath the mantel of a sculpted fireplace; a soft and voluptuous scent was the soul of things.

My companion took off her cloak and I looked at her. I doubted my eyes, however, for they beheld Blandine. It was her! On my soul, it was her! Emerging from the heavy fabric like a flower from its envelope, her poetic beauty enchanted my gaze. How could I be mistaken? Her image was the troubling joy of my memory…it was her. The expression on her face was the identical dreamy and candid expression that had impassioned me so many times when I had studied it on the features of the young woman of my own country. She was wearing her habitual costume—that long dress of bright silk, tumbling in regular creases like the inverted corolla of a flower.

Meanwhile, she held out her hand for money. In the midst of the foolish stupor that possessed my unhinged mind, an obscure desire to satisfy her caused me to throw a handful of gold into a cup. Blandine—no, the woman who was in front of me!—smiled. Then I took hold of the woman's hands. I shivered with a frightful fever as I contemplated the charming face. I searched the large eyes for the luminous gaze that the shadow of the lashes attenuated, and I read in those large eyes all the memories of our love. On her left hand was the gold and silver ring that I had given her. I plunged my devouring gaze once again into the depths of those large, sad and tender irises.

"Blandine," I said, "what are you doing here?" And at that moment, I pitied myself. How could I believe that that was my fiancée?

I burst into irresistible laughter, which faded out in the groan of distress.

She spoke to me in an unknown language, and it was her voice—her voice, which awoke all the echoes of my memory;

her tender voice, as if sometimes steeped in tears, which had once sung in my heart the hopes and fear of its young love.

I don't know how I didn't die then, and I wish to God that I had! Overwhelmed, I sat down by the fireplace. I let my gaze wander around. Meanwhile, my companion began to undress. Something more frightful than despair tore my entire being apart. I wanted to get to my feet to kill her. I saw her flesh. The cowardice of desire seethed within me and enslaved me. With lascivious mystery, her movements revealed her intimate beauty to me. She was naked. I thought: *She is even more beautiful than I dreamed.* And that had referred to my fiancée, to Blandine herself, whom, in moments of sensual reverie, familiar to any love, no matter how pure it may be, I had pleased myself by imagining thus, unveiled.

And thus she came to me, dazzling with grace, in the exquisite glory of her nudity. She lay in my arms, my hands touched her skin, she inclined her marvelous head toward my face and hr breath intoxicated me....

I shall not attempt to describe that night of love. The woman I possessed then was a virgin and a prostitute. Her body had not yet known the act itself, but, outside of that, she was more expert than any courtesan I had ever encountered. Her caresses were adorable and vile. I experienced frightful sensations. I moaned with love and jealousy. *Where, then*, I asked myself, *has she learned such things?*

And I begged her to reveal her enigma, to tell me the secret that was wringing my heart. I interrogated the amorous harmony of her sighs, and I bathed my soul, tortured by doubt, in her large passionate eyes. And then, furiously, I sought one again the philter of her burning lips, the ineffable languor of her palpitating and perfumed flesh, the supreme voluptuousness of her embrace, as profound as the abyss....

Finally, I went to sleep, exhausted, holding her, nude, against my breast.

A brutal contact woke me up. I heard a deep voice. My eyes, partly open, were dazzled by the light that a lamp directed at my face. My thoughts were vacillating and memory remained numb within my brain.

I tried to move, but it was in vain, because I was retained by bonds. I was gagged.

Astonishment brought me to my senses. I saw several black-clad men surrounding me, and filling the narrow cell where I now was, chained to the wall and lying fully dressed on straw. The wan morning twilight, falling through a barred ventilation-shaft, rendered things even more sinister.

Meanwhile, one of the men read aloud from a parchment baring a seal. I could not grasp the meaning of his words. Another man, who had remained at the back until then, came to place his hand on my shoulder and made me get up. At his gesture, two other approached, untied me, and set me between them. Without understanding, without daring to understand, I let them do as they wished, looking in anguish at the expressions on the human faces that pressed around me—but I found nothing but cold firmness or brutal indifference. In a few gazes I saw pity, and that frightened me.

I was dragged sideways through long vaulted corridors and empty rooms. We formed a lugubrious procession. An old man joined us. He took me by the hand. He contemplated me with tearful eyes and blessed me. A heavy door creaked and opened....

I cannot say whether, deep down, I had suspected it, whether I had envisaged that most odious of possibilities, but I really was not astonished when, in the cloudy and moist light of the sunrise, in the middle of a square from which howls were rising, I saw the gibbet.

No, I cannot say that I was astonished, but an inexpressible distress took possession of me. I shuddered profoundly. It was to this, then, that I was destined? Why? Why?

I applied myself unconsciously to study, with eyes troubled by terror, the scaffold, the rope, the ladder. I saw the serried ranks of soldiers, and behind them, everywhere—on roofs, in trees, at windows—thousands of convulsed, howling faces: the odious visages of the savage multitude. I tried in vain to believe that it was a nightmare.

The hand of the executioner shoved me forwards. Then, I seemed suddenly to understand fully the maddening horror of my situation. I struggled furiously, until my bonds were partly broken; beneath the gag I howled like a beast in agony; I fell to the ground, sobbing and sniggering. I no longer had any moral energy within me; courage and human dignity had abandoned me; horror—the unmatchable horror of my fate—was the mistress of my muscular strength, and I found myself more cowardly than a child....

I was overcome by my guards and solidly tied. They carried me to the gibbet. I was groaning with terror; I implored, with words of despair, those people who could not hear me...and then, again, I laughed and howled in frightful torment.

I came nearer, nearer...and a bleak stupor then overwhelmed me. I was hypnotized by the rope....

I was scarcely breathing, already sensing the noose around my neck...an immense self-pity invaded me. Without being conscious of it, I found myself on the ladder. I climbed one step, and another, and another, and suddenly tried to throw myself down. I made a frantic effort to break my bonds. I raised a horrible clamor toward the sky...and the moment had come.

The rope gripped my neck. Convulsively, I opened my eyes, in which visions of the world were spinning; I stiffened my muscles to the point of twisting them; I breathed in desperately for the last time. The hand of the executioner shoved me toward death....

And it was then that I saw once again, in the first row of the filthy crowd, upright and attentive, more adorable than ever with her dreamy eyes and her soft smile, her—Blandine.

THE MAN WHO HAS SLEPT

Strange, oh, strange! What does that tale mean? But Companion, if you are dead, how can you be talking to us?

THE THIRD COMPANION

Don't ask questions. Only listen, until the moment when you will be listened to in your turn. Listen to me.

It was autumn. The man was asleep. A voice shook his hut, sounding in his ear like the angel's trump.

It said: "Get up, laborer, the time has come! Get up; harness your oxen to the plough, drive your plough to the large field. The time has come!"

The man trembled with fear. He got up and went out. In front of the door of his hut there was a column of flame, which spread no light in the surroundings. He prostrated himself. The voice cried: "Stand up! Work, laborer! What are you waiting for now?"

The man stood up. He went to the stable, took the oxen to the plough, put the yoke on them, and went out with his team.

"March!" cried the voice.

He marched, following the column of flame, going in that manner to the big field surrounded by hills, where multitudes had been massacred and which he had never dared put under the plough, so much more redoubtable was the solitude there than the ordinary solitudes of that country, where humans no longer lived. He marched, praying to God, regarding his life, whose sins and pride he was expiating in humble retreat and patient labor. Clouds were building up in the sky. The oxen pulled the plough at a slow pace. Unknown noises emerged randomly from the shadows.

The plain appeared. The mountains limiting it were covered in forests. A river flowed to the south. A light mist covered the expanse. It was cold; the breath of the oxen emerged vaporously from their nostrils.

The voice said: "Drive your oxen! Work the field!"

The fiery column disappeared and the man worked. A supernatural force had entered into him. Without pause, without fatigue, he pushed his plough through the field. He went from the river to the hill, and then from the hill to the river, tracing the profound furrows.

And he saw on one side the labored extent in which the raised earth seemed to form regular waves, and on the other side, the extent still intact, which stretched out its brow uniformity.

On the first night, the laborer was troubled by the vision of delightful mirages in which magical cities were reflected in the light of the dawn.

On the second night, armies battled in the sky, and he dared not slake his thirst at the river, for its waters were stained with blood.

On the third night, which was the last of his labor, he unearthed bones and there were fire-follets in front of him and the skeleton of a laborer behind him, who was driving fleshless oxen on his heels and burying the blade of his plough in the furrow already traced.

As morning came, the last furrow was completed. Then the oxen lay down on the ground and died. The man lay down beside them; he wept with anguish and fatigue, and then went to sleep.

The voice of the Spirit woke him.

"Get up! There is work to be done. Rest will come after the labor. Climb the hill to the summit, and bring back what you will be given."

The man climbed the hill. At the summit he saw a vast flat black stone. Four rocks surrounded it, each reproducing a human face. When the newcomer was in their midst, he was insulted and threatened. He was afraid, but remained nevertheless.

After a time, two great eagles came from the Occident and the Orient. Each of them was carrying a leather pouch in its claws, which it dropped on to the stone table. With piercing cries, they hurled themselves at one another, and tore at one another until they died. Then the man picked up the two leather bags, in which there was grain, stained black and white.

The bag that came from the East was black, and the man put it on his right shoulder; and the bag that came from the West was white, and the man put it on his left shoulder.

The four stone faces seemed to be agitated by rage and dolor, but they were no longer speaking.

He went down the hill, but he had to defend himself against the assaults of a huge pig, which knocked him to the ground with his bags. The grains scattered in the mud, and the man had a great deal of difficulty in gathering them up. After that he was permitted to reach the bottom of the hill.

The Spirit, reappearing, said: "Take the black and white grains, and sow them in the furrows. Sow to the left that which was to the left and to the right that which was to the right."

The man took the grains, which were all soiled with mud. The man wanted to wash them in the river, but the voice cried: "Sow without delay! They are good as they are!"

Thus, the sower walked along the furrows, and his hand threw the white and black grains into the air. And the grains shone in the shadow of the night and plunged profoundly into the shifted soil. And there were signs in the sky, and the column of fire rose up in the middle of the expanse....

He sowed, and the furrows were fecundated one after another, and the time passed.

When the sower was in the middle of the field, the first bag being empty, he took the other, and the bag that came from the East was sown to the right, and the bag that came from the West was sown to the left.

When the labor was complete, there were glimmers floating over the waves of the plain, convulsed like the sea in a tempest. And unknown words were pronounced by celestial voices, and echoed between the hills.

Now, when morning came, the laborer saw human beings who were growing in the earth.

To his right there were men, to his left there were women. And all of them were rising from the ground, naked and vigorous, with their arms folded and their heads held high.

Now, the Spirit had returned to the sky, and these new creatures were extracting their feet from the nourishing earth, when the man who had worked so hard to give them life emerged from the rocks where he had hidden. A boundless pride and a prodigious joy dilated his heart. He breathed in the inebriating morning breeze, and paraded his gaze tenderly over the host that animated the desolate plain and he said to himself: "This is my work."

He went down toward them and cried: "Humans, I am your father! I have created you; I want to teach you life! You shall know from me how humans may live, defend themselves, nourish themselves, shelter themselves. I shall teach you just laws and divine precepts. You shall remain free and virtuous. Concord and love will reign among you and you shall be happy, my dear children!"

As he concluded these words, overflowing with delight and love, he advanced toward them, his arms open. The human beings looked at him gravely. Then, they came to meet him, without saying anything, and, as the man as weeping tears of delight, they seized him in their arms and strangled him. He could not defend himself; he did not even think of it. As he emitted his last breath, one of the women leaned over and kissed his bloody lips....

Such is the story of the laborer. It is very ancient.

The soul of the man thus killed was tortured by a horrible stupor. In the brief moment during which it passed from life to death there was room for long meditations, into which the fear of the beyond certainly did not enter, but in which hypotheses were formed concerning the cause of his ambiguous fate. He remembered the words spoken to him by the Spirit: *Rest will come after the labor.* He thought that the humans might not have understood the meaning of the words pronounced by his mouth and that they had believed him to be an enemy. Perhaps they did not know what their victim had done for them.

That is possible. It is also possible that they acted as they did without any other motive than the primordial malevolence of humankind, avowed to evil from birth.

That is possible. However....

THE MAN WHO HAS SLEPT

However?

THE COMPANION

However, that story is mine. I was the laborer, and that work I have described was my work, and those to whose creation I contributed put me to death as I have reported.

That story is my story, and at troubled moments when the soul meditates in disgust for itself and everything that exists, I cannot help being certain that, if those human creatures did what they did, it was surely because they knew what labor I had been given to do, and what work my arm, commanded by the Spirit, had accomplished. And because, plunged since their first moment in the irremediable horror of existence, and wanting revenge, they had been unable to reach any higher Creator, those creatures had avenged themselves on me, their brother, the instrument of their creation.

Thus, the hand of the executioner, which is only the executor of the sentence pronounced, is hated by the condemned man, who sometimes seizes him in his teeth and bites him cruelly, with all his rage and all his despair.

THE MAN

I can't say anything about that story. Certainly, the story of the man who saw his reflection at the end of the magical corridor is cruel and singular, and the adventure of Blandine's lover in the unknown city is more strangely horrible than any other adventure, but there is in the parable of the laborer something supernaturally frightful for the human soul. However, my story, which I must recount now, surpasses all of that.

When I emerged from the forest where I had been wandering for such a long time, without being able to count the days, enveloped by the eternal shadow of the ensorcelled woods, I thought

I was coming back from Hell. I wept on seeing the daylight again and I knelt down to glorify the sun.

I was in a delightful valley, partly covered by dense woodland. Thick and flowery grass carpeted the ground. Springs were singing under the grass and forming streams that flowed into a transparent river. There were clumps of trees laden with fruit and aromatic bushes. Shady arbors invited repose; charming birds lived there. There were flowers everywhere, of a beauty that I had not suspected, expanding their incomparable corollas, from which delicious perfumes spread and on which vast butterflies perched, which also resembled flowers. A group of children, emerging all of a sudden from a pathway, ran up and surrounded me curiously.

They were pretty and cheerful; the bigger ones were leading the little ones by the hand and they were speaking in deep voices, with silvery laughter.

I questioned them, but none of them wanted to reply at first. They seemed to be making a game of my embarrassment. I repeated my questions. They drew away, singing gaily, without paying any further heed to me.

I was tired and astonished, and I sat down on the ground. However, a gracious little girl came back. She was brown-haired, with very white skin and bright eyes. She said: "What do you want, poor man? We can do nothing for you. We have no idea what you mean. There are no roads or houses. Are you hungry? Would you like fruits?"

I was very astonished, you understand, I think. I spoke again, and she said: "There are no big people."

But I persisted and she replied, quite sincerely: "I assure you that I cannot. I don't understand the things you're talking about. There are no other things than those you can see. We eat fruits, we drink water, we sleep on the grass."

And she went on: "I don't understand at all, I tell you. Why do anything? We play! There is no winter, there is no rain, there is no cold; it's always the same. There is no village, there are no big people. There's nothing at all. We don't need anything else.

We're little children and we love one another. We're very happy. You're ridiculous in not understanding."

Then she became impatient. "We don't grow up—how stupid you are! We can't grow up, you see, we're little children. I'm going—*au revoir....*"

Already she was fleeing, at a run, but I asked her to show me the path to take me out of the valley, for I couldn't see any way out and I sensed that it would be better for me to get away without delay.

"There is no path, I believe," she said "I'll be glad to take you to the mountain, but after that, you'll go on alone; I won't go. We can't go there. It's terrible. You won't be afraid? Come...."

She walked in front of me, eating a fruit she had picked. The wind stirred her dress and her hair. We went up the first slopes of the hill, and the place became darker and bleaker as we left the valley. When we were half way up the hill, I saw high bare rocks and a narrow defile between them. The landscape was frightfully desolate, under a black fog. The child stopped.

"Look, I'm tired," she said, "and I'm afraid of the big stones. Adieu!"

She held out her arms and offered me her pretty face, I leaned over to kiss her forehead, didn't I? But she put her arms around my neck and it was her lips that....

Well, I've obtained many sensual pleasures from the love of women in many lands, and I've learned many enjoyments, but there's one thing I can tell you, because it's the truth: nothing in the world can be compared with what I experienced at that moment. And I'd gladly accept a new life, full of misery, in order to have that again. But then that delight disappeared in a sentiment that I can't describe—for in my arms, there was a child's skeleton, and beneath my lips, the cold and little teeth of the white skull....

And I ran, fast, and for a long time, through the gap in the mountains, chased by terror. And I traversed immense distances before coming to fall down here, with no more strength. And this place, where we are, is unknown to me....

You know my story, travelers. I've related it to you with a spirit that isn't mine. Another is speaking through my mouth...I perceive that I'm no longer similar to myself. I've forgotten what my life was and I know many things that I didn't know before. However, I don't understand my story, as I've remembered it. I'm tortured by anguish.... Tell me, I beg you, if you know it, what these things mean!

To respond to that urgent plea there is now, in the midst of these individuals, an individual who has not yet appeared. He is sitting on a stone facing the man who has slept, and his appearance presents a perfect resemblance to the appearance of the man. The identity is absolute. And his eyes plunge into the eyes of the man, which are exactly similar, the same gaze that emanates therefrom, and his smile is the same haggard smile that trembles on the lips of the man. A voice, which is the same voice that has just been heard interrogating those who cannot respond, responds to the last words pronounced:

The story of the monk was singular and significant, and also that of the traveler, and that of the laborer even more so. But see: the story of the man and the child—your story—is the most astonishing. It is an image and a reflection. It is, itself, its own mirage....

I shall not attempt to explain it to you. It is necessary not to try to understand, for that is vain. I shall only tell you that it would have been better, for you, not to have lived that adventure if you love your human existence. What is, however, cannot not have been. You have kissed your death on the mouth beneath the gentle smile of your last dream; you have come to sit down on the stone of the sepulcher; you have slept in the autumn wind; you are looking into the face of your own double. It is the end of your carnal destiny.

Lean backwards, stretch out your arms, fall into the paludal water in which the mobile clouds are mirroring their indecisive faces. Many bodies, since distant times, have been buried there, many bodies will be buried there in ages to come....

Those who have come to relate their supreme adventure to you have spoken with the same spirit that has guided your speech, and of those adventures, the issue was analogous to the present issue of your adventure....

And once again, it is accomplished....

That voice ceases momentarily. The sepulchral stone is empty, for the body of the man has been swallowed by the paludal water, among the reeds and the reflection of the mobile clouds.
And the voice continues:

Thus we retain the simulacrum of our human aspect, in the illusory vanity of existing for the eyes of the person whom fate leads here by the hand. I am like you, O resigned specters. We are weary; the lamps have no more oil; the labyrinth has no exit; the masks have, for us, quit the face, but that face remains a Cimmerian shadow....

I am what you are, O phantoms! I am what I am, and that is all that I know of myself...I know nothing more. No one knows anything more. No one ever knows anything....

THE ANTISOCIAL MAN OF
THE QUAI BOIS-L'ENCRE
A Historical Summary,
with Reproductions of
Original Documents

At ten past eight on Quasimodo Sunday[8] in the year XXXX, Monsieur Méandre, a family man and senior bureaucrat, was with his wife and four children, eating their evening meal in the comfortable dining-room of the fourth-floor apartment that he occupied at number 3 Quai Bois-l'Encre in the Raisin-Sec quarter.

The maidservant Anna, a young provincial of nineteen, who was serving, had just set a steaming plate of duck and turnips in the middle of the table.

It was then that the first initiating phenomenon occurred of the most extraordinary sequence of events that had ever unfolded in the bosom of a civilized nation and had ever impassioned the minds of any nation to delirium, disrupting the progress of business, engendering the most profound religious, political and financial perturbations, and causing the print-runs of all the newspapers to increase by prodigious proportions, until the fervently-desired denouement that brought relief to all the nations.

8. The first Sunday after Easter, named by conflating the first two words of the mass sung on that day; by 1901, of course, the term was indelibly connected with the outcast hunchback in Victor Hugo's classic novel *Notre Dame de Paris*.

The phenomenon in question was this. Suddenly, without the slightest preliminary sign giving any warning, the white-painted hook that supported the light suspended over the table tore free of the situation that it had always occupied in the ceiling. Obedient to the law of gravity, the lamp fell vertically.

Its formidable weight, as it shattered into a thousand pieces, crushed the duck and turnips, smashing the plate and cracking the table, destroying the glassware and launching a clowd of solid and liquid debris, greasy or flaming, into the air, which fell upon the entire Méandre family. About a liter of a green syrupy substance, like some kind of stinking mud, then poured through the hole left in the ceiling.

Meanwhile, on the table, the flaming oil started a fire, which Monsieur Méandre succeeded in smothering beneath the folds of his jacket, which he took off in order to employ it for that purpose, not without the garment suffering considerable damage.

Naturally, there was a scene of tumultuous consternation in the bosom of that placid family. Madame Méandre suffered an attack of nerves, and her youngest child struck his head on the fireplace, which rendered him infirm for life. The maidservant Anna fled, with the aim of fetching a policeman, and the demoiselles Méandre, under the direction of their older sister, recently emerged from boarding-school, uttered a long series of piercing screams.

After the extinction of the fire, Monsieur Méandre, understandably prey to a furious anger, shouted: "It's that swine upstairs again! This has to end! How dare he, with a man of my character!"

These words related to certain trivial events that had previously occurred, including an unusual note, emanating, in all probability, from the aforementioned "swine upstairs"—the tenant of the apartment above—to which we shall return at the appropriate time.

Monsieur Méandre then ran downstairs in his shirtsleeves and forced the concierge, Armandine Vane, to come up and bear witness to the facts. That functionary only lent herself to the task with a rather ill grace, and did not manifest all the indignation that he had a right to expect. (It subsequently proved that she was inclined to be prejudiced in favor of the fifth-floor tenant, who constituted a source of monthly income for her.) She even dared to suggest that it might have been an accident, as anyone could see. But Monsieur Méandre knocked down this theory by exhibiting the note mentioned above, which consisted of a small piece of hard wood on which a red-hot needle had traced the words: *Stop playing "A Maiden's Prayer" on the piano. Otherwise, punishment.*[9]

This piece of wood, without anyone knowing by what means it had been introduced, had been found the day before on Mademoiselle Adélaide Méandre's piano. Having just left boarding-school, as previously mentioned, and anxious to complete her musical education, she devoted all her leisure time—an average of seven hours a day—to the study of the celebrated piece reproved by the author of the wooden plaque.

Naturally, no notice had been taken of that insolent injunction, and Mademoiselle Adélaide Méandre had persisted in practicing her art, while her father, in accordance with his character, had avowed a strong resentment against the upstairs neighbor, to whom he imputed—in view of certain details that will be related in due course—the outrageous communication.

The fall of the hanging lamp, which the family was inclined to envisage as the threatened punishment, fully corroborated this opinion. "And thus, the two events, acting in concert, prove their common source." Those were the terms in which Monsieur Méandre spoke to his concierge, Armandine Vane. The latter shook her head and, without any other reply, went back down

---

9. Boutet could not know in 1901 that this piano piece by the Polish composer Tekla Badarzewska-Baranowska, taken up but many Parisian students after its publication as a supplement to the *Revue et gazette musicale de Paris* in 1859, would subsequently be adapted as a country-and-western standard in the U.S.A. According to Wikipedia, it is also played by garbage trucks in Taiwan.

to her lodge.

And that was the end of it, for that evening.

The next day, Monsieur Méandre, still in a towering rage, went to see the Commissaire of Police of the Raisin-Sec quarter, Monsieur Églantine—the same one who was later to play an active role in the second act of the drama.

The magistrate listened with considerable interest to the strange tale that he was told. He promised to send a report to the Hygiene Committee, and advised Monsieur Méandre to take legal action. The senior bureaucrat had already decided to do that, and took his leave of Monsieur Églantine in order to go to his Ministry, where he took pleasure in telling everyone about the intolerable insult that a man of his character had received—and everyone, from the directors to the office-boys, offered ardent commentaries on that new subject, thus breaking the dull monotony of the hours of work.

Monsieur Méandre launched his legal action, the first step of which was an affidavit taken by Maître Cormoran, bailiff, of 1 Rue du Clou-dans-le-Mur. A suit was instituted and a demand made for damages and compensation. The accused tenant did not respond to the citations, however, and another event occurred, which required a new affidavit and added a serious grievance to the man who had registered the complaint.

On the morning on the seventeenth of May, the young maidservant Anna, on going into a dark room that served as a lumber-room, noticed some tangled and twisted filaments on the ceiling, which she assumed to be cobwebs.

Oh well, she thought, *I'd better get rid of them. Madame will complain if she sees them.* And she went out, in order to return later with a feather duster of the sort known as a Turk's-head. Her efforts at clearance were in vain. The unknown filaments were tenacious, resistant and flexible in nature, and defied all attacks. They were emerging from the ceiling itself and had caused the plaster to disintegrate, which fell upon the young maidservant in abundant flakes. Astonished and vaguely anxious, the latter went in search of her mistress and came back accompanied by that lady and Mademoiselle Adélaide, who, driven by curiosity, had abandoned "A Maiden's Prayer," which she had been playing on her piano.

With the aid of a chair and a candle, the ladies realized that they were dealing with the roots of some unknown tree—and thus was annihilated the opinion of young Anna, who believed that she was in the presence of the devil's tresses.

The astonishment of the three women was boundless, however, and the maidservant departed in haste to inform Monsieur Méandre at his Ministry. That gentleman came home at top speed, prey to a violent anger, and accompanied by one of his friends, Monsieur Barnabé Cruchot, a journalist working for the newspaper *Le Plein-Jour*, which had already published an item about the first incident. The two individuals called in at the Rue du Clou-dans-le-Mur to collect Maître Cormoran, the bailiff previously mentioned, whom they brought up to date with the new insult offered to a man of Monsieur Méandre's character.

The facts were confirmed and the affidavit sworn, while young Anna, left to her own devices, could not resist going to recount the story to her friends and acquaintances, who had already been informed of the earlier events, and via which channel the story spread throughout the entire Raisin-Sec quarter and its neighboring districts.

Everyone then became inflamed with curiosity with regard to the mysterious tenant of the fifth floor of number 3, Quai Bois-l'Encre, about whom the most fantastic rumors were already circulating, with regard to the singular silence opposed by him to Maître Cormoran's citations—not to mention various previous and passably remarkable singularities that had been noticed, the rapidly-multiplying details of which were circulated clandestinely. At the same time, at the Ministry, whose staff Monsieur Méandre had naturally informed, with a degree of exaggeration, bets were laid regarding the causes of the phenomena. Vaguely, people conceived that serious events were in potential.

The next day, however, a rather long article entitled *The So-Called Mystery of the Quasi Bois-l'Encre* appeared on page two of the *Clairvoyant* and calmed minds somewhat. In that article, the author of which remained carefully anonymous, Monsieur Barnabé Cruchot gave extensive details about the unknown tenant whose attitude was so enigmatic and who constituted the evident and responsible cause of the agitation.

He was, the article said, a misanthrope who almost never went out or received any visitors—men, women or children—or letters, had forbidden his concierge to furnish any information, and had instructed her never to let anyone whatsoever go up to his apartment—save for the usual suppliers—in order to make sure that he would not be disturbed in the course of his important work, which consisted principally of research into the existence of God. It was not excessive to suppose the gentleman had not received Maître Cormoran's citations in time. Undoubtedly, he would appear in court. His name was Dubois; he was known to honorable men—the author of the article seemed to be insinuating that he was one of the honorable men who was acquainted with Dubois—and, in sum, there was no proof of his responsibility for what had happened and of which he had been accused, perhaps wrongly.

By means of this vague and fallacious information, Barnabé Cruchot—who had discerned at the first glance that enormous interest was latent in the poignant mystery of the affair, and had weighed in the reliable balance of his clear professional judgment a few prodigious advantages that he might be able to obtain from it by working appropriately and reserving it for himself to the extent that was possible—quieted the curiosity of the public and deceived the vigilance of his colleagues, who were always in quest of some sensational event. At the same time, he isolated the concierge Armandine Vane—with whom no one could suspect him of sleeping—entered further into the confidence of Monsieur Méandre and introduced himself into the intimacy of the bailiff, Cormoran and the Commissaire of Police, Églantine, by playing cards with them for high stakes.

Thus, the cunning fellow, giving free rein to his genius, prepared his means for the not very distant day when he would raise the professional trumpet to his lips in order to blow with all his might a fanfare that would resonate throughout the world, finding faithful echoes everywhere, immediately animating all of his readers with a frenetic curiosity to know what would happen next, and making Barnabé Cruchot the uncontested king of reporters, and the *Plein-Jour* the dazzling mirror which, for the duration of the extraordinary affair, would enjoy sales ten times more considerable than any of the competing papers.

The day arrived when the so-called Dubois was summoned to appear before the law of the land.

The day arrived, but Dubois did not.

By default, he was sentenced to pay the ten thousand francs in damages and compensation demanded by Monsieur Méandre, notification of which was made to him at the prescribed times by Maître Cormoran, speaking to a woman in his service—who was, in fact, the concierge Armandine Vane.

Did Dubois receive that document? And having received it. did he read it? No one knows. In any case, he acted as if he had neither received nor read it, in the sense that he did not do anything at all.

Now, in the dark room, the roots were still growing, and sometimes, especially when the "A Maiden's Prayer" had rung out more than usual, the stinking green mud fell through the hole in the ceiling on to the dining-room table, while Monsieur Méandre stubbornly refused to take his nourishment elsewhere, because that would have been unworthy of the dignity of a man of his character.

It is necessary to note at this point the very lively practical intelligence of which the young maidservant Anna gave proof. She was able, at the time when curiosity was particularly excited by the causes of the complaint, to amass a rather considerable sum of money by permitting curiosity-seekers to enter the apartment while her employers were out, to contemplate the hole left by the hanging lamp and examine the roots, in return for a down-payment of one franc. For an extra franc, people were allowed to touch, and one Englishman paid two hundred francs for a twisted fork, which he subsequently had mounted on a tie-pin and sold for five hundred and fifty francs to a foreign prince.

This industry was interrupted by the indiscreet request of a entrepreneur of spectacles, who, believing that Monsieur Méandre had a share in the scheme, in view of the continual and seemingly obliging absences of Madame Méandre and her children, offered to take over the enterprise, take charge of advertising and share the benefits that would accrue from the manufacture and sale on a large scale of fragments of artificial roots mounted on amulets. Needless to say, the honorable senior bureaucrat refused indignantly. If Madame Méandre went out, it was because she had to go out. It was inconceivable to make such a proposition to a man of his character. And to prove his point, he disavowed such practices and kicked Anna out. Subsequent reflections permitted the thought that the influence of Barnabé Cruchot was no stranger to that resolution, for the cunning reporter justly feared the unfortunate effects that such fame might have on the personal advantages that he expected to obtain from the affair.

The time came for the execution of the judgment condemning Dubois to put the sum of ten thousand francs into the hands of Monsieur Méandre.

The time came, but the money did not.

At about the same time, the report made to the Committee of Public Hygiene by the Commissaire of Police, Églantine, also produced its result. The committee charged two of its members to go and carry out an investigation on the spot, and those gentlemen, vaguely anxious, began with a visit to Monsieur Églantine, the Commissaire of Police.

That step was taken on the eleventh of June. The magistrate informed the visitors that in two days' time, on the thirteenth, he was, at the request of Maître Cormoran, the bailiff, to accompany the latter in the seizure to be carried out at the domicile of Monsieur Dubois, the prior notification of seizure having had no effect. Monsieur Églantine invited the delegates of the Committee of Hygiene to join him.

The gentlemen accepted.

One might have thought that the clarification of the mystery was imminent, and Barnabé Cruchot knew that the moment had come for him to go into action. The following day, therefore, Sunday the twelfth of June, an explosive article, the fruit of Monsieur Cruchot's labor, appeared in the *Plein-Jour*. The article in question took up half the newspaper's front page and the whole of page two. Photographs reproduced views of the house in the Quai Bois-l'Encre and the door of the fifth-floor apartment, as well as the ceiling blurred by roots and the martial physiognomy of Monsieur Méandre, senior bureaucrat. A large black headline imperiously forced the exciting title to enter into all eyes and brains.

The effect, as noted above, was immense. Curiosity rose to the point of delirium. There were battles to acquire the issue, and one of the vendors, an expert newsmonger known by the nickname of Oeil-sans-Os, made enough in one day to buy a house in the country. All the midday and evening editions reproduced the astonishing revelations, with additional notes, and the foreign papers, in their respective languages, spread them through the entire world.

This is the article:

THE ANTISOCIAL MAN
OF THE QUAI BOIS-L'ENCRE

At number 3 Quai Bois-l'Encre in the middle of the Raisin-Sec quarter, events have occurred that are extraordinary to a degree so excessive that the memory strives in vain in seeking pale precedents, no matter how distant, and the best-equilibrated mind, in relating them, vacillates anxiously, fearful of entering into dementia. Is there any need to say that we refused to give them credence when our general information service gave us a brief summary of them? A personal and detailed investigation, however, has fully convinced us of their reality, which is far beyond what was initially related, and which the most insensate suppositions could not have glimpsed. We are bringing them to light, in the belief that it is our duty to report without commentary and as succinctly as possible what we know—the truth.

Yes, an Antisocial Man exists among us! In our epoch of science, progress and justice, when we are finally reaping the fruits of the bitter labor of the last century, when we live equally, free and fraternal, according to our conscience as modern, strong and reasonable men, in our enlightened and civilized epoch, a human being exists who, rejecting all the advantages that can be drawn from commerce with his fellows, maintains himself in our midst like an enigma and a challenge!

Yes, a human being that no one has ever seen, the sound of whose voice is unknown, who has refused for many years any relationship with other humans and who, trampling social conventions underfoot, tends indirectly to arrogate, over those of his fellows that evil destiny has placed within his range, the rights of a master over slaves—not to mention the confirmed facts and horrible possibilities that allow certain significant details to be suspected, of which the injudicious police should have taken an interest long ago.

But let us be precise and return to the events....

(At this point we have omitted two columns repeating various facts previously published, refuting his own optimistic and anonymous article in the *Clairvoyant*—declaring that the author was obviously in the pay of the government—in which Barnabé Cruchot related the facts that we have already reported, from the discovery of the piece of wood and the fall of the hanging lamp to the judgment of seizure, passing via the roots, the mud and a few other apocryphal incidents evidently invented by Barnabé Cruchot.)

Struck by so much singularity and by such an obvious baroque element in the mystery, suspecting some strange adventure, but without suspecting the extent of that strangeness, suspecting above all what had been related to us second-hand, we devoted ourselves, as noted above, to a personal and detailed investigation, which—corroborating the investigation undertaken in parallel by the amiable, energetic, sagacious and active Monsieur Églantine, the Commissaire of Police of the Raisin-Sec quarter—has revealed to us the following facts, which defy all commentary and only render more opaque the tragic darkness that has accumulated around this sensational affair and its mysterious and perverse protagonist.

The property bearing the number 3 on the Quai Bois-l'Ence belongs, we are told, to the Society for the Protection of Animals, and it is rented in sections. The apartment situated on the fifth and topmost floor of the house is the only one occupying that landing, and its windows overlook the river. Its annual rent is five thousand eight hundred francs. The person who occupies it at present took possession of it six years ago, signing the lease in the name of Dubois, which is obviously assumed.

Details are lacking with regard to the installation, because the present concierge, a lively and sprightly woman of thirty, was not the occupant of the lodge at that time. Her predecessor, a worthy old man decorated with the colonial medal, whom she replaced four years ago, was content, according to his military expression to "pass on the standing orders" relating to the fifth-floor tenant. Those standing orders are worth reporting. They are pinned up in the lodge and drafted as follows:

ORDERS RELATIVE TO THE FIFTH-FLOOR TENANT

1. Never even think about allowing anyone to knock or ring, for any reason whatsoever, on the door of the fifth-floor apartment, much less go into it.

2. Go on every settlement day to Maître Gemissant, notary, 51 Rue Poire-Pourrie, who will pay the rent and pay an additional fifty francs for the inconvenience, plus an additional two hundred francs on the January due date. Act likewise relative to contributions and other demands.

3. Go at the beginning of every month to the same Maître Gemissant to collect the sum of seventy-five francs necessary for the acquisition of three kilograms of tobacco (ordinary scaferlati). There will be an extra twenty-five francs for the errand, which will not be confused on due dates with the special recompense. The tobacco is then to be taken up to the fifth floor on that same day, and on that day only, there will be a right and a duty to approach the door. It must be exactly midday. Blow into the bugle that is passed through the little spy-hole to the left of the door the well-known refrain: "Long live wine, love and tobacco!/That's the song of the bivouac!" Afterwards, put the tobacco through the flap that opens lower down to the right and leave. Then cease immediately, for a month, to give any thought to the existence of a fifth-floor tenant.

*4. Send away insistently all beggars, fraudsters, col-
lectors (religious and otherwise), cesspool-drainers
and other analogous vermin who request entry.*

*5. Any infringement of the present regulations will be
cruelly punished.*

We have reproduced this strange document in its
entirety—which, until now, has been, and continues to
be, carefully obeyed.

The concierge has never seen her tenant. She is
completely ignorant as to their life. People go up with
morning provisions, but she knows that they never enter, acting as she does with regard to the tobacco, but
sounding different refrains according to their profes-
sion, and that they are paid in the same way by Maître
Gemissant.

Not daring to take up Maître Cormoran's writs herself, nor to keep them, she took a middle course and
confided the first to the butcher's boy who delivers
meat every day to the fifth floor, and who included the
paper with a consignment of beef. The following day,
however, he received a forceful jet of dirty water on
his head and in his mouth when blowing into the bugle
the refrain: "Toreador, take care...." before making his
delivery; he took that as punishment for his indiscre-
tion and refused angrily to take the subsequent writs,
which remained in the lodge on sufferance.

Sometimes, deceiving the surveillance of the concierge, mendicants or domiciliary collectors go upstairs, but the door on the fifth floor does not open to
them, and they undoubtedly have nothing for which
to congratulate themselves. The neighbors have never
been inconvenienced by any excessive noise, but
sometimes, in the nocturnal silence, distant muffled

groans seem to emerge from the mysterious place and fill their souls with terror.

We have been able to learn from shopkeepers established in the quarter for a long time that the unknown individual had moved in to the apartment at night. He directed the operation personally, four creatures that are believed to be negroes unloading carrying and handling a host of enormous crates from which unhuman plaints occasionally escaped. It is truly extraordinary that the police, who generally involve themselves so zealously in what does not concern them, and who are certainly not unaware of these facts, have never intervened.

A visit to Maître Gemissant was imperative and, postponing the continuation of our investigations on the spot, we went to 51 Rue Poire-Pourrie.

We found Maître Gemissant at home, but, to our great disappointment, he could not give us any precise information. He admitted having as a client a gentleman resident at 3 Quai Bois-l'Encre, whom he had not known at all before having received a very large sum of money from him, the income from which was intended to pay the quarterly invoices presented by the Society for the Protection of Animals and monthly bills for meat, poultry, wood, vegetables, pastries, wine, tobacco, etc. There was always a considerable tip for the employee who brought the bill. Maître Gemissant's honoraria were also included.

The unknown individual, in handing over the money—bearer bonds and cash—had made no secret of the fact that it was to his position as a city notary that Maître Gemissant owed his clientele, for absolute security was necessary.

We then interrogated Maître Gemissant with regard to the size of the sum and about the appearance of the individual Maître Gemissant replied to us that he was a middle-aged man of average build, who gave the impression of being a traveler. The name given—Dubois—was evidently assumed. The sum was very large, although there were evidently even larger ones, and also lesser ones, without ceasing to be very large.... Maître Gemissant really could not say. He stopped—hindered, we understood, by the professional secrecy behind which he eventually retrenched himself, and giving evidence of the vague anxiety that troubles all those who are connected, in any fashion whatsoever, with the recluse—which we did not escape ourselves when, an hour later, we were in front of the door of his apartment.

A faint hope of learning more took us to the butcher cited by Maître Gemissant, who is one of the most notable in the quarter. The visit was in vain. The owner, a surly and taciturn colossus, declared that he too was bound by professional secrecy, and refused to give us any information at all, "not wanting at any price to displease a client with whom he had nothing but satisfaction, and might perhaps find out about it somehow." When we persisted, the brute threatened to beat us with a leg of mutton that he was holding, and we left, understanding that the impolite tradesman, like all the other suppliers, did not know anything about the mysterious individual.

At the greengrocer's, to which professional duty took us next, we learned that every morning, fifty salad vegetables, fruits and three dozen fresh eggs were taken to the fifth floor of number 3, Quai Bois-l'Encre, and that, in order to receive them, the procedure was the one already described. Someone went up at eight o'clock precisely, and blew into the bugle passed through the little spy-hole on the upper left; the greengrocer's tune was "Do you know the land where the oranges grow...." The foodstuffs on order were pushed through the large flap lower down on the right, and the delivery man went away.

The baker willingly declared to us that every morning, in the same fashion, he delivered forty éclairs, as much coffee as chocolate, and twenty-five rum-babas (!), but he refused flatly to tell us what melody he had to produce in order to make his delivery.

We then returned to number 3 Quai Bois-l'Encre. The concierge consented to accompany us as far as the fifth floor landing, albeit with great difficulty and only on our formal promise not to make any noise.

The staircases have twenty-five steps, are broad, comfortable and clad in a yellow and red carpet retained by copper stair-roads.

On the fifth floor, the apartment door is at the back, facing the stair-head. It is dark, made in heart of oak, seemingly solid enough to resist any proof. Two loopholes are cut into it, sealed with metal shutters. One is situated to the left, about one meter fifty from the floor; it presents the form of a square, twenty-five centimeters on each side. That is the one through which the bugle is passed. The other is cut into the right-hand batten at floor level. It resembles a small door two feet high, which opens wide. It is by that route that the place is supplied. There is no doorbell to be seen. The whole presents a solid, grim and resolute appearance, well-designed for intimidation. We stuck our ear to it, but its thickness is evidently considerable, and it must be padded, for no sound reached us.

In spite of the promise made to the concierge, we could not resist the temptation to knock on that menacing door with our cane, but the concierge, who was watching us from the middle of the stairway, where she had prudently remained, took fright, annoyed by our audacity, and ran downstairs, enjoining us to follow her.

Obedient to that injunction, we went into Monsieur Méandre's apartment. He was at the ministry. The amiable Madame Méandre welcomed us and allowed us to observe that the roots were still growing, now occupying the entirety of the little dark room—which is not, as has been falsely suggested, a laundry-room, but a lumber-room. We were able to ascertain that a frothy and malodorous juice is now trickling incessantly from the dining-room ceiling. A basin has been place in the middle of the table to receive it, Monsieur Méandre not wanting to resolve himself to abandoning the dining-room, which would seem to be a making a concession to his cowardly and, in sum, unknown enemy.

In response to a question from us, Madame Méandre admitted to us that, unknown to her husband, she has put a stop to the piano sessions, and that Mademoiselle Adelaide Méandre now studies "A Maiden's Prayer" in town.

Taking our leave, we went down to the quay in order to determine the exact position of the windows. Unfortunately, they are equipped with large balconies garlanded with climbing plants, which renders it impossible to see in. On the other hand, the river prevents moving further away, and the houses on the far side of the water are much too distant for anyone to be able to attempt an investigation from their rooftops, even with the aid of a telescope.

As we were looking up, considering matters, a bearded man clad in a locksmith's leather apron approached us, emerging from a wine merchant's shop. He tapped us in the belly, laughed sardonically and, launching a jet of saliva almost at our feet, exclaimed: "All solid, eh, that door? They don't make 'em like that any more. I'm the one who fixed it up! And worse—there's a grille behind it that'd keep elephants out. It's beautiful work—there's not a hope of forcing it!"

Hoping for significant revelations, we took the man back into the wine-merchant's from which he'd emerged. There, leaning on the counter and smoking a stinking mouth-burner, he allowed us to understand, under the influence of a dozen small glasses of alcohol, that his name is Panari, that he is a locksmith, and that six years before, he had fitted the door of the fifth-floor apartment, with was then empty, with steel plates and bars. He had placed a grille behind the door and had carried out various other tasks. The work had been generously remunerated by the individual who rented the apartment and who is, according to his expression: "A truly decent sort, strapping and straight up."

That was all that we could get out of the drunken, mocking and familiar proletarian, who ended up shoving us outside and repeating: "I'm the one who fixed it up, and there's not a hope of forcing it!"

That incident was the last of our investigation.

Such is, at the present moment, the situation. Any commentary would be vain. Any recrimination regarding the incuriosity of the authorities would be illusory. Tomorrow the mystery will be elucidated. Tomorrow, Maître Cormoran, Monsieur Églantine and a few other individuals, whom we are not authorized to name because of the high social positions they occupy, will penetrate into the mysterious apartment. They will include a journalist—one only—and, without mentioning his name, we can promise our readers that they will be the first to be informed and in a definitive fashion.

These representations of civilization will be able to see the Antisocial Man, will be able to speak to him and obtain from him the compensations and explanations to which the whole of society has the right.

We hope so—but shall we say that we can scarcely believe it? A vague peril seems to us to emanate from that enigmatic apartment. One can expect, in our estimation, the worst resistance. Will we be in the presence of a furious maniac whom an intrusion will render frantic, or one of those cold and pitiless lunatics who, invaded by the obsession of a science or an art, would march unflinchingly over the ruins of the world, eyes glued to their enigma? We dare not venture an opinion; we hope with all our heart that everything will work out well—but in the end, nothing can prevail against force but force.

Will it be necessary to come to that?

Barnabé Cruchot.

We have reproduced this article in an integral fashion, in view of its historic importance and the almost-complete veracity of the details it contains. All our readers will certainly have taken cognizance of it at the time of its original publication, for one can say that it was read by the entire world. The next day, the most important organs—the *Synoptique*, the *Cent Bouches*, the *Tonnerre*, the *Clairvoyant*, the *Sursum Corda*—with rage in their heart at not having been the promoters of so much agitation, published special editions with photographs of the house, the door, the roots, the concierge, etc. All their efforts were, however, in vain, for the one paper that remained in the eyes of the public the uncontested master of the true beacon in the affair was the cunning *Plein-Jour*, whose print-run went up from a hundred and thirty-eight thousand to two million nine hundred and forty-seven thousand overnight.

On the morning of the thirteenth of June, the day on which the seizure was to be carried out, an immense crowd gathered around the house bearing the number 3 on the Quai Bois-l'Encre. A significant police presence had to be organized in the vicinity of the building, whose door had been prudently locked since the previously day. Shortly after two o'clock the individuals arrived who were to penetrate into the apartment. There were eight, to wit:

Monsieur Truie, Senator, Commander of the Légion d'honneur, former Minister of Public Works, President of the Society for the Protection of Animals, and, as such, effective owner of the building, who was wearing a dress-suit with his commander's cravat and all his foreign medals;

Monsieur le Docteur Volière, Vice-President of the Committee of Hygiene, whose co-vice-president, Monsieur Cousse, had sent his apologies, being ill;

Maître Cormoran, bailiff, due to proceed with the seizure, and his clerk;

Monsieur Églantine, the Commissaire of Police, wearing his sash and accompanied by two police inspectors, Andréas and Trolay;

and finally, the locksmith Panari, who had established the metal reinforcements of the door and had been summoned to force it.

Added to that official company was the journalist Barnabé Cruchot, who had been in the concierge's lodge since the previous day and who had been permitted to join the group, thus obtaining a considerable advantage over his colleagues—a hundred and fifty-eight of whom, as many national as foreign, and after stubborn insistence, had only been able to obtain permission to occupy the stairwell up to and exclusive of the tenth step of the flight leading up to the fifth floor. They were getting their own back by taking photographs of everyone.

Madame Armandine Vane, the concierge of the building, was able to join those who were going in, driven by curiosity and protected by Monsieur Églantine, the Commissaire of Police. The absence was noted of Monsieur Méandre, the plaintiff and senior bureaucrat. The gentleman in question had not wanted to take part in the visit, fearing that he might not be able to contain the fury of a man of his character, if brought into the presence of that detested enemy "the swine upstairs."

When the group composed of these various elements occupied, in its integrity, the fifth floor landing and Maître Cormoran advanced, a trifle green around the gills, and knocked on the door with his cane, there was a perfect silence and an anguished expectation.

But there was no reply.

Then Monsieur Églantine, the Commissaire of Police, approached, and when he pronounced the solemn words: "Open in the name of the law!" there was an even more perfect silence and an even more anguished expectation.

But there was no reply.

The demands were legally reiterated, in vain. Then Monsieur Églantine, the Commissaire of Police, gave the locksmith Panari the order to begin work. Murmuring between his teeth: "There's not a hope of forcing it—I'm the one who fixed it up!" the man set to work without ardor.

After laboring fruitlessly and superficially for three-quarters of an hour, Panari declared flatly, and with an evident satisfaction, that neither he nor any other locksmith could finish the job like that, with his hands, and that in his opinion it would require "elephants" because there "was a grille behind it, and worse." He added, not without pride: "It's me who fixed it up, and it's beautiful work!"

Monsieur Truie then came forward, majestic and firm, to negotiate with the obstinate battens. He made a touching speech in which he talked about just laws and the forbearance of judges, the horror of rebellion and the advantage of being decorated with the Légion d'honneur, the joys of family life, the happiness of being free and on good terms with everyone. He was eloquent and poignant, and there were people there who wept as they listened to him.

The door, however, was unmoved; it did not open.

Vexed, Monsieur Truie changed his tone. He talked about the strength of the government, supported by an immense majority, about the number of men serving in the active army, about cannons and gendarmes. He evoked cells and their padding. He spoke about convict prisons, the probability of dying there, and the necessity of severe punishments. He was redoubtable and impressive, and there were people there who were afraid.

The door, however, did not tremble; it did not open.

"Very well," said Monsieur Truie then, with a majestic firmness. "I have come hoping that my authority might influence an insensate resistance. I see that it counts for nothing. All indulgence is extinguished within me, and nothing remains but the public man who must ensure that the law is respected. I shall not fail in that duty. Since, today, unprepared for such inconceivable resistance, we lack the necessary means of victory, and it is getting late, we are going to retire. We shall return tomorrow, and we shall enter."

Then the door opened.

The right hand batten opened half way, very quietly, and through its narrow gap, nothing was perceptible but a profound darkness.

The batten resisted a vigorous shove that attempted to open it more fully.

There was a hesitation, as to who would go in. However, a reporter from the American newspaper, the *Wireless Telegraph*, having shouted from the stairwell that he was prepared to go in immediately and alone, a forward movement began.

It was then four twenty-eight. Outside, the weather was fine and the birds were singing.

The first person to go in was police inspector Andréas, then Commissaire Églantine, then Monsieur Volière, then the journalist Barnabé Cruchot, preceding Monsieut Truie, and the concierge, following Panari, and, a modest eighth and last, the bailiff Cormoran. The clerk, suddenly taken ill, had been obliged to run precipitately down to the lower regions of the building. Inspector Trolay was left to guard the door, the stairway and the journalists, with fourteen uniformed police officers under orders to block the steps.

Thus, the troop entered, and Inspector Trolay remained on

the landing in front of the door.

But the door suddenly slammed shut, almost in his face, with a loud bang, and those who had gone in could not longer be seen.

No clamor was heard, no movement occurred, no reply was made to the knocking, timid at first and then furious, that Inspector Trolay, after a time, took it upon himself to order two uniformed officers to deliver with the aid of the butts of their weapons.

Nothing was seen or heard, but the people who had gone in did not come out again; the door remained closed.

That various group of citizens, from the minister to the locksmith, had thus disappeared, and no longer existed so far as exterior life was concerned.

Those who witnessed the disappearance, when it was understood to be definitive, experienced a strange anguish, and discerned that something had changed—that a new era was dawning in the world, since such phenomena were possible.

Finally, some of the journalists, shaking off the torpor that was holding the in place, dazedly, their eyes on the door, went downstairs to transmit the news to the crowd and throughout the world.

Others remained, and bivouacked on the stairs. Inspector Trolay sent a uniformed policeman to inform the Prefect of Police, while he stayed to guard the door and prevent any journalists who desired to do so from going up, for that was his duty.

MAÎTRE CORMORAN'S NOTEBOOK

(We are reproducing Maître Cormoran's notebook in its entirety, intercalating within it succinct notes recalling the external events engendered by or consequent upon the tragedy, then unknown, that was unfolding within.)

Tuesday 14 June. I am Cormoran, bailiff, and what you are about to read is a faithful account of everything that has happened to us in the domains of the Antisocial Man since yesterday, 13 June, when we entered them.

I am devoting myself to this task in order to distract myself a little from the horrors of my situation, and above all, in order that no one should be unaware and that the entire world should know—if this manuscript is not buried along with me in some catastrophe—what destiny befell us in this place.

I shall begin by declaring that my dearest hope is that the nation should rise up without delay in order to save us, if we are found alive, or to avenge us, if the course of our careers is interrupted by a horrible and premature death.

Let no one attribute any literary form, perhaps insufficient, to these vague notes cast in the spasms of mental agony on to hazardous paper. Let it merely be known that I am writing while being, with the exception of my arms, completely trussed up and suspended from the ceiling of a virgin forest, if I might put it thus. I have my notebook in my left hand and my pencil on my right. The rest of my body no longer exists in the capacity of a free man. As one can imagine, this position is unfavorable to intellectual labor. Furthermore, the horrors that I have witnessed and the torments inflicted upon me by a boa constrictor, not to mention that the frightful perils that menace us constantly by the mere fact of our situation, have driven me half out of my mind....

But I shall resume my story at the moment of our entry into this deadly apartment.

Everyone knows in consequence of what events I and my companions in misfortune—for none of us escaped except for my clerk Sidoine, who, betraying his duty, went back downstairs, on the pretext, which I believe to be false, of a sudden indisposition—found ourselves together on 13 June on the landing of the fifth floor of the house bearing the number 3 on the Quai Bois-l'Encre.

We were, as everyone knows, to penetrate, by permission or by force, into the apartment of the so-called Monsieur Dubois, in which, at the request of Monsieur Méandre, senior bureaucrat, I was to execute a warrant of seizure. There were eight of us—eight members of society more or less elevated on the scale of civilization but all honorable. Among us shone Dr. Volière, Vice-President of the Committee of Hygiene, and, highest of all, the venerable Monsieur Truie, the former Minister and well-known Senator.

When I think that it is against such notable individuals, such profoundly respectable people, official personages whose mission dressed them in an august luster, that the most monstrous crime has been committed—and is still being committed—I wonder why our fellow citizens, in order to save us, have not already demolished this house stone by stone, and I doubt Providence!

But let's get back to the story....

Everyone surely knows about the futility of my knocking on the accursed door of this detested apartment, and how vain were the summons issued by Monsieur Églantine, the Commissaire of Police, as well as the attempts to break in legally undertaken by the locksmith Panari. It was only after two eloquent speeches by Senator Truie that one of the battens opened, a satisfaction granted to us that we attributed to a fearful submission, when it was nothing but the manifestation of the most atrocious of perfidies.

The door opened, then—or, rather, half-opened—and we passed through one by one, myself, modestly, eighth and last. And behind me, the door closed again, with a loud and sinister crash. Then I heard a snigger in my ears like that of a demon, and suddenly, before we had been able to see anything, something threw itself around the group that we had formed, griping us around the midriff and drawing us tightly together with immense force.

Instinctively, I put my hand on that unknown bond; it was thick, round, cold and scaly. I opened my mouth to cry out; a soft and sticky mass filled it. The appeals, coughs and imprecations that rose up were stifled with a similar rapidity.

I had Monsieur Églantine's beard in my ear, and the handle of Dr. Volière's umbrella in the hollow of my stomach, the considerable thighs of the concierge Armandine Vane pressing on my abdomen. I was choking, the bond cutting me in two, and I fainted....

When I recovered consciousness, the daylight was fading, and my stupor knew no bounds for I found myself in mid-air, completely trussed up, save for my arms, with strips torn from my own frock-coat, and suspended, so far as I can tell, by the buckle of my belt, from a hook, evidently designed for hanging things on, fixed on the middle of what I recognized with a certain difficulty to be a ceiling—but my God, in what condition!

The strangest thing of all—which filled me with amazement, fear and stupidity, and made me doubt the state of my wakefulness and reason until I remembered the incidents motivating Monsieur Méandre's complaint—is the spectacle that surrounded me, and which is still surrounding me while I am writing these notes, and will surround me until the Lord knows when!

I finally understand. The tenant of the apartment, the so-called Monsieur Dubois, the Antisocial Man, has made the rooms that he has rented into a reproduction of the jungles of India, the virgin forests of Mexico, the African veldt or the Australian bush. I can't be more precise, being a peaceful and well-balanced man, averse to ferocious beasts and long voyages.

In this environment, returned to its primordial destination, which was intended to shelter the virtuous existence of some honorable family, all the partitions have been demolished, with the result that all the united rooms form an irregular area of wilderness.

The floor, which is a thick layer of vegetal earth, is covered by thick grass and nourishes a host of vegetation of every size and nature. Recalling some faint botanical knowledge, I recognized a coconut palm, a tamarind-tree, a date-palm, a catalpa, a magnolia, a baobab and a cedar, not to mention better-known species such as a plum-tree, a cherry-tree, a quince-tree, an apricot-tree, an apple-tree, an orange-tree and a laurier, almost all laden with ripening fruits.

The equatorial forest giants whose branches were bent against the ceiling, forming a dense vault, are interlaced with a host of lianas and other climbing plants in which bright corollas open here and there. Giant ferns, melons, spiny cacti, azaleas, camellias, wild rose-bushes and a host of vegetable species unknown to me are growing freely, verdant and vivacious, beneath the domes of greenery.

A spring is emerging from a rock to my right and a fountain is elevating its musical and limpid sound behind me, in the distance of the apartment, where there is, it appears, a kitchen garden. Thus is formed a babbling brook, invaded by reeds.

I understand now where the mud comes from that is trickling into Monsieur Méandre's apartment, and I'm astonished that the infiltrations that are inevitably being produced have not yet damaged the house further.

And this apartment ought, according to the conditions of the lease, to be inhabited by a respectable family man!

A host of animals, mostly ferocious, inhabit this forest and live here in complete freedom. I shall talk about them shortly, as well as the master of the place—the Antisocial Man himself.

The windows, I ought to note, have been blocked up for half their height, two movable panes opening at the top to let in air, which do not show the sky.

The large glazed bay that advances, so far as one can see from down below, on to a terrace, has been left free. Always open, draped with verdant garlands, it produces a permanent current of air that is not useless for ventilation, but which might prove deadly to people whose lungs are as sensitive as mine.

Suspended as I am, I find myself almost in the middle of the whole space. Gilded cornices, although dirty and invaded by greenery, indicate to me that I'm occupying the place of the drawing-room chandelier.

The drawing-room chandelier!!! I think I'm dreaming!!! A chandelier, in the very heart of the most savage nature, where birds are flying, where mosquitoes buzz and bite, where plants are growing along my limbs and where I can hear the splash of water beneath the belly of a hippopotamus! For I ought to mention that a relative large space has been transformed into a pond for the use of one of those pachyderms—young as yet, it's true—and the other inhabitants that like swimming. It's doubt-less one of the rooms that has been lined with metallic sheets. The stream coming from the springs aliments it, and the sink in the kitchen—or what used to be the kitchen—collects the overflow.

The watery room is fertile in plants and reeds. Aquatic animals—rats, snakes, turtles and otters—live in it, not to mention newts, mollusks, mudworms and other vermin of every sort.

To my right is the door that connects the drawing-room (the drawing-room!) to the antechamber where we were captured. That antechamber is the only room in the apartment that has kept its original appearance. The door that leads to it has been cut half way up, as is customary in stables to allow the animals to get some air without their being able to get out, but here it's the top part that serves as a passage and the bottom that retains the soil....

Such is the place in which we've been living since yesterday, if one can call this living....

I need to arrive now at the most odious subject, which is the population of the apartment and the fate that awaits each of us, as miserable captives of nameless monsters, as insolent as they are brutal, as devoid of delicacy as they are well-provided with cruel ingenuity, but estimable when one envisages their leader, the Antisocial Man himself.

Here I might be permitted a very important remark: given the monstrous facts, for which I do not hesitate to assume respon-sibility, one could believe that this gentleman is insane. It is necessary to banish that idea: the Antisocial Man is not mad; I proclaim that loudly. It is sufficient to see and hear him to be convinced of that. It is sufficient to be in his presence to recog-nize, at first glance, that he enjoys a perfect mental certainty, a clear and frightful intelligence.

He is not mad, he is merely pitiless; he cannot be moved, and before him, it is necessary to abandon all hope. As can easily be imagined, several of us, from the very first moment, have begged him to set us free. Prayers were addressed to him that would have softened the heart of a tiger, and tears flowed that would have melted a rock.

It was in vain.

The Antisocial Man, without saying a word, extended his hand and showed us, nailed to the trunk of a baobab, a small piece of wood analogous to the one that was found in Monsieur Méandre's home. A red-hot needle had traced: *Stop talking. or eat mud.* And when Monsieur Truie persisted, majestically invoking the just reprisals of a society so cruelly offended in our persons, the Antisocial Man made a gesture, and one of the brutes that are his slaves, abruptly shoved a sticky, green-tinted, fetid handful into the venerable senator's mouth. I understood then how we had been gagged during our capture. But I'll get back to my story.

The Antisocial Man, as I've said, is not mad. At the very moment when I am writing these lines I can see him through the foliage, a short distance away. He is sitting on the edge of the spring. He is thin, beardless, muscular, sardonic and calm. He is smoking his pipe. His clothing is simple. He rarely speaks. Sometimes he reads books. At his feet is his favorite goat: a very young, very pretty, very affectionate and very capricious goat, which never leaves him for long and for which he appears to have, doubtless in imitation of Robinson Crusoe, an excessive tenderness.

The other members of this pandemonium are:

1. Three or four creatures of vaguely human form, sometimes bipeds but more often quadrupeds or quadrumanes. They are black, hairy, bearded and mute. Their vigor, agility and dexterity are boundless. They serve the Antisocial Man fanatically, and seem to venerate him and love him beyond expression. One of them is called Zephirin, another something like Venceslas,

the others I don't know yet. Perhaps they are negroes, but more probably gorillas.

2. A baboon of tall stature, as cunning as he is vicious: the most hateful being I know.

3. An enormous brown bear, hiding beneath a mild appearance an immoderate penchant for the most cruel jokes.

4. The ant-bear Samuel, a large hairy beast with formidable claws, which has a long trailing tail and a disgusting tongue like a black worm, which hangs out.

5. The hippopotamus already noted, hardly existent outside his bath.

6. A demented jumping kangaroo that causes me mortal anguish and frightful heart-stopping moments when it suddenly launches itself from one side of the area to the other, bumping into me for the express purpose of making me oscillate, which amuses it.

7. The goat, which is called Angèle.

8. A boa constrictor, which is my personal cross and to which I shall return in due course.

9. An armadillo, a kind of small scaly pig without paws, which sometimes emerges spasmodically from a crevice in the rocks and goes straight back in.

10. A bearded vulture, a hideous monster with pale blue eyes covered with leucomas and a bald neck.

In addition to these principal inhabitants there is a host of other, lesser creatures, either comestible and domestic—rabbits, guinea-pigs, chickens, pigeons, etc.—or wild: hummingbirds, flamingoes, lizards and insects of every sort, among which I shall cite a swarm of strident and enraged mosquitoes, which make no small contribution to rendering our life intolerable.

I should also make mention of the fireflies that are reminiscent of fat glowing winged worms scintillating everywhere at night like stars. That's quite pretty and inoffensive.

All of this swarming, active, turbulent population exists quite naturally in the forest, delivering itself in total freedom to its needs and its passions without worrying about us—or rather, alas, not worrying overmuch, for we serve it as playthings. Each of us is prey to one of the monsters, which, occupied with one individual in particular, renders his hours of captivity, by any and all means, increasingly punishing.

For my own count, I'm the slave of the boa constrictor. That ophidian does me no harm, but from the first minute we were introduced it has developed an immense affection for me and cannot bear to be separated from me for an instant. It is always enlaced around a portion of my anatomy, and its weight, its contact, the sight of it and its presence are more odious to me than I can say. When I push it away, with gentle insistence, as if I were reproaching a misconceived devotion, it draws even closer, fixing me with its cold, unctuous and languid eyes, which give me vertigo. And I dare not persist, for it scares me.

Senator Truie's fate is more especially horrible. He is nearby, in his shirtsleeves, with neither waistcoat not hat, secured by the waist to the trunk of a baobab. The baboon is his master and seems to have taken it as its mission to make his life a constant stream of shame and pain, by means of refined tortures, of a nature so disgusting, cruel and satanic that I cannot dwell on them even for a second. Can you believe that the monster has gone as far as to deprive its victim of his Commander of the Légion d'honneur's cravat, in order to put it on itself, wearing it upside-down, and that, at this very moment, it is sitting astride Monsieur Truie, who has been knocked down, and smoking one of his cigars, which it has stolen? It is attempting to produce musical sounds by beating two bones on the Senator's belly, as if on a drum.

I cannot hold back my tears in the face of such a spectacle, and in thinking that it is a rich and highly-considered man—a senator who was once a minister and might become one again in the not-too-distant future—whom that unspeakable brute is torment and humiliating thus.

And when I think that the infamy in question is taking place under the eyes and with the consent of another man—a citizen who is governed by the man he is allowing to be outraged to the point of death—when, I say, I think of that, a limitless fury grips me, and although I am religious and easy-going by nature, I would like to tear the Antisocial Man's eyes out of their orbits with my own fingernails....

The fate of Barnabé Cruchot is also cruel. At dawn, this morning, one of the gorilla slaves dragged him before the Antisocial Man. The latter was holding in his hands an issue of the *Plein-Jour* dated 12 June and containing the article that caused such a sensation. With a diabolical smile, he presented that unfolded newspaper to Barnabé Cruchot, whose teeth I could hear chattering.

"Eat!" said the Antisocial Man—and his voice did not suffer any hesitation.

With a deathly expression, Barnabé Cruchot received the newspaper and ate the eight pages. Since then the kangaroo has taken possession of him, pulling his hair during each of its furious runs and prodigious bounds.

Dr. Volière, the Vice-President of the Hygiene Committee, was given to the ant-bear. That uninventive brute has contented itself with digging a hole in the ground and burying its victim so that only his shaved head protrudes. Sometimes, the vulture comes and sits on it.

Monsieur Églantine's fate is somewhat kinder. The brown bear accords him a relative liberty, contenting itself with keeping him on a leash improvised from his own sash, and making him rid it of fleas twice a day.

Of the locksmith Panari I have no news and I have not seen him. I tremble to think what fate must have been reserved for that unfortunate proletarian, doubtless suspected of treason with regard to the affair of the door, and whose life is not protected, like ours, by the importance of the positions we occupy in society—something of which, in spite of everything, I am sure, the Antisocial Man is well aware, and which is perhaps the only thing preventing him from massacring us.

About the female concierge, Armandine Vane, I shall say

nothing. That unfortunate woman no longer has any vestige of honor. All of them have violated her. I blush in writing those lines.

It is still necessary for me to record the deplorable situation of Police Inspector Andréas. He has been immersed in the pond—as a punishment, as I understand it, for the desperate resistance that he put up at the moment of his capture, in the course of which he fired three revolver shots at the gorilla Venceslas. The bullets only killed a guinea-pig, and Andréas, although he is endowed with a famous vigor, was knocked down in less than no time by his adversary, whose muscular power seems truly limitless. Andréas was then tied up a set to soak under the surveillance of the hippopotamus, which is called Jocko.

Our nourishment consists of meat that is almost raw—it is, it appears, too warm to take the trouble of having everything cooked—and a few raw eggs. This morning I was permitted to browse some vegetable leaves. Those of us who are deprived of the use of their hands are hand-fed twice a day by the monsters that look after them. As for myself, Monsieur Zephirin stuffs odious comestibles into my mouth with the aid of a rod. What nourishment for a man with a delicate stomach! Brackish water is our beverage....

I shall stop for today. It's light and the sunlight is fading. I'm tired from having written for such a long time, but I thank the Lord for having always given me a taste for literature, which permits me to find a distraction from my sufferings of every kind. I shall continue this journal for as long as our incarceration lasts—not long, I hope. My notebook is thick and new. I shall extract great consolation from these pages, and eventually, I hope, some glory from their publication.

Wednesday 15 June. I don't know how I'm finding the strength to write. The most horrible, most inhuman, most insensate peril has been suspended over our heads since this morning. Really, those who desire to rescue us and who, in pursuit of that end, are adopting the most extreme means, ought to weigh their determination a little more carefully, and think about the frightful results that they might have for us, lamentable victims.

I do not know what baleful intelligence thought of imposing an embargo on the provisions that ought to have renewed this place's food supplies. He has acted as our worst enemy. He has made our situation, which was already cruel, into a gridiron on which the most intolerable anguish is searing us.

It was today, Wednesday 15 June, that it happened. Throughout yesterday evening a few faint noises seemingly coming from the stairwell, had given us some hope, but they ceased without any result.

(The "faint noises" to which Monsieur Cormoran refers were the roars and terrible blows of the steam-powered battering-ram with the aid of which attempts were made, without success, to break down the door. That attempts, as is well-known, was the first one made to liberate the prisoners, whose capture and unknown fate caused such universal horror and curiosity. The failure led the Minister of the Interior to attempt famine, in spite of the opposition of the suppliers, who, supported by the leaders of the extreme Left—the leader of the opposition, Ganglion, made a famous speech on the subject—protested against what they called an "attack on the liberty of labor." The disastrous effects that nearly ensued, as we shall see in due course, led to the fall of the Ministry. It was replaced in power by the combination known by the name of the "Combat Ministry" because it was under its reign that violent means were employed, and because it was presided over by General Crampon, the Minister of War.)

This morning, when the time drew near to receive the provisions, the negro gorilla Zephirin, who was then in service, went as usual to open, first the grille, and then the little loophole high on the left of the exterior door. Then he passed the bugle through.

Soon, that instrument produced an uncustomary fanfare; the

tune played was: "Open up, fatal door,/Intoxicate me with space and air!"—which informed the prudent monster that it was not the peril-free blowing of one of the suppliers. Not opening the larger loophole, he withdrew the bugle and looked outside. A man then approached and shouted in the name of the law things that I could not hear in their entirety but in which the communication was sufficiently discernible that food-supplies would be suspended until the end of the rebellion, or at least until the liberation of the prisoners.

Already my heart was leaping with hope, but a dull sound interrupted the voice. It was Zephirin, who had reached through the upper loophole and struck the government's messenger with his fist.

(The man struck by the monster Zephyrin was the honorable Monsieur Druide, the deputy head of the Sûreté. That functionary fell dead, a victim of his duty, under the terrible blow, which fractured his skull and caused the brain to spurt out. The immense emotion caused by that unspeakable murder will be remembered, as well as the splendid funeral held for the victim, with which the entire population was associated.)

Then everything was closed again, and two minutes later, the Antisocial Man stood in front of me, taciturn and smoking his pipe. He fixed me with his cold stare. I had no idea what was going to happen. Was he about to steal my notebook, curious about my literary activity, read it, and take offence at a few slightly sharp expressions dictated to me by ill-humor? Drops of sweat dripped from my forehead on to the floor.

The Antisocial Man took a step back to avoid getting wet. He took his pipe out of his mouth.

"Write, Bailiff!" he said to me—and the deliberate calmness of his incisive voice chilled me with terror.

I brandished my pencil as a manifestation of obedience. He was the master, after all, and perhaps, in his intellectual superiority—for one cannot deny that he is intellectually superior—a humane and philanthropic objective was acting.…

The Antisocial Man then dictated to me the following ultimatum:

"If, tomorrow morning—put the date," said the Antisocial Man, and I obeyed, inserting 16 June—"the embargo placed on foodstuffs is not lifted, which are to be delivered as usual, we shall begin eating the prisoners."

I trembled violently, nearly dropping the pencil, but the Antisocial Man's gaze hypnotized me. I continued:

"The first to be eaten will be Monsieur.…"

The Antisocial Man darted an investigative glance over us. "What's the name of that fat one?" he demanded, indicating the Commissaire of Police, who was listening open-mouthed.

"Églantine," I said.

The Antisocial Man resumed his dictation. "The first to be eaten will be Monsieur Églantine, because he is still young, plump and succulent. Then Andréas, who is marinating. After that, Senator Truie"—on hearing his name, the baboon leapt upon its victim, who was sobbing, and shook him, grinding its teeth—"and then the rest of them."

And I wrote that atrocity, scarcely able to conceive the reality. Groans, soon stifled, went up in various directions, for my unfortunate companions had heard. Monsieur Églantine, on the eve of such a frightful fate, felt ill, but the discontented bear recalled him to life by clawing him.

"Sign it," the Antisocial Man told me.

And I put: "Signed, *The Antisocial Man*, written according to his dictation by *Cormoran*, bailiff."

I could not help adding, underneath my signature: "For the love of God, re-establish the provisions. He will do what he says. C."

Then I dissolved in tears.

(The effect produced outside by this ultimatum, thus drafted and thus signed, with the touching additional request, was immense. The entire world was shaken by a prodigious emotion.

All governments felt shaken by it. All parties in all countries took possession of it, in order to make it into a weapon against their adversaries. Civilization was struck by a kind of dementia. Caravans were organized everywhere, which set off for the Raisin-Sec quarter, while pleasure-trains and boats, chartered expressly, started arriving from all points of the globe at full steam, with innumerable catastrophes, to disgorge variegated crowds speaking unfamiliar languages, anxious to see, from a distance, the celebrated house, which was guarded night and day by an army corps.

The Press, on that occasion, showed what it could do, when moved by something that was worth the trouble. It was then reaching the apogee of its power, and its reporters worked wonders, launching news every day more sensational than the day before and exciting the readers of all nations to the point of incessant delirium, like a furious sea rising higher and higher every day, and multiplying the print-runs of the papers....

O Barnabé Cruchot, however, the most illustrious of all and the progenitor of such a fine affair, you were no longer there to reap the fruit of your labors, and so much glory was lost to you!)

The note passed from my hands into those of Monsieur Venceslas, who went to throw it through the small loophole high on the left. We shall see the effect tomorrow morning. Today, rabbits and chickens will appease our hunger, but afterwards? Will I have to see Monsieur Églantine, with whom I have so often played cards and backgammon in our little café, the Bock Rafraichisant, fall victim to the most odious of fates? Will I have to participate in a meal composed of his palpitating limbs, his raw flesh? Horror! Will I be obliged myself, later....

No! Superlative of horror! Will my turn come? The last, doubtless. I'm thin and already old. And then, too, I can serve as a scribe...and I've never offended anyone here; if I came, it's because my job compelled me to do so...the Antisocial Man, in his magnanimity, wouldn't hold that against me....

Alas, I sense, deep down, that he would—that a moment will

come when, immolated and butchered, Cormoran, the master of my office, will know, as an illicit tomb....

I'm shivering; I'm burning; I can feel a cold sweat running over my ardent skin. An immense anguish, worse than death itself, is clawing at my soul...my immortal soul! It is immortal, my soul! That's understood....

I'm going mad.

But what about my body? My mortal, carnal, comestible body? Ha ha ha!

A convulsive and perverse gaiety, a tortured gaiety of the damned, is hallucinating me! I see myself roasted, boiled, stuffed, in a pâté, braised, in a sausage...

But no—they'll eat me raw!!!

I've come out of a long faint. I recovered my senses only to fall back into indescribable horror. I can't tear my thoughts away—a contrast that excites I don't know what bitter delights in me—from the exquisite stews that my maidservant Pulchérie cooks for me. I caress the boa distractedly to attract its benevolence to me. I feel ready to remain suspended like this for years on end. I'll do anything anyone wants—but I don't want to die! I don't want to die!

Thursday 16. We're saved! A few moments ago—O thrice adorable and adored music, more delightful than that with which the sirens charmed Ulysses!—the bugle resounded, playing: "Toreador, stand up...!"

It was the butcher, with the meat. The other suppliers followed.

The first moments were a delirious joy. Afterwards, however, I couldn't help retaining a bitter thought: were the forces of civilization expiring, then, on the threshold of that fatal apartment? Did the external world deem itself so incapable of recovering the members—us—that had been stolen from it? Did not a submission so complete and so perfect to the orders of the Antisocial Man indicate the extent of their uncertainty of liberating us in the short term?

At any rate, let us not be ungrateful to Providence. I shall not be eating Monsieur Églantine…and above all, above all, will not be eaten! That's the main thing!

10.30, same day. They've just fed us. The brute Sylvain—one of the gorillas—with the aid of a rod, stuffed my share into me in such a hurry that I nearly choked and remained for a little while within an inch of death, with a piece of raw veal in each hand and another in my mouth, which was so big that I couldn't catch my breath.

The baboon is amusing itself making Senator Truie jump after every mouthful. It has tied his hands behind his back and, posting itself on a branch, is letting the morsels dangle on a piece of string that the unfortunate senator has to seize in mid-air with his teeth. At the same time the monster is gorging itself on coffee éclairs, a consignment of which it has taken up into the tree. The spectacle is heart-rending, but I'm experiencing a great joy in thinking that we won't be eaten.

The boa is annoying me considerably, however; taking the attentions that I lavished on it during my anguish for the signs of a sincere affection, it no longer leaves me a moment's peace.

(It was on that same day, the sixteenth, that the Council of Ministers, having met in an extraordinary session, decided, in response to the proposal of the engineer Monsieur Dozamy, the director of naval construction, to attack the place from below by means of a perforation made in one of Monsieur Méandre's ceilings.

It was also at about this time that, with the subscription of Janathan Carnyby, the billionaire known by the nickname of "the Sturgeon King," the great gambling agency was founded in Chicago that took, at very good odds, all the sums that anyone wanted to wager *against* the Antisocial Man. Mr. Carnyby declared that he was utterly convinced that the Antisocial Man would hold out until the end.)

Friday 17. Today, for the first time since the beginning of our captivity, I've seen Panari, the locksmith. He was free, dressed only in a pair of underpants and his leather apron. He appeared to be on very good terms with the negro gorillas, who were playing leap-frog with him.

Some time afterwards, as he was passing beneath me, alone and smoking his pipe, I asked him in a whisper whether he was working for our liberation. Having taken his filthy pipe out of his mouth, however, and spat in the face of Senator Truie, who was laid low by the effects of indigestion, that creature, which I refuse to call a human being, replied brutally: "Leave me in peace, you old fool! We're doing fine here! And anyway, there's not a hope of forcing the door. It'd need elephants! I'm the one who fixed it up!"

He seemed to be drunk. He went to sit down on the edge of the stream and started fishing with a line, humming a licentious refrain.

I didn't persist, reserving myself the right to criticize such revolting conduct and denounce such a monster to the abomination of every civilized person on Earth.

P.S. The detestable serpent never ceases to overwhelm me with its attentions, which render it impossible for me to sleep. Knotted around me, it is now licking me with its little cold and viscous forked tongue, and its glassy, metallic and languorous eyes are staring at me, imploring me passionately for I don't know what.

What a life!

Saturday 18. Last night, as a solemn silence reigned, troubled only, as usual, by groans—our groans—until, at about two a.m., I believe, a roar of pain suddenly sprang from the hippopotamus' bath, where Andréas, the police inspector, is still immersed. It was that unfortunate who had uttered it. By the tremulous light of fireflies, two negro gorillas came running and pulled him out of the water. It was evident that he had been grievously wounded in the right foot.

A vague sound of running water was heard then and the level of the little lake dropped abruptly. After a quarter of an hour or so, the noise ceased and the water, renewed by the stream, gradually recovered its former level. Andréas was bandaged by the Antisocial Man himself and was laid on the ground, but he soon became delirious and I fear that he might die in spite of the care lavished on him by Dr. Volière, untied for that purpose. I don't understand what has happened.

(Monsieur Cormoran could not know about the attempt made to gain entry via Monsieur Méandre's ceiling, which was mentioned above. Unfortunately, the drilling was undertaken in the very center of the ceiling situated beneath the pond-room. As is well-known, the Chief Engineer of Bridges and Highways and the Colonel of Firemen, who were jointly in charge of the operation, were drowned along with fourteen of their men by the muddy deluge that descended with prodigious impetuosity, and which proved very difficult to stop by blocking the hole in order to avoid further damage.

Not knowing whether the entire apartment above might be a lake, it was considered unwise to persist. It was the following evening when the proposal of the Swedish mathematician, who proposed entering through the roof wearing diving suits, was received telegraphically. The inexplicable opposition of the Society for the Protection of Animals, which declared that its building had already suffered enough damage and refused to allow any further demolition, forced the rejection of that plan.

It was then, in despair of the cause, that the idea was raised of one last and furious attack on the door with the aid of mountain artillery.)

Same day. It's now about three o'clock in the afternoon. The weather outside is very fine.

How I would have loved to be in the garden of my little house in the suburbs, wearing a panama hat and watching the trains go by. Such delights are not for me—alas!—but even dreaming about them is pleasant.

An unspeakable spectacle brought me back to reality, however. Senator Truie, still the prey of the abusive baboon, is suffering unparalleled tortures. I cannot describe what I have seen. It is unimaginable how far the horrible, evil genius of that quadrumane can go. Would you believe that, assisted by the infernal locksmith, it has laid its unfortunate victim on his back and tied his limbs to four stakes, and that it is now mounted on a high branch, occupied—I scarcely dare write it—in blowing mashed-up paper pellets at his face through a hollow reed?

In the meantime, the infamous Panari, smoking his eternal pipe, is reproaching Monsieur Truie for his millions and his corpulence, for so-called embezzlements and filthy debauches— entirely imaginary, I'm sure—which he describes in the crudest possible terms. He is mingling all that with philosophical arguments about the inequality of society and taking large swigs from a bottle of cognac that he has dug up somewhere.

Monsieur Églantine, the Commissaire of Police, is sitting some distance away, occupied in killing fleas in the thick fur of the bear, which is asleep at his feet. The magistrate sometimes raises his eyes toward the odious spectacle that I have just described, and tears of pity and impotent rage run down his thin face, as they are running down mine at this very moment.

The odious locksmith can see them, those tears on my cheeks, and he is feigning a violent emotion. By means of a grotesque pantomime he is mocking my pain. Putting one knee on the ground, he strikes his breast and prostrates himself, putting on a semblance of imploring forgiveness. Then, as if enlightened by a revelation, he leaps up, gestures a summons to Venceslas, who is scratching himself on the edge of the spring, and, using him as an improvised ladder, succeeds in reaching my height. Then he stuffs the neck of the bottle—which he has not put down—between my teeth and forces me to swallow a large dose of cognac. What an unspeakable brute!

The alcohol produces an effect on my unaccustomed and debilitated organism that is as prompt as it is intense.

I feel nebulous…my head is spinning.…
I'm content.…
We'll soon be getting out. How nice the weather is!
How nice it is on the grass with a girl-friend.…
At the request of Monsieur Méandre.…
Aha! I can see the concierge…she's a lovely woman.…
Me too.…
Everything's spinning…spinning.…
My heart hurts.…
Oh la la! The Antisocial Man.…
I haven't has anything to drink.…
The boa.…
He's drunk.…
Liberty.…
Equality.…
I'm going mad!
I need a drink!!!

(The last few lines had been crossed out by Monsieur Corcoran himself, but as they are legible in spite of the scribbling it has been thought worthwhile to publish them, in order to demonstrate the extent to which an honorable man, in such a frightful position and under certain influences, can act out of character. The provenance of the alcohol is explicable by the fact that several bottles had been added to the provisions in the hope that drunkenness might favor a surprise entry into the place. That did not succeed. The method of general poisoning proposed by Dr. Bain, Professor of Comparative Philanthropy at Monaco, was rejected because of the high social status of some of the prisoners. Also rejected for the same reason was the proposal made by Captain Souffle that the house should be bombed.)

Sunday 19. I've slept badly and for a long time, perturbed by the alcohol that the detestable Panari forced me to drink.

I feel full of emptiness and bitterness. My sufferings are ignoring the weekly day of rest, and a frightful grief has struck us this morning. The unfortunate Andréas died at dawn, in the horrible convulsions of tetanus, in spite of the cares lavished on him by Dr. Volière, who, I must say, seems to be suffering our ordeals with a singular constancy. He opposes nothing but a serene calm to all the misfortunes that are being heaped upon us, and, after Andréas' death, he allowed himself to be buried again by the ant-bear without saying a word.

Folowing the Antisocial Man's orders. I wrote these words on a piece of paper: YOUR HANDIWORK IS RETURNED.

The piece of paper was attached to the breast of the deceased police inspector. Afterwards, without even permitting Monsieur Églantine to address a final adieu to his worthy and unfortunate subordinate, the body was shoved out on to the landing through the large loophole low down on the right. May people give him a glorious Christian sepulcher…and may Providence extend its protective hand over all of us who are still alive. For our fellows seem to have abandoned us.…

Same day, five o'clock. I've just understood, after days and days of utterly enigmatic supplications addressed to me, what the boa constrictor wants. It wants me to scratch its head and neck with my fingernails. It's insane, but that's the way it is. Its mime, initially persuasive, then furious, has left me no alternative, and I'm scratching it. I, Cormoran, sworn bailiff, citizen, elector and eligible bachelor, am hanging by my belt-buckle and scratching the neck of a boa!

Monday 20. I'm ill. The raw meat I'm eating is causing internal perturbations. In my position, that's terrible. May heaven forgive me, but I'm beginning to wish for death.…

Senator Truie has just rebelled against his torturer. He tried to punch it, knock it down and run. At the same time, he insulted it.

"Baboon! Riff-raff! Extortioner! Senator!" he yelled.

The vexed quadrumane bit him cruelly.

Tuesday 21. The obstinate constrictor is still hanging round my neck. Exhausted by its weight, the intense heat and my sufferings, I scarcely have the strength to write. Strange visions traversed a nightmarish night.

The vulture came to perch on my head. It flapped its wings, launched a jet of guano down my neck, gave me a sharp peck on the left ear and said: "You're funny, you are, and that's why I love you!"

Then it flew away. I don't have the energy to meditate on that bizarre incident. I sleep, I wake up, I suffer. I can no longer see my companions in misfortune. I'm scarcely alive.

Same day, six o'clock. Hope is giving me new strength. A slight noise is coming from the stairwell. Will a new attempt be made to rescue us? It's high time. Senator Truie is down to his last breath. Monsieur Églantine, held on a leash by the bear, has just passed beneath me, saying: "Monsieur Cormoran, I bid you adieu. I sense that I'm about to die."

At that, tears sprang from my eyes. Anyway, I can't do any more.

The heavy boa is asleep on my back, digesting a rabbit that I can feel descending along its intestine. What a life, Lord!

Wednesday 22. Another hope disappointed. The noises heard yesterday were indeed the preludes to a desperate attempt made to rescue us. Alas, thwarted by the genius of the Antisocial Man, it had hardly begun when it was miserably aborted, without giving us any hope and leaving us even weaker and more discouraged, with a clearer and more forceful consciousness of the immense power of our master. I'll describe what happened.

This morning, when the butcher came to deliver the meat, some unknown person shouted at us with a megaphone, through the little loophole high on the left, which had not yet been closed: "Two big guns have been set up on the landing. They'll fire in five minutes."

(This attempt, which Monsieur Cormoran justly considers desperate, was only made as a last resort, and to satisfy public opinion, which had been enraged by the restitution of Andréas' corpse by the Antisocial Man. The entire house had been evacuated in advance.)

The sensation was general. The baboon stopped polishing the cranium of the recumbent Monsieur Truie momentarily, and the locksmith Panari came running from the far end of the space.

"It doesn't matter!" the drunkard growled, in a thick voice. "The door will hold! I'm the one who fixed it up!"

Meanwhile, the Antisocial Man had come to stand beneath me, still calm, his face creased by his habitual sardonic smile.

"Bailiff," he commanded, "Write." And he dictated: "There are seventy-one melinite bombs behind the door. If the cannon fires, they will all blow up. Signed: *The Antisocial Man*, written in conformity with his dictation by *Cormoran*, bailiff-clerk."

I couldn't see any bombs, however, and no one brought any. Even so, the hair was standing up on my head and my tongue was utterly dry in my mouth.

The paper passed into the Antisocial Man's hands and he presented it to Senator Truie, who was lifted up for the purpose.

"Certify," commanded the Antisocial Man.

Poor Monsieur Truie, to whom the excess of his terror had rendered some strength, looked around in bewilderment.

"Where...where...are they?" he stammered.

"What?" demanded the Antisocial Man, coldly, hypnotizing him with his gaze.

"The...the bombs?" groaned his victim.

"That's none of your business, you disgusting specimen," howled Panari, intervening. "They exist! I've seen them! And anyway, even if there aren't any, it's all the same!"

And Monsieur Truie, bewildered by this singular argument, wrote in a trembling hand: It's true. *There are seventy-one melinite bombs. For pity's sake, think of us and the quarter.*

Signed: Truie, *senator*.

And he began to weep.

"Chicken!" murmured the infamous locksmith, scornfully, while the baboon leapt on its victim.

The note was thrown through the small loophole high on the left. Immediately, everyone outside ran downstairs precipitately. I assume so, at least, given the racket whose echoes reached me.

But the loophole closed, and all communication with the exterior ceased. We heard no more mention of cannon and remained alone with our torturers, our executioners.

(It was in the wake of this attempt and Monsieur Truie's dolorous postscript that the leader of the opposition, Ganglion, asked General Crampon, the President of the Coucil, a question that was transformed into a challenge. In his speech, which was very violent, he went so far as to accuse the government of complicity with the Antisocial Man and of desiring, with his aid, to get rid of Senator Truie and the compromising secrets that the individual in question was assumed to possess. The Ministry was in a minority by 517 to 12 (its own votes). The coalition that succeeded it was formed and presided over by Monsieur Sorgue, the Minister of the Interior. He received an imperative mandate from the Chambres to reckon with the Antisocial Man within forty-eight hours.)

Thursday 24. An exhausting heat has reigned since this morning and is contributing more than a little to the augmentation of our suffering. Half of the inhabitants of the apartment are spending their time in the pond. I've begged the Antisocial Man, in the most touching terms, to return me to civilized life, but his only response was a negative shake of the head, and the abominable locksmith, who is our cruelest enemy and now wanders completely naked through the forest, has directed my attention the plaque bearing the prohibitive injunction: *No talking, or you'll eat mud.*

At the same time, he brandished a handful of horrible mud

mixed with dung.

I shut up, with rage in my heart, and Venceslas was kind enough to throw an entire bucket of water over me as he went past. It is necessary to believe that all sentiment of pity is not dead in him.

The night of the same day. I don't know what time it is. The darkness is profound. I'm writing by the vague light of a firefly that has perched on my piece of paper.

Something has just happened that has filled me with an immense emotion, which is agitating such contrary sentiments in me that I can't wait for daylight to confide it to this notebook, my only friend, as if, having written it, I shall had unburdened my soul, alternately and tortured by poignant doubt, terror and delirious joy....

Just now, suffocated by the boa, which, having slithered in its sleep, was strangling me, I was woken with a start from a slumber full, as usual, of nightmares and frightful visions.

Then I heard voices and I caught a glimpse in the shadows of the Antisocial Man, sitting by the spring and chatting with someone sitting beside him. That individual was not one of the inhabitants of the apartment. *It was someone from outside*—a rather stout man dressed in gray and wearing a straw hat. His face was broad, clean-shaven and resolute. He was smoking a big cigar, which, every time he took a pull, lit up with a red glow, and he had offered another to the Antisocial Man. They were talking in a foreign language with the greatest cordiality and seemed to be perfectly in accord.

I was amazed. I thought at first that it was a hallucination, the continuation of a dream—but no; I could smell the odor of Havana tobacco, and I pinched myself hard, which hurt, so I wasn't dreaming.

Who could that strange individual be who was talking to the Antisocial Man? What wouldn't I have given to understand what they were saying! Did the individual represent deliverance? But why all the mystery, then? Was it not more likely to represent some frightful new peril? How had he got in? What was he going to do to us? Had he come for us? The white slave trade crossed my mind. Was he a slave-trader…or…? Oh God, was it possible? No, not that! Anything…but not that! It would be too horrible.… Anguish suffocating me, I hung there, fainting.…

It only took a few seconds for me to come to my senses, still in complete darkness. Everything has disappeared now and I can no longer see the unknown visitor. However, I can still smell the odor of his Havana tobacco, and as I've said, I'm writing this to soothe my mind.…

At present I'm trying to go back to sleep and not to think about it any longer—it's too horrible, and at the same time, so full of a radiant hope.…

(The incident to which these lines of Maître Cormoran's relate is not one of the least singular in this strange affair. On the afternoon of Thursday 24 June a gentleman presented himself to the competent authorities and requested to enter into negotiations with the Antisocial Man. When, taking him for a madman by virtue of that request, they were content to reply that it could not be done, he declared that his name was Jonathan Carnyby, the American billionaire known by the nickname of the Sturgeon King, and that for him, nothing was impossible.

The owner of several islands in the Pacific, he wanted to offer to grant one or two of them to the Antisocial Man, with free transport for him and his companions, in exchange for his accommodation in the Quai Bois-l'Encre, such as it was. He, Carnyby, had the intention, after having bought the building, of making it into a warehouse for his tinned sturgeon. The only reply to this extraordinary proposition was laughter; it was taken to be that of a hoaxer or a lunatic, even though Jonathan Carnyby had provided all the desirable proofs of his identity. The gentleman, annoyed, then declared that he would take the measure directly to the Antisocial Man, and that once his consent had been obtained, they would see.

He came back the next morning, saying that he had spoken

to the Antisocial Man, and that the latter, who was a perfect gentleman in every respect, consented. Naturally, no one believed him, and Jonathan Carnyby—if he really was the person in question—was asked to take his hoaxes elsewhere.

Mr. Carnyby went away then, prey to a keen irritation, calling the general secretary of the Ministry of the Interior a "fat belly on legs"—a wounding allusion to the functionary's conformation—and "a rotten sturgeon in a tin." He then went to London, where, in the newspaper *Liberty Enlightening the World*, he published a detailed account of his attempt, with the appreciation that the only reasonable and courteous person he had encountered in the course of his trip was the Antisocial Man, whom he was honored to call his friend. The story was generally considered to be a lie, but it must be observed that it is entirely in accord with Maître Cormoran's journal, and that the latter has given an exact description of Mr. Carnyby and places his visit on the day when that gentleman claims to have made it. Did Mr. Carnyby really get into the Antisocial Man's abode, then?)

Friday 25. The heat no longer knows any bounds and our suffering is intolerable. The debris of my frock-coat is weighing on my shoulders like a lead mantle. My sweat is dripping on to the ground, and the inexorable boa keeps demanding that I scratch it, relentlessly and mercilessly. I began this morning at five thirty-five and I was still scratching at eleven thirty. Now it's having a bath.

While scratching, I recalled with frantic sentiments what I had seen last night, but I dare not dwell on that....

A battle has broken out beneath me. Barnabé Cruchot, weary of being dragged by the hair after the bounding kangaroo, has torn himself free from its paws. Then, having taken his wallet out of his pocket and a press card out of his wallet, he stuck it under the marsupial's nose, demanding in the name of the press of the entire world, that the door be opened in order that he could deliver his copy. His adversary threw him to the ground, and stole his wallet, which it put it in its abdominal pouch, and his watch-chain, of which it made a necklace. Then, gripping its victim by the hair again, it launched itself through the air with a mighty bound, to fall back in the middle of the pond, where they both disappeared in a muddy splash.

At the same time, the boa came out of the bath, all sticky and viscous. It is now climbing up toward me again, in great haste to be scratched, and I'm resuming that ridiculous task....

Two hours have gone by, and now it's asleep. I'll do the same. I'd love to drink a large tankard of cool beer, without my false collar on....

Same day, six o'clock in the evening. Another attempt made from outside. In vain, naturally. So far as I can tell, they tried, with immense ladders, to effect an entry through the windows. As soon as the Antisocial Man was alerted by the abject Panari, on sentry duty on the veranda, he came to me.

"Cormoran," he said, "write."

And he dictated: "There are still the seventy-one melinite bombs. Don't forget them. If you persist, everything will be blown up. Signed: *The Antisocial Man*, written in conformity with his dictation by *Cormoran*, bailiff clerk."

The paper was taken from me and Panari, having attached Monsieur Truie's watch to it as ballast, threw it out of the window at the feet of a group of people that the detestable lock-smith declared to have recognized as ministers "by their dirty mouths."

Thus the disrespectful blackguard expressed himself, and, almost immediately, the ladders disappeared from the horizon they had occupied. With that means of defense, the Antisocial Man is beyond reach, and there is no hope that the place will ever be taken by force. The most frightful thing of all is that I firmly believe that there have never been any bombs, and that it's an imaginary means of intimidation employed with the greatest success to terrify the people outside and us. For, after all, one never knows...perhaps there are bombs—and what a catastrophe that would be!

(That attempt, made with floating ladders maneuvered by electric cranes, was the last effort made to enter the place by force. The further advertisement of the seventy-one melinite bombs produced a sudden and supernatural effect of terror, such that all the citizens within a radius of a kilometer deserted their dwellings. Strangely enough, however, the number of curiosity-seekers crowding around the perilous building increased, in considerable proportions, doubtless attracted by the possibility of witnessing the advertised catastrophe.

It was the following day, 26 June, the Parliament overthrew the Ministry presided over by Monsieur Sorgue. The succeeding coalition, with Monsieur Caressaie as President of the Council and Minister of Justice, received a mandate to negotiate immediately and to study the means to do so—bitterly regretting the absence of Jonathan Carnyby, to whom ten telegrams full of apologies and offers were addressed, signed by the Secretary General of the Ministry of the Interior.)

Saturday 26. Monsieur Églantine has disappeared. I have just discovered that, on waking up after a few hours of painful sleep, more exhausting than insomnia. This morning, the bear no longer found the Commissaire of Police beside him, who had been there the previous evening.

That's all I know. That's all that we know, I could say, for no one seems to know the truth. I tremble at the thought that one of the ferocious beasts that surround us might have killed our unfortunate friend in a fit of rage.

I remember that he had a violent altercation the day before yesterday with Samuel, the ant-bear. Has the latter monster taken advantage of the shadows of night to murder him and bury his body in some unknown abyss? I shudder at that odious thought and I prefer to believe that Monsieur Églantine, successfully carrying out an escape plan doubtless prepared over a long period, has got outside. Outside! Oh, my God, what a dream! What a deceptive and torturing dream!

What corroborates that idea is that everyone—except, naturally, for the impassive Antisocial Man—seems quite astonished by the disappearance. Furthermore, I've just seen the ant-bear that attracted my suspicions going past; it seemed perfectly serene and quite incapable of being stained by innocent blood. Perhaps the escape of Monsieur Églantine, whom I delight in imagining free and making speeches everywhere in favor of our deliverance, will be the basis of our definitive salvation?

(This hope had no solid foundation, since Monsieur Églantine, the Commissaire of Police, was no more outside than inside, and no one ever saw him again. His disappearance was complete and definitive. It constitutes one of the most dolorous mysteries of the affair. It was impossible to elucidate, and the most contrary suppositions were advanced by everyone without persuading anyone, especially because the fact only came to light subsequently, when no investigation was any longer possible. It is generally assumed, however, that Monsieur Églantine attempted to escape through one of the windows with the fallacious complicity of one of the monsters—the locksmith Panari has been named, without any proof—fell into the river and drowned, and that his body, carried away by the water, has gone to nourish the fish somewhere in the deep sea.)

Sunday 27. Today will take its place among the most frightful. From outside, nothing new. Inside, unspeakable torments. First of all the boa, the infernal, uncomfortable and obstinate boa constrictor. Then Monsieur Truie, fallen completely into senile dementia, howling at the absent moon, like a dog weary of life, while his executioner continues to torture him, without my being able to tell whether it is trying to shut him up or increase the force and duration of his plaints. Then the tropical heat, crushing, stormy, driving the mosquitoes mad, which are driving me mad....

And then a long nose-bleed, come to weaken me further....

And then, always and above all, the monotonous and heart-rending screams of Monsier Truie, imbecilic, tortured....

Truly, oh, truly, I turn an affectionate gaze toward liberating death!

Monday 28. I believe that we're approaching the end of our ordeal. While I was surrendering to an impious desire for death, Providence was preparing the way for our deliverance. This time, I think, we won't be disappointed—but I no longer have the strength to be enthused, or even to hope with any ardor. I've so often done so in vain....

Proposals of peace, however, have definitely been made. People must have decided to make a start on that instead of letting us suffer a thousand deaths for such a long time and covering the entire civilized world with ridicule by so many fruitless attacks, which demonstrate all the forces of civil and military science to be impotent....

Let us not recriminate, however, and recount the facts.

This morning, by the intermediary of the butcher's boy, we were sent, along with our ration of meat, a ministerial envelope and a telegram from London. The Antisocial Man, opening the telegram, read it with a calm satisfaction.

As he was underneath me and I had, in spite of everything, retained my excellent spectacles on my nose, I was able to read over his shoulder.

This is what the telegram said:

London 27-6-19-22-23
Jonathan Carnyby enchanted victory signaled Antisocial Man honored to call most dear friend. Offer Pacific island still vehement. Preparing means transport will guide himself and remove at moment Antisocial Man will please telegraph by return.
                    Jonathan Carnyby, Sturgeon King.

The Antisocial Man then opened the ministerial envelope, which contained forty-six octavo pages containing the Government's offers. The Antisocial Man merely glanced at them and threw them to the kangaroo, which ate them, thus removing them from the curiosity of Barnabé Cruchot, who tried in vain to take possession of them.

The Antisocial Man smiled, however, and dictated the following ultimatum to me, with the locksmith Panari to his left and the goat to his right, and Venceslas behind him, astride the hippopotamus streaming with mud. The armadillo also emerged from his hole in order to listen.

ULTIMATUM
General Conditions

Article One. There will be no further mention, in any fashion, of the ridiculous lawsuits brought against the Antisocial Man, nor of the petty incidents that prompted them.

Article Two. The Antisocial Man will be free to go, without being trouble, to the island that Jonathan Carnyby, the Sturgeon King, is putting at his disposal in the Pacific. On that island, he will live with his friends without being the object of any civil or military action, and will be left perfectly tranquil there.

Article Three. The cravat of a Commander of the Légion d'honneur, the rank of Corporalcy of the Armies of Land and Sea and the passports of a Consul General in the Pacific will be placed at the disposal of the Antisocial Man, in order that he can make use of them to recognize the graciousness of Jonathan Carnyby.

Article Four. The sum deposited with Maître Gemissant, notary, Rue Poire-Pourrie, by the Antisocial Man will be returned integrally to the hands of the latter in current legal coinage.

On which general conditions the Antisocial Man will undertake to abandon forever, by the aerial route, the apartment rented by him from the Society for the Protection of Animals on the fifth floor of the house bearing the number 3 on the Quai Bois-l'Encre. He does not wish to claim any indemnity for the anticipated annulment of his lease. He makes a gracious gift to the invalids of the hospital of the comestibles and furniture filing the apartment. He will, however, take away with him the seventy-one melinite bombs, which he reserves the right to drop on the crowd at the moment of his departure, if it does not proceed smoothly.

All under the following additional conditions:

1. Monsieur Méandre and his daughter who plays "A Maiden's Prayer" on the piano, will be put in the hands of the Antisocial Man in order to be delivered to the beasts.

2. Monsieur Panari, locksmith, who refuses to quit the company of the Antisocial Man and his friend, will receive the settlement in good and due form of all of his debts, including those contracted in the establishment of the wine-merchant Foutré, whom he informs once again that he has supped from his bottle and slept with his wife.

There will, furthermore, be delivered to the aforesaid locksmith an official attestation to the effect that he was the one who fixed up the door, and that there was no hope of forcing it.

3. Senator Truie will remain the exclusive property of the baboon that has surrounded him with care during his sojourn in the home of the Antisocial Man, on several occasions snatching him from the jaws of death in the course of quotidian indigestions provoked by the gluttony of that member of Parliament, and who loves him so much that he would prefer death to a separation.

4. The concierge Armandine Vane we not return to her husband or her lodge. She prefers to stay in the new circle of relationships that she has been able to form, the mores of which suit her better. Moreover, she will soon be a mother. Her divorce will therefore be granted immediately, in order that she can re-marry, should she wish to do so.

At this point the voice of Dr. Volière, still in his hole, interrupted. To my knowledge, it was the first time he had spoken, and his voice, although half-stuffed by the feathers of the vulture, which was carefully and scrupulously brooding his skull, was clear and grave.

"Monsieur!" he called.

"What?" said the Antisocial Man.

"Monsieur," said Dr. Volière, "I want to go with you to your island in the Pacific. I was to study the flora, fauna and pomona of those austral lands Then again, you seem to me to be a gallant man and your hygienic procedures interest me. I would be flattered to be your companion."

"That would give me pleasure," said the Antisocial Man.

"Thank you," Monsieur Volière replied. "Can someone disinter me, then, and can the vulture cease sitting on me—it's giving me a headache."

That was done immediately. I'm still flabbergasted by such a request on the part of a man that I had always thought to be well-balanced and reasonable. I fear that, by dint of treating him like an egg, the vulture might have rendered the honorable vice-president of the Committee of Hygiene mad.

Meanwhile, the Antisocial Man resumed his dictation.

5. Dr. Volière will also stay. He desires that he should be brought, as soon as possible, all his instruments and apparatus, as well as his complete wardrobe.

"Tell them not to forget the detachable collars," remarked the doctor, half-disinterred.

I added that remark, and the ultimatum was concluded thus:

6. The attached telegram will be transmitted to its addressee immediately.

7. A response to the present ultimatum will be made before midnight today, by way of the small loophole on the upper left, which will be opened for that purpose.

Signed: The Antisocial Man

Written in conformity with his dictation by *Cormoran*, bailiff-clerk

For approval of the articles concerning:

Dr. Volière, Vice-President of the Committee of Hygiene;
Panari, locksmith-libertarian who fixed up the door;
Armandine Vane, ex-concierge;
On behalf of Senator Truie, unable to sign, *X* (the Baboon).

The Antisocial Man took the ultimatum from me.

(The passionate debates occasioned by the articles of this ultimatum are well-known. They were discussed, point by point, in a Parliamentary session that lasted from six-thirty in the morning until six-thirty in the afternoon, in the course of which session three Ministries succeeded one another and were brought down in their turn, until the desirable result was achieved and the response was drafted, which was dispatched immediately to the Antisocial Man.)

"Now the telegram," he said.

Jonathan Carnyby, Sturgeon King
London W2

Antisocial Man thanks dear friend Carnyby. Accepts. Desires means transport midnight Tuesday 29. Sincerely

Signed: The Antisocial Man

Carried away by habit, I added: *Written in conformity with his dictation by Cormoran, bailiff-clerk.*

"Imbecile," said the Antisocial Man, on reading it, but left it all in.

(Mr. Carnyby had this telegram framed in platinum, encrusted with rubies and opals, in order to display it in a place of honor in his curio collection. In a duly-made will, he made a gift of it to the Museum of Great Discoveries recently inaugurated in Chicago, on Lake Michigan.)

These papers were transmitted outside, and we were fed.

I'm awaiting the response with feverish impatience. My heart, I confess, is swimming in joy. Free! Tomorrow evening we shall be free!!! My every thought and my every action is a gesture of thanks. An immense delight is enveloping me—enveloping everyone, it seems to me....

Only Monsieur Truie is downcast, but I think that's imputable to senility and not consciousness of the fate that threatens him, for he is certainly incapable of understanding anything whatsoever outside of the cruelties of his torturer, the baboon.

The hippopotamus also seems to me to be in a bad mod. The character of that pachyderm, moreover, is exceedingly peevish. The goat is utterly joyful. The boa is demonstrating even more affection toward me than usual. It's no longer demanding that I scratch it, but it's licking me all the time with its little cold forked tongue and viscous and imploring me with its glassy, glossy and languid eyes, When I think that I'm going to abandon that detestable companion forever, my joy no longer knows any bounds.

The following night, time uncertain. I'm in the midst of taking part, much against my will, as one can imagine, in an insensate Saturnalia. It seems that it's the baboon's birthday, and we're having a party. A powerful electric lamp brought from God knows where has been hung on the trunk of a baobab, and by its dazzling light the Sabbat commenced shortly after midnight.

The baboon, which was pretending to be asleep, was woken up by the bugle, blown by its dear friend, the filthy Panari. The negro-gorillas were there, surrounding Monsieur Truie, who was forced to gather a bouquet and who came trembling with senility and drunkenness, to offer it to his torturer. The baboon, feigning surprise, confusion and tenderness, kissed him on the cheeks three times while pinching him, and then leapt on to his back in order to greet the various individuals who arrived at that very moment to present their good wishes. The impudent quadrumane, grimacing with great joy, welcomed them, expressing its emotion and gratitude by means of diabolical contortions. In the meantime, the infamous locksmith extracted the most frightful sounds I have ever heard from his bugle, the gorillas danced a frantic bamboula, and I am being forced to beat time with a rusty key on the lid of a chamber pot, which obliges me to stop writing temporarily....

Alcohol, needless to say, is flowing in rivers....

After a demented scene, they have finally gone to bed, exhausted and snoring, leaving the baboon to sleep off its heavy drunkenness on Monsieur Truie, who is serving as its pillow. I shall try to get a little sleep....

Alas, no! Not yet. The boa is dragging itself toward me as, having drunk, it has taken it into its head to smoke a pipe, in which it has not succeeded, it is suffering from sea-sickness and I have to care for it. What a life! Anyway, it's the last night...."

Tuesday 29. Six thirty a.m. The response to the ultimatum had just arrived when the storm broke, in its full fury, shortly after daybreak. I saw the storm born, the boa not having permitted me to sleep until the moment when the thunder forbade it! The Antisocial Man, naked on the veranda, allowed himself to be soaked by the rain. He took cognizance of the response and I saw a slight smile on his lips.

"Cormoran," he said to me, "write: *Accepted. I depart this evening, at midnight. Signed:* The Antisocial Man. *Written in conformity with his dictation by* Cormoran, *bailiff-clerk*."

I thought I should add: *Thank you, dear friends outside who are returning us to our functions, to freedom, to civilization, to life. Thank you from the bottom of my heart! C.*

My note was transmitted outside and the Antisocial Man returned to his shower.

I am prey to a mad joy. I can say that I am savoring my last moments of captivity. Everyone around me seems radiant, and the delight is universal. Only the boa seems to me to be a little sad. That's because it's leaving me. In spite of the torments it has inflicted upon me without realizing it, it affects me to know that it loves me so much!

Would one believe that even Monsieur Truie is asleep, smiling and drooling like a little child. I feel very sorry for that poor old man, thus condemned to dwell with so many monsters—for his fate is certainly sealed—but in sum, it's necessary that one of us should sacrifice himself for the others. Then again, he's so accustomed to his torments that if he were deprived of them he would doubtless miss them. And then again, truly, he's so senile....

I'd be curious, all the same to discover what the reply made by our governors—by our liberators, whom I can never glorify enough—was to the ultimatum that I wrote. That response—a duly signed ministerial document—is lying directly beneath me. Barnabé Cruchot, who seems to me to be very agitated, has already attempted to take possession of it several times, in order to read it, but his tyrant, the kangaroo, has taken a malign pleasure in preventing him from doing so. Perhaps Panari, in passing, might consent to hand me the object of my curiosity....

I've just addressed my request to him. That brutal being initially gave me an instruction to "plaster my crack"—which is to say, to shut up—but he picked up the piece of paper to read it himself....

Suddenly his face lit up with a snigger, and he exclaimed: "Certainly I'll pass it to you. It's too superb!"

He handed me the liberating letter and stuffed his pipe. I thanked him warmly for his unexpected graciousness. I opened it. I read:

29 June

RESPONSE OF THE GOVERNMENT
TO THE ANTISOCIAL MAN'S ULTIMATUM

In the name of the Nation, the Law and Parliament.

Unique article: The conditions imposed are accepted en block, save for the following exceptions:

A. Monsieur Méandre and his daughter Adelaide, who plays the "A Maiden's Prayer" on the piano, will not be placed in the Antisocial Man's hands to be delivered to the beasts.

He is offered instead thirty-five cases of extra-dry champagne of the highest quality.

B. The rank and uniform of Corporalcy of the Armies of Land and Sea will not be put at the disposal of the Antisocial Man in order to be awarded to the honorable Jonathan Carnyby, for they are already in the hands of the present title-holder, who does not want to be separated from them at any price. There can only be one Corporalcy of the Armies of Land and Sea.

He is offered instead the rank of Academician with the green-embroidered coat, tricorn and épée (this distinction confers the title of Colonel.)

The position of Consul General in the Pacific and the cravat of Commander of the Légion d'honneur are accorded.

C. We cannot agree to abandon Monsieur Truie; that would dishonor the government.
We offer instead...AAAH!

(The following lines are in the handwriting of the locksmith Panari.)

Old Cormoran—who seized me in the old days, which I still hold against him—has just dropped his notebook on the coffee-pot while fainting. So I'm sticking on his paper what has got him steamed up, but I'm laughing so much I don't know if you can read it. Two minutes ago he asked me to pass him the paper with the response. I told him to piss off, naturally, but I wanted to read it and then I gave it him to see his face. This is what it says—I'm copying:

We cannot agree to abandon Monsieur Truie (what a cheek—an old slob like that, a senator!)
We offer instead Maître Cormoran, bailiff....

No, I'm splitting my sides! That's when he fainted. It disgusts me a bit to have him with us, but all the same, seeing his ugly mug cracked me up! I'll never forget it. It's better than the twenty-five smashed glasses! He's waking up...better give him back his paper and sit down, because I'm laughing too much....

Anyway, I'm well content to get out of here with Monsieur Antisocial Man, who's the nicest fellow I ever saw—and to hear no more talk of the dirty cows who govern us. Long live welfare!"

PANARI, *locksmith libertarian, who fixed up the door, which'd need elephants.*

(The notebook resumes in Maître Cormoran's handwriting.)

God, isn't it a nightmare? There are beings bearing the name human who would be cruel enough to condemn one of their own to such a terrible fate! They're throwing me, Cormoran, to the dogs! They prefer to cast me out of the bosom of civilization than abandon that wretch Truie, a senile and useless rag who's soiled himself with every infamy! While I, virtuous and upright, am in the prime of age and talent!

Shame! Shame! It was necessary to rescue everyone or let us all die…we form a single homogenous whole. It was necessary to recover the whole, at the cost of no matter what sacrifices… only to save one part is not to save any.…

Vile men that have sold me, may you be sold in your turn. New Judases, I want you to suffer for such a sin the same hideous expiation as the old one. Yes, cowardly criminals, base hypocrites, I call down upon your heads all misfortunes, all vengeances, in awaiting the judgment that posterity will inflict upon you!

Alas! Alas! It's true, then, that I shall remain in such company.… With that Antisocial Man who hypnotizes me and dictates things to me…when once, it me who dictated.… With these brutal and libidinous monsters.… With that boa, above all! That accursed ophidian, more tenacious than a whore, more demanding than a taxi-driver, more affectionate than an employee in search of a rise!

Horror!

I shall no longer live in my little villa in the suburbs, from which one can see the trains passing by. I shall no longer eat the delicious onion stew cooked by my maidservant Pulchérie, who is so obliging.… I shall no longer drink the large tankards of cool frothy beer. I'll never seize anyone again! I'll no longer play cards or backgammon! I shall no longer be, in a word, the bailiff Cormoran! I shall be a deplorable specter marching through a nauseating life toward an ignominious tomb!

Oh, let's leave it there, let's let our tears flow!

They have flowed, those bitter tears, and now I no longer have the strength to rebel. My furious despair has changed into a bleak depression. In the course of my sobbing, I having been taken down. I'm sitting on the ground because my legs refuse to carry me, but that's all the same to me—everything is all the same to me. I no longer have any hope for the future, any hope of escape. And I'm writing this to distract myself, in order not to think, to finish what I've begun. At the last moment, before saying adieu forever to the civilized world, to an ingrate fatherland, to the traitors who have sold me and to everything I love—I'm weeping again—I'll get these lines outside, by some as-yet-unknown means.

Barnabé Cruchot, liberated from the kangaroo, which is making its preparations to leave, has just approached me to make a request that I consider to be monstrous: he has asked me to confide the present work to him in order that he can publish it himself, once at liberty, as a collaborative endeavor. I'd have half the authorial rights!

"No, Monsieur," I've replied, indignantly, "this notebook is the fruit of my sleepless nights and the flesh of my flesh, and I won't tolerate you attributing it to yourself! I'd rather lose all the authorial rights, if anyone is unjust enough to steal the price of so much pain from me. I'll employ a sure means, with which inspiration will furnish me when the time comes, in order that the document will come into the hands of those who will give it the immense publicity that it merits. I still desire that posthumous glory. I want people to know what soul was mine. It's necessary that no one is unaware of it!"

"Monsieur" he cried, then, "You're reducing me to despair! What! I, Barnabé Cruchot, will have done everything to launch such a beautiful affair, and the glory will be stolen from me by another? I, a journalist, will have deceived all my colleagues thanks to ruses worthy of a Redskin, lost innumerable hands of stupid card games at high stakes to you and the vanished Églantine, listened to the tiresome speeches of that cretin

Méandre, slept with a fat and repulsive concierge—me, who only likes thin and distinguished women—eaten an indigestible newspaper, been brutalized incessantly by a furious marsupial for an interminable fortnight spent in a direly uncomfortable place among lawless and faithless rabble—will, I say, have endured all of that with the most perfect constancy, only for it to be, at the end of the day, a bailiff who relates everything that has happened and obtains universal glory thereby! What might the vague descriptions be with which an infidel memory will furnish me, what will my wittily made—dare I say?—assertions be, and even my most beautiful inventions, compared with the pages that I have seen you writing, day after day and hour after hour, from the height of your incomparable observatory, and which have, for sure, the vigorous and scrupulous veracity of a definitive and indubitable report...?

"Reflect, my dear Maître Cormoran, reflect....I'll let you have three quarters of the authorial rights, and put your signature ahead of mine. Come on, consent...."

"No, Monsieur," I said, firmly.

"Very well, Monsieur," he said, then. "Very well...you're ruining my career and dishonoring me. I shall never forgive you...."

And he went away.

I hate that man. When I think that he dares to dream of stealing a success that will be immense, I'm sure, according to his own words, I boil with indignation. Then again, he'll be free, while I....let's pass on...let's pass on....

3 p.m. The Antisocial Man has just received a telegram thus conceived:

London, 28-6-19-7-50.
Will arrive midnight exactly. Sincerely. Carnyby.

It's settled, then. The last preparations are being made. The cases of champagne offered as a replacement for Monsieur and

Mademoiselle Méandre have just arrived. Also just arrived, in begs, are the sums deposited with Monsieur Gemissant, as well as the crate containing the Academician's coat and accessories destined for Jonathan Carnyby. Let us also note forty pipes for Monsieur Panari, may the devil take me.

Dr. Volière, with perfect calmness, is packing his wardrobe, which has just been sent to him, and explaining to the Antisocial Man the working of the esophageal probe. Monsieur Cruchot is striding back and forth and giving me dirty looks. Monsieur Truie has been untied and his jacket has been returned to him, but the baboon has taken him to the far side of the apartment in order to torment him more at his ease until the last moment… one can hear the screams from here…damn you, you old swine! When I think that he's been preferred to me.…

6 o'clock. The official papers have just arrived. I'm opening the envelopes with the aid of the brown bear and Sylvain. There's the entire treaty between the Antisocial Man and the Government, Monsieur Panari's receipts and certificate, the concierge Amandine Vane's divorce certificate. Let's add the diploma of Consul General in the Pacific and that of Commander of the Légion d'honneur. The Government, in its cowardice, has added a diamond-studded cross and another certificate of that ridiculous order in the name of the Antisocial Man, in order to mollify him.

10 o'clock. The darkness is profound. While awaiting the departure, everyone is singing, laughing and dancing. They're swilling champagne joyfully. I'm drinking too, of course. I'd be very stupid to deprive myself of it. Armandine's larking about with Sylvain. The vulture's eating a rum-baba. The fireflies are spreading a phosphoric light.…

The boa is coiling up, full of joy, at my feet. Dirty beast!

Why that dirty beast? Dear friend, rather. It's glad to keep me, that's all, and if it's at my feet, it's to keep me warm. My moral dolor is beginning to ease. Perhaps it won't be as bad as all that on this island. In sum, the society we're quitting isn't all that attractive. A policeman gave me a caution last month because Pulchérie shook a carpet too hard.…

Then again, the job of bailiff doesn't bring in very much. Perhaps this Pacific island is utterly magnificent…and interesting.… If Dr. Volière, who's a man of profound and accurate sense, has decided to go there, it's obviously because serious reasons have led him to it. Perhaps there's a means of making a fortune out there…coal mines…or…one never knows.…

Anyway, we shall see.…

11.40. The hour of departure is approaching. Only one thing still worries me seriously, and that's the means of transport we've been offered. The Antisocial Man said something about the aerial route. As long as there isn't any danger.… My eyes are searching the sky in every direction.…

11.50. Nothing yet. A feverish expectation is raking all of us, except, naturally, the Antisocial Man, the insouciant Panari, who's smoking his pipe, and the baboon, which, having dragged Monsieur Truie back into our midst, is too busy tormenting him to think about anything else.

One can understand that—after all, the old chap is so ugly!

11.58. A luminous dot has appeared on the horizon and is growing with prodigious rapidity. It looks like a powerful searchlight that can fly. I can hear the roar of the crowd, which has seen it, rising from below.

Midnight. As that lugubrious hour was chiming, in the bosom of the beautiful summer night, the thing that is to take us away settled on the roof, with an impact so formidable that the entire house shook.

A large hole was pierced in the ceiling in no time at all. A ladder unfurled from above. The luggage was hoisted up in the blink of an eye. We followed. As, after a last glance at the place where I've suffered so much, and where I lost my last illusions regarding the human heart, by virtue of an infamous treason, as I set foot on the first rung I felt a tug on what remained of the tail of my jacket. It was Barnabé Cruchot, imploring: "For the last time, Maître Cormoran!"

"No Monsieur," I said, pulling free.

"Heart of stone," he murmured. And he added, in a dull voice: "Well, I'm going too."

"No, Monsieur," said the peremptory voice of the Antisocial Man, who was there.

"Yes, Monsieur," affirmed Monsieur Cruchot, who had started.

"No, Monsieur," replied the Antisocial Man, even more curtly.

"Yes, Monsieur, or I'll hurl myself out of the window to smash my skull on the pavement. I can't live in society with my dishonor. I'm in the world to inform. If I can't inform, I can only die."

I thought I saw a shadow of pity in the Antisocial Man's eyes.

"Come, then," he said. "But you'll never write again, in that case."

Barnabé Cruchot made no reply.

I climbed the ladder and, reaching the roof of the house, found myself in front of our means of transport. It's some kind of gross flying machine, which has two large wings and the general form of a cucumber. One climbs inside with the aid of a metal stairway, and it's equipped with powerful electric search-lights, switched off for the moment.

Mr. Carnyby—I recognize my vision of a heart-rending night—is here, with three negroes, who are working on the moorings, assisted by four gorilla slaves that they immediately embraced like brothers.

The departure will take place in a few moments. I'm waiting, full of calm and philosophical intrepidity, which leave me astonished. To pass the time I'm looking around. The immediate vicinity of the house is guarded by troops, but beyond them, in all the streets, as far as the eye can se, there's an immense crowd. The river is covered with boats of every sort. The vast Place du Raisin-Sec is particularly crowded. The part nearest to the Old Bridge, and, in consequence, nearest to us, has been partitioned off. A ten-deep row of bayonets is holding back the human tide, which is trying to break through with various howls, or rather to pile up, in a compact, motionless block. There are numerous groups in the empty space—members of the Government, generals in brilliant uniforms and scientists aiming telescopes and cameras at the unusual company we form.

(Everyone knows that it was impossible, in view of the darkness, to obtain anything passable by way of photographs. No one dared direct any kind of luminous beam toward the roof in order to illuminate it, for fear of attracting melinite bombs in response.)

Everything is ready. The Antisocial Man, who had stayed down below until the last moment, has just appeared on the roof. He and Mr. Carnyby are congratulating one another. We're about to leave.

One more moment. Monsieur Zephirin has been obliged to go back down to fetch the baboon, who can't bear being separated from Monsieur Truie....

He's coming back up with the quadrumane, which is still holding a fistful—the last one, I think—of its victim's hair. Everyone has embarked. We're going.

A brief order.

We're off.

I'm going to throw....

Not yet. I have a moment. Incidents are occurring.

Firstly, the demented intervention of Monsieur Méandre, who, just as we're taking off, has sprung from who knows where on to the roof, drunk with rage, and is rushing forward to stop us howling: "I haven't signed any treaty! What about the law? My money! A man of my character!"

He tries to gab the Antisocial Man, misses his clutch and finds himself grabbed by the hair. It's Panari who's lifting him up in his powerful hand. He makes him follow our flight momentarily, swaying in mid-air, and lets him go over the river, sniggering.

"A man of your character, one sends for a bath. And it's me who's fixed it...."

And Méandre falls with a great scream, and is immersed in the muddy waves, choking and splashing.

(The honorable senior bureaucrat had never consented to abandon his claims for compensation and, as he put it, "to make dross of the sentiments of dignity of a man of his character." He often declared that one could kill him, if that were necessary, but that he had to have the money that the tribunal had legally awarded him. He addressed several petitions in that sense to the Head of State, the Ministers, the Chambres and the whole world. As he was passed over, and also learned of the request made for him by the Antisocial Man, desirous of handing him over to the beasts, he became almost made with rage, and resolved to take action himself: a decision that led to his insensate attempt on the roof—which only brought him, apart from the sensations of the fall and the bath, a pleurisy that put him in bed for fifty-eight days and ruined his constitution forever.)

Then our pause above the Place du Raisin-Sec, with electric searchlights on the crowd, the dispersion by the Antisocial Man and Mr. Carnyby of handfuls of gold coins, which provoke jostling.

(The jostling of which Maître Cormoran speaks were the furious battles that everyone, without exception—from the meanest people to the official dignitaries—undertook in order to pick up the gold, in the course of which nine hundred and forty-one people, not to mention the wounded and the crippled, found an unproductive and inglorious death.)

Finally, and suddenly, as we're contemplating that spectacle, the Antisocial Man's command: "Go back. We've forgotten the armadillo!"

We return then at high speed, our collision with the veranda so violent that this time, the house lurches with a sinister crack and all the windows break, allowing us to see Monsieur Truie sitting on the floor next to his baobab, and covering the armadillo, which he is holding in his arms, with kisses.

Zephirin rushes inside and brings them back—just in time. The building bearing the number 3 on the Quai Bois-l'Encre crumbles into chaotic rubble, an indescribable ruin.

We leave again. The baboon, grinding its teeth, seizes its victim again, whom the Antisocial Man, mindful of his sworn oath, decides to abandon on the roof of the Ministry of Commerce, which also offers us a convenient surface to rectify our tangled mooring-ropes.

We are there at thus very moment. Truie has been disembarked, although he no longer wants to leave us, and tied to a chimney. That gives me a magnificent idea. I shall hang this notebook around his neck. He's so senile that he won't even know what it is. My work will thus be safe and will reach posterity....

I prepare the string and moor the precious document, which I'm completing hastily in pencil. We're about to leave the roof. Truie is waving his hands at us like a little child, weeping and drooling, and stammering: *"Au revoir...au revoir...."*

"See him again?" objects Panari, as he goes back to the machine. "Fat chance! It'd need elephants!"

I'm following him.

Adieu, cruel fatherland.

(There Monsieur Cormoran's notebook ends. The document was found the morning after the departure, suspended by means of a piece of string around Senator Truie's neck, whose presence was noticed by a tiler on a nearby roof.

The senator—who was so demented that it was necessary to send him to an asylum immediately, where he ended his days—was asleep, attached to his chimney. In his sleep he was weeping, and agitating his senile hands toward the horizon toward which the great flying machine had drawn away, carrying the Antisocial Man.)

(31 March 1901)

ABOUT THE TRANSLATOR

BRIAN STABLEFORD has translated more than a hundred volumes of French prose into English. His principal interests are the French Romantic Movement and its Decadent/Symbolist aftermath, with particular reference to the evolution of the *conte cruel*, and the evolution of the *roman scientifique* from its origins in the eighteen-century *conte philosophique* to the aftermath of the Great War of 1914-18.